APACHE KISS

Branded Wolf stepped forward, the look in his dark eyes putting an end to any and all of her thoughts. He pulled her into his embrace and she knew she should fight him. She should shove him away. She raised her hands, but instead of pushing him, she rested her palms on his wide chest.

His eyes burned with a passion she'd never witnessed before in her life. It held her mesmerized, fascinated, excited. Her mind told her to push away; her body stayed still. Her mind told her to tell him no; her lips said absolutely nothing at all.

She could feel the beat of his heart beneath the palm of her hand. His bare, sun-bronzed skin was warm under her fingertips. As she stared up at him, she felt his heartbeat quicken and she knew hers raced right along with his.

Branded Wolf's hold on her tightened and he drew her closer. And closer.

Pulling her to his chest with one arm, he slid his other hand down and pressed her hips to his. She gasped and then he took her lips in a hungry kiss that stole her next breath clean away from her.

One thought crossed her mind: *She'd never been kissed like this before.*

Books by Joyce Adams

REBEL MINE
GAMBLER'S LADY
MOONLIGHT MASQUERADE
LOVING KATE
TEMPTING TESS
DARLING CAT
APACHE PRIDE

Published by Zebra Books

APACHE PRIDE

Joyce Adams

Zebra Books
Kensington Publishing Corp.
http://www.zebrabooks.com

ZEBRA BOOKS are published by

Kensington Publishing Corp.
850 Third Avenue
New York, NY 10022

First Printing: August, 1999
10 9 8 7 6 5 4 3 2 1

Printed in the United States of America

*This book is dedicated to John Scognamiglio,
editor extraordinaire. Thanks for believing in me.*

ACKNOWLEDGMENTS

I would like to extend my thanks to the following people for their assistance with my research and sharing their knowledge.

Suzanne Moody of the Chiricahua National Park Service (Arizona). Thanks for your generous sharing of your wealth of information.

Barbara Reese of the Fort Bowie National Historic Site (Arizona). Thanks for checking obscure facts.

Chuck Rand of the National Cowboy Hall of Fame— Research Center. Thanks for your help in researching and photocopying.

Marty Rogers and Shirley Rolf of the National Cowboy Hall of Fame, Oklahoma City, Oklahoma. Thanks for your information and special tour.

Greg Ames of the St. Louis Mercantile Library, St. Louis, Missouri. Thank you for your knowledge of transportation in the 1870s.

Chapter One

Spring 1879

She tried. She honestly tried, but it was hopeless.

Oh, stars and heavens, she couldn't stop it.

As another whiff of dust tickled her nose, Regan McBain daintily covered it and its sprinkling of freckles with her gloved hand. Springtime in Philadelphia was nothing like this. She took a breath and sneezed loudly.

Then chaos broke loose on the train.

The little white ball of fur leapt from her lap as if the sleeping dog had been shot out of a cannon. As the Maltese pup bounded down the narrow aisle, barking at everything in sight, Regan jumped to her feet and gave chase. Thankfully, Mama wasn't here to scold her.

"Sweet Pea, come here," Regan ordered, unconcerned with the looks she drew with her unladylike run down the aisle in her stylish blue traveling gown.

The furry pup listened and obeyed the way she always

did. Not a whit. Instead the dog leapt up onto the seat beside a woman passenger and right onto the bonnet resting on the seat, crushing the brim of the hat beneath her paws. The woman screamed, and Sweet Pea took off in the opposite direction, bonnet held firmly in her mouth. Two yellow ribbons trailed the floor in her wake.

"Oh, no," Regan moaned.

The conductor stepped forward, making a quick grab for the dog, but the little pup ducked between his legs. The stout man lost his balance and landed on the seat atop the irate woman.

Regan closed her ears to the shouts and chased after her wayward dog. Dodging the conductor's legs, she rushed past him with a murmured apology and tucked a strand of auburn hair out of her eyes.

Sweet Pea slowed to a halt and looked back as if waiting for someone to catch up and resume the game, the bonnet still held firmly in her mouth. Dusty yellow ribbons dragged the floor of the railcar. She wagged her plumed tail back and forth.

Regan lunged forward and her fingers skimmed the dog's silky fur, but the train chose that moment to sway to the side. She straightened and tried valiantly to regain her balance, flailing her arms. Her action sent her blue drawstring bag sailing from her wrist.

It struck the back of a man's head, knocking his dark hat from atop his head. Regan winced at the low sound coming from the man's throat.

Oh, stars and heavens, she'd done it this time.

Raising her chin and putting out a hand to the back of a seat to steady herself, she did the only proper thing possible. She walked up to the stranger to offer her apology.

"Sir, I . . ."

As the man turned his head, her words stuck in her throat. Straight dark hair the color of deepest midnight hung to his shoulders. She stared openmouthed as his hair brushed his buckskin shirt. High cheekbones and an angular jaw added strength to his face, not that he needed it added. She'd never in her entire life seen anyone who radiated strength and power like this man.

His buckskin breeches molded his legs, outlining his firm muscles, and moccasins reached nearly to his knees.

"A . . . an . . . Indian," a woman passenger gasped from behind her. "In our railcar."

Regan mouthed the word "Indian," but not a sound came out.

The man's only outward reaction was a slight narrowing of his blue eyes on her. He held her drawstring bag out to her.

Regan felt the heat of a blush stain her cheeks at her impudence. She'd just insulted a savage, but she couldn't utter a word in her defense. The only thing she could do was stare at him in amazement.

He reached out and cupped her chin with his fingertips. His fingers were warm and calloused against her skin. With a firm but gentle touch, he pushed her open mouth closed. Then he trailed his thumb over her lower lip for the space of a heartbeat.

She jumped back at his intimate touch. Her cheeks heated to scorching under his intent gaze, and her lip almost burned where he'd touched it. The skin retained the warmth of his thumb. She snatched her reticule from him.

With a wicked smile he dropped his hand to his side.

Regan was rendered speechless. No man had ever touched her without first asking permission. She wasn't certain what to say. Her usual confidence and assurances had completely deserted her.

While she continued to stare at him in fascination, he flicked her a dismissing glance, then bent down and scooped his hat off the floor. As he lifted it upward, a ball of white fur lunged and snapped small jaws over the brim.

He muttered something she didn't understand but was certain wasn't a compliment to her or her pet.

"I beg your pardon." Regan raised her chin in her best insulted-Philadelphia-society gesture.

Her cool affront bounced right off his angular chin. He gently shook his hat, dislodging the pup. Sweet Pea tumbled to the floor at the conductor's feet and set up a din of barking.

"Why, you—" Regan sputtered.

"Ma'am," the conductor cut in through gritted teeth, his fear of the Indian showing clearly. "Would you please take your dog and return to your seat." He held the little fluffy, slightly soiled dog out to her.

Regan didn't wonder at the man's fear. The Indian exuded a powerful force, even standing perfectly still. She turned away from him and offered the conductor a smile as repentance. The poor man couldn't help being abrupt. This was the third time Sweet Pea had slipped loose and ran through the cars since their prior stop. The last time, she'd shredded the poor man's pant leg before Regan retrieved her.

The conductor kept his lips in a thin, firm line. It was obvious he wasn't falling for her smiles again.

Before Regan could reach for her pet, Sweet Pea nipped the conductor's hand. He yelled at the dog and then at Regan. Sweet Pea kicked free and jumped—right onto the Indian's chest.

The Indian wrapped one hand around the dog's neck, then shifted his grip and caught the wiggling creature by the scruff of the neck. As he held the dog out, the pup's tongue snaked out and left a wet puppy kiss along his cheek. He stiffened but didn't utter a sound.

Regan tried to bite back her laughter, but a giggle slipped out.

The dark-haired man turned his attention to her, and she

nearly swallowed her next breath down the wrong way. He had the most startling, intense blue eyes she'd ever seen. And right then their full force was focused completely and totally on her.

He looked her up and down with a hooded gaze that gave nothing away, then he reached out and dropped her dog into her arms. Tipping his hat, he shoved it on his head and turned away from her. She'd never been so insulted in her entire life.

She'd been dismissed by an Indian. A savage. And the most handsome man she'd ever encountered.

"Well, I never."

Regan whirled away, her cheeks heating. She caught up her skirt in one gloved hand and returned to her seat with as much dignity as the swaying railcar allowed. She couldn't get to her father's fort quickly enough now.

The wheels clicked monotonously on the rails, lulling her temper. As the minutes slipped past, she couldn't seem to keep her eyes from straying to the back of the man's dark head again and again. It was most unladylike. The one time he looked back at her, she lifted her nose into the air and turned to stare out the grime-covered window.

As the train slowed for their next stop, she saw him stand to his feet. Pausing a moment, he looked back over his shoulder directly into her eyes. Regan couldn't force her gaze away from his blue-eyed stare no matter what.

Then he did it again. He tipped his hat, turned, and, dismissing her, strode from the train.

"Well," she grumbled to herself. She rubbed her pet's soft fur. "Sweet Pea," she bent down to whisper, "I do believe we've both been insulted."

The pup flicked a kiss across the bottom of Regan's chin. She patted the top of her head absently, unable to look away from the scene outside the window.

She watched the dark-haired man through the dusty window. He moved with a pantherlike grace, and she could almost imagine that his footsteps were silent, dangerous.

"Ma'am." The conductor stopped a safe distance of three seats away.

She turned her wayward attention to the stout man.

"Best not be setting your cap for him, ma'am," he warned her.

Affronted, she sat up ramrod-straight in her seat. "Whatever do you mean by that?" Insulted dignity tinged her every word.

"That there's Branded Wolf. He's a breed." His lips curled in disgust. Now that the safety of the train wall separated them, his earlier fear had disappeared.

Regan wondered at his remark. She'd never heard such a word before. "A what?"

"A half-breed Apache." He almost spat out the words.

She thought on his statement a moment, and as comprehension dawned, her mouth formed an O. So that explained the Indian's startling blue eyes.

Imagine that. She'd met her first Apache warrior. And he was half white.

"Ma'am," the conductor interrupted her silent contemplation. "Your stop is the next one. You'll be catching the stage there, and then the two-horse covered coach for Fort Bowie."

Regan truly wasn't looking forward to her upcoming time on the stagecoaches, but the train didn't go far enough into the Arizona Territory yet. Something about it being too uncivilized, she imagined.

As the conductor turned away, Regan could have sworn she heard him grumble "Good riddance."

Was there no end to the conductor's rudeness and nosiness?

She hugged Sweet Pea close and lifted her nose in disdain.

Turning, she gazed out the window again. And right into the blue-eyed stare of the Apache warrior.

Branded Wolf let his eyes drink in their fill of the woman. She was a beauty. And as spoiled as she was beautiful. Sun-streaked hair the shade of a handful of Arizona soil, bow-shaped lips made for kissing, and a pair of enticing green eyes the color of a Chiricahua mountain meadow in spring. Those eyes insulted and tempted at the same time.

She hadn't acted as he'd expected. She'd shown neither fear nor a white woman's disgust. When he'd cupped her chin, she hadn't shrieked in terror as he'd thought she would. Instead, she'd stared at him, her eyes wide with sudden anticipation.

And she had enough arrogance for three Apache braves.

He recalled that her skin had been silken beneath his thumb. He'd resisted the urge to stroke her like a wild horse. She reminded him of one—untamed and unbroken.

He shook off the sudden surge of raw desire. He had many miles to cover before nightfall. The stagecoach and its confines were not for him. Leave the rocking box to the white-eyes.

Once again the white beauty with her green eyes claimed his mind. She was different. But he had more important things to attend to than a beautiful woman. Much less a beautiful *white* woman. As much as he tried, she remained in his thoughts even as he prepared to leave the station, overshadowing his eagerness to return to the territory and resume his hunt. He turned his back on the train, awaiting the arrival of his mount.

Regan continued to watch, her nose pressed against the glass. As the man walked up to a bay horse being led from the train, she leaned closer, nearly sliding out of her seat. The Indian swung onto the horse's back, and Regan released an "oh" of admiration. Both were magnificent specimens. She lightly brushed her gloved hand across her chin where he'd touched her.

As the train jolted forward, Regan was thrown backward. She landed on the floor of the railcar in a flurry of petticoats and jostled bustle. Sweet Pea yelped and planted both paws on her shoulders. Before she could stop her, the dog administered a half dozen moist puppy kisses.

Catching the dog close in one arm, Regan wiped her cheek and pushed herself up onto the hard seat. Her stop was next, then the stage. Soon she'd reach the fort.

At the thought of the upcoming meeting with her papa, she bit her lip. During the trip she'd tried to push her constant worries about her stricken father to the back of her mind but without success. One encounter with that Indian had driven all thoughts of her dear, dying papa from her mind.

Guilt and shame rushed over her. Here her dear papa was lying near death, and she had been thinking of that . . . man.

She covered her mouth with her hand and sent up a silent prayer for her father. She hoped he lived long enough for her to see him again. It had been nearly ten years since Mama had left him, taking her to Philadelphia. She hadn't seen him since that tearful day. And she'd heard from him only infrequently in a few letters. Until . . .

Then she'd received his last letter. In it he'd asked to see her "before he met his maker."

Holding back a sob, Regan caught her pet close. Sweet Pea let out a yelp of protest.

"Oh, please, let me see Papa again," she whispered the prayer into the dog's lush fur.

She'd give practically anything to see her father well again.

Fort Bowie, Arizona Territory

Regan repeated her prayer while she followed an officer across the sloping parade grounds to her father's quarters as commanding officer. She didn't even bother to take in the garrison he commanded. Her thoughts were filled with her father and his horrible illness.

As Captain Something-or-other—she'd forgotten his name—showed her into her father's quarters, Regan steeled herself for the worst. She brushed dust from her skirt. Oh, how she hoped her dear papa still had the strength to speak with her.

In the first room she clenched her gloved hands tightly together. Decorum demanded she face this meeting with dignity. And with fresh gloves firmly in place.

Taking a deep breath to prepare herself for the worst, she handed Sweet Pea over to the officer, then nodded to him to open the door to her father's bedroom. She couldn't wait to rush to his bedside. The man she'd worshipped as a child had been tall and strong. Poor Papa, to be so weakened and bedridden . . .

The door swung open to reveal a tall man dressed in his calvary uniform standing by the window. He turned to her with a smile of greeting.

Regan stared in shock and disbelief at her father. Her very healthy-looking, robust father.

"Regan?" He stopped and stared at her. "You're the image of—"

He strode toward her with firm, strong steps. Why, this man was no dying invalid. By some miracle he'd gotten well. Relief rushed over her, and she felt the sting of tears filling her eyes.

"Regan, how beautiful you've grown up to be. Captain Larkin, isn't she a beauty? Didn't I tell you—"

"Papa!" She ran forward, throwing her arms around him.

He stiffened at her action and pushed her away. "My dear."

She winced at the stab of pain his rejection caused. Studying him, she noted his healthy color then narrowed her eyes. He didn't even have the look of a man who'd been ill. No paleness marred his strong-featured face. Not a single cough interrupted his commanding voice. Her comprehension grew, but she refused to accept what her eyes told her.

"Father." She cleared her throat. "You're . . .you . . . appear to be looking quite well. You've recovered from your terrible illness?"

He brushed a finger absently over his mustache. "Well, I am sorry for the slight deception." He looked uncomfortable with the admission. "Something needed to be done, what with you nearly past marriageable age."

Regan gasped. She was nineteen—not matronly at all.

As her father smiled, her shock and relief began to turn into anger. Acceptance of the full truth struck her. He'd tricked her without a care for her feelings.

"You said you were dying." Her voice was tight with emotion, quivering on the last word.

He brushed a finger across his mustache again in a gesture she recognized as guilt. "Now, my dear, I never actually said that."

"You did," she fired back at him.

Anger thoroughly replaced her relief at finding him well, instead of at death's door as she'd been led to believe.

"No, I wrote that I wanted to see you before I died."

Regan stomped her foot and clenched her hands into fists. "You never were ill. You lied to me."

"Now, dear, I may have exaggerated a little—"

"Lied," she corrected him. Her lower lip quivered, a sign of impending tears. Unwelcome tears. She hated crying. Hurt and betrayed, she crossed her arms over her chest in an unconscious gesture of self-defense and pride.

"My dear girl. I wanted you to meet my captain. Get acquainted with him."

She shot a fleeting glance to the uniformed man standing beside her. In an instant she took in his medium brown hair and pale blue, emotionless eyes, then turned back to her father. She didn't attempt to keep the anger from her eyes.

Her father cleared his throat. "Surely you can understand—"

"What's there to understand? You deceived me." She understood perfectly now.

"Regardless, now that you're here, you'll stay out the month."

Regan faced him in defiance. At the look of disappointment that came over her father's features, her rebellion evaporated. It was a look she'd become well familiar with through her early years. Her eyes burned with hurtful memories.

If she didn't get out of there soon, she absolutely knew she'd cry. And she refused to do so in front of him. This is what she got for defying her mama and sneaking off in the middle of the night to visit him.

"Are my quarters separate from yours?" She asked the question but knew the answer. Her father had kept himself quartered separate from her and her mother throughout their last few years together as a family. She'd accepted it as the norm until she'd seen friends' parents living together in Philadelphia.

"Yes, dear. Your quarters are across the parade ground."

Whirling around, she snatched her pet from the startled officer's arms. The dog gave a yip of protest.

"Captain, would you show me to my rooms?"

"Well, ma'am—"

"Now." Regan caught up her skirt in one hand and walked out the door.

Captain Larkin reached her side in two long steps. "Ma'am, please reconsider—"

She cut him off with one look.

"Do I need to ask someone else to show me?" she asked with all the dignity she could muster.

"No, ma'am. This way." He opened the door for her and led her outside.

Behind her, her father's silence hurt worse than any words he could have said to her. His disappointment followed every step she took as surely as if he'd walked alongside her.

Regan could almost hear the question he'd asked so many times while she was growing up. *Why couldn't she have been the son he'd so baldly wanted instead of the daughter he didn't want?*

Regan slammed down the lid of her camelback trunk. It bounced back open, evidence she'd packed one too many things inside for the trip. She never should have opened it for another change of clothes. She administered the trunk a solid kick, wishing it were a particular someone's knee. The act didn't lessen her anger one bit.

"The low-down, dirty, rotten, conniving . . ." She whirled away, pausing to suck in a breath between clenched teeth, and shoved the silk flounce of her cream gown out of her way.

Throwing a disparaging glance around the quarters her father had issued her, she blew out her breath. Her sun-streaked auburn hair fluttered, then dropped back down into her eyes. She brushed the curls away.

She'd dearly love to plop down onto the bed, but the thin mattress sagged on the poor excuse for a bed. How could he do this to her?

"Oh, da—" She remembered just in time that her mama wouldn't tolerate a lady swearing and changed it to "Oh, stars and heavens."

A little bundle of white fur disentangled itself from a half-mauled pillow and launched itself into her arms. She caught the small Maltese dog close.

"Oh, Sweetie. I can't believe he's done this. Look at this place." She spread one hand out to encompass the dismal room. "We're stranded in a fort in the middle of the wilderness."

If she weren't so mad, she'd have given in to the dog's comforting licks and cried into her soft white fur. She couldn't believe her father had done this to her. Her own father.

She'd trusted him. And he'd lied!

Regan smoothed the hair away from Sweet Pea's dark eyes. The little dog had lost her bow somewhere in this awful place. Reaching out, she pressed down on the lid of her trunk again. They were getting out of there as fast as she could manage. Her father could take his demand of a one-month stay and . . .

She wouldn't stay there. She absolutely refused.

How could she have been so gullible? She'd believed his letter, argued with her mama, slipped away alone to make this awful trip. And she'd even shed tears over his pitifully sad request to see her again before he "met his maker."

Why, she'd wasted time worrying about him, and all the while he . . . he . . .

The old scoundrel was in perfect health. And likely intending to marry her off to his favored officer. Was that his way of acquiring the son he'd never had? Pain and anger collided, but her temper won out.

"The low-down, sneaky . . ." She took up her tirade again and strode to the window to stare out at the barrenness of the fort with its earth-colored adobe buildings.

She couldn't see one bit of beauty in the landscape. And there were Apaches out there. At least that's what the driver of the stagecoach had told her on her way there. She shuddered and held her comforting dog closer.

Her mama had told her the same thing and warned her

against her papa. But she'd refused to listen to her mother. But she should have paid attention to her mama's dire predictions of her father's treachery. But no, instead, she'd run off to see her dear, dying father.

"Dying, ha!"

Mama had been right. Papa had lied to her. Deceived her. And now she was stranded in a fort out in the middle of the wilderness.

Regan stomped her foot, and a cloud of dust rose around her satin slippers.

"Regan?" A knock sounded at the door seconds before it flew open.

She shrieked and spun around to see her father standing in the doorway. The top of his blue cavalry hat nearly touched the lintel. Why hadn't she inherited his height instead of her petite mama's stature? Then she'd feel better suited to the coming argument. It was going to be a good one too.

"Regan, now, listen to me—"

"I'm not speaking to you." She raised her nose in the air with haughty indignation.

Sweet Pea mimicked her mistress with a sniff and a lifting of her black nose.

"You will not behave as your mother. Now, see here—"

Regan wrapped her arms around her pet and turned her back on her father. Her skirts swirled around her legs, her petticoat brushing across her ankle. She kicked at the fabric in frustration.

"I think we've had enough of your temper, daughter." Colonel McBain's voice took on the commanding tone he used with his regiment.

That was his mistake. Regan stiffened her back in instant reaction and drew in a breath of fury. Mama never used that tone, and she didn't issue orders either.

Temper? He hadn't seen anything yet. Mama always said

she was a termagant when angered. Just then she was as mad as she'd ever been in her life. Why, she could almost spit—if she weren't a well-bred lady.

Instead, she did the next best thing.

Whirling around, she picked up the nearest object within reach, a tin pitcher of wildflowers. Mere weeds. Her father hadn't even had the common decency to buy her real flowers. She threw the pitcher without pausing to take aim. It bounced off the wall beside her father.

Colonel McBain took a quick step to the side and shouted at her. "Regan, that's enough."

"I am not something to be given away to your favorite officer as a reward for a job well done." She grabbed up the metal washbasin and sent it sailing through the air. It landed at his feet.

"Now, stop that this instant. Given time, you will come to appreciate Captain Larkin."

The third time she took aim. The silver-backed hairbrush skimmed the bottom of her father's mustache.

The colonel stiffened in anger. "You are intolerably spoiled. This is what comes from your living with your mother. I never should have let her take you. Look at what she's done to you—"

"Don't you talk about Mama that way."

Mama had always told her what a hero her father had been, and what a terrible husband he turned out to be. Her mama had finally left him in frustration, taking Regan with her back to the precious civilization of Philadelphia society.

"You're just like your mother. If that woman had exerted some control over your actions—"

"If Mama had anything to do with this, I wouldn't be here," Regan shouted back at him.

Why hadn't she listened to her mama and stayed in Philadelphia instead of running off to brave the wilds to see her father before he died?

"I've already dispatched a telegram informing her of your arrival."

"I sent her one from a town myself, so she wouldn't worry," Regan snapped back.

The coming affect of his remark struck her. *He'd* sent a telegram. Oh, no.

Oh, dear stars. A telegram from her father would guarantee her mama's trip to the fort. She was certain a wilderness war wouldn't create half the havoc as her parents in the same room would.

Regan sighed deeply. "You do know she'll come."

Her father smiled. "I'm counting on it. We can't have a wedding without your mother's attendance," he stated matter-of-factly.

Regan gritted her teeth into a smile before she spoke in a syrupy-sweet voice. "There isn't going to be a wedding. Not once your precious captain encounters the real me." She patted a curl into place and tossed her head.

"Daughter, you will behave yourself."

Her only answer was a smile.

"And you will attend the dinner party I've planned for tonight in my quarters," he ordered, but she noticed that his blustery voice faltered the smallest bit.

"Of course, Father." She flashed him a look from under lowered lashes that should have warned him.

"Daughter."

"Come on, Sweet Pea, we need to get ready." Regan turned her back on her father. "Good day, Father."

"Regan, you will behave," he ordered before he shut the door.

Regan turned and glared at the wood door.

Oh, she'd behave all right—only in a manner her father had yet to see. Her first true smile of the day graced her lips.

Chapter Two

Branded Wolf bent low to study the riders' tracks leading away from the long-cold campfire. The men wore boots, the heels leaving indentations in the dirt unlike the soft partial print of an Apache moccasin.

The white-eyes' trail would be easy to follow. Sure of themselves and their disguise, they hadn't even tried to cover their tracks. It didn't take a skilled warrior to see this. He scornfully flicked away the broken arrow lying beside the last bootprint, a poor trick to make anyone tracking them believe the men were Apache.

Scooping up a handful of sandy dirt, he clenched his fist around it until his knuckles whitened with his hatred. A faint breeze blew his shoulder-length hair back away from his sun-bronzed face.

He was close to his prey. Very close.

The taste of revenge filled his mouth. It was bittersweet on his tongue. Once again he smelled the stench of blood and death in his mind. His heart filled with hatred for the killers of his father, uncle, and Soaring Dove, his wife-to-be. They'd all been killed the morning before the wedding.

He shoved away the memories and the guilt. Nothing would bring Soaring Dove back, not even the scalps of the white-eyes masquerading as Apache. But the men would die anyway. As slowly as she had died.

His honor as an Apache demanded it.

Branded Wolf swung back into the saddle of his bay, his buckskin pants brushing against his moccasins. His shirt chafed his shoulders, reminding him yet again of his hated half-heritage. His life as a bounty hunter commanded he wear a shirt to dress in part as the white men—the half of himself he hated.

Shading his blue eyes against the scorching Arizona sun, he stared off across the desert. Heat rose in ripples from the ground. His people's land. He paused and let his gaze take in the majestic beauty around him. The cactus and yucca stood tall and proud, enduring heat and adversity like an Indian warrior. Like his people.

He would not let his band, now running free from the hated San Carlos Reservation, take the blame for these killings. He stood alone in his belief of their innocence. The nearby fort was even then preparing to take action with the next killings. He had to bring in the true killers before that.

No matter what.

A faint breeze of unease blew across the back of his neck. The killers knew of his determined hunt ever since he'd nearly captured them in New Mexico following Soaring Dove's murder. He wouldn't rest until they paid for it.

If he ever let his guard down, they'd trap him. Sometimes he felt like the hunted instead of the hunter, but he would triumph. He must fool them into believing they had him, then spring on them unawares.

He turned his mount in the direction of the fort tucked in the eastern corner of the Arizona Territory. The men would eventually return there to the protection it offered them. To the safety the foolish white colonel provided.

Time was slipping away. He could not fail.

That night he'd watch and wait outside the fort. He had the patience of a trained warrior. His prey would show up sooner or later.

And he'd be willing to give up the last bounty he'd collected it would be sooner.

The appointed time for her father's wilderness dinner party came too soon for Regan's wishes. Outside her father's quarters, she paused to draw in a deep breath for the courage she'd need to carry off her farce.

Before the evening ended, her dear, deceitful papa would regret bringing her there under false pretenses. She'd see to it.

"Here we go, Sweet Pea," she whispered, bending low and giving the little dog a pat of reassurance, more for herself than for her pet.

She took a moment to straighten one of the pink bows holding the pup's hair away from her eyes. Then she straightened, stiffening her spine. Now was not the time to show any softness.

With all the haughty dignity she could gather, Regan knocked on the door, then strolled into her father's quarters, leading her white fluffy pup on a leash made of pink ribbon. It matched the rows and rows of ribbon trim on her flounced skirt perfectly. She knew every eye was on her and her little dog, and she raised her chin a slight bit to meet the challenge.

The stares held a mixture of shock and disbelief. And they were exactly what she wanted.

She held back her triumphant smile. She couldn't look more out of place for a common meal at a fort in the wilderness—the gown with its yards of exquisite watered silk had been a perfect choice. She knew any woman present would give her soul to own the lavish gown. And the ribboned leash tied around Sweet Pea's neck offered a flash of inspiration.

The other two women present wore attractive gowns but hadn't bothered with a bustle. Regan knew she looked woefully out of place, but she reminded herself that was her intention. She felt slightly ashamed when the other two women greeted her with sincere smiles of welcome.

Her father turned to her with a mere glance that carried a distinct hint of coolness to it. He was obviously still angry. For an instant, a stab of pain cut through Regan. Once again she'd disappointed him. But then, hadn't she always been a disappointment to the proud father who had wanted a son and practically ignored the daughter he'd been given instead?

Cutting off the hurtful memories, she narrowed her eyes in defiance. Her father had gotten a daughter he'd never wanted; let him deal with the consequences of bringing her out there with his lies and deceptions.

Oh, yes, she'd *behave* all right. And let her father beware the consequences.

With all the dignity she could muster with the hurt eating at her, she caught up her skirt with her right hand and crossed into the middle of the room. She paused, waiting until she knew she had a full audience.

"Good evening, ladies and gentlemen," she greeted them with a voice dripping with sweetness. "Sorry if I'm late."

A uniformed officer inclined his head. Captain Larkin, her father's favorite. She caught the faint disdain in his eyes before he hid it behind a stiff smile of welcome. The man was all officer—stiff and formal as could be. Not to mention ambitious; she'd spotted the give-away look in his eyes when he watched her father.

She could tell the type even from a distance. Stiff manners, smooth words, and cold ambition ran through their veins.

Hadn't she met enough of them in Philadelphia? Men whose main interest lay in finding a wife of position to further their own rise in position.

She'd had more than enough of the type to last her a lifetime. When she chose to marry, it would be for love. And hopefully to a man who had a spark of life inside him.

If Captain Larkin thought he'd be acquiring a docile wife suitable to aid his ambitious climb to commanding officer, she was about to prove him wrong.

Let him stand back and enjoy the performance, along with her father.

Regan felt a momentary twinge of guilt over what she was about to do, but she didn't have a choice. She had to make her father change his mind. He had to see she didn't belong there. She'd only disappoint him again if she stayed out the month. Swallowing down her trepidation, she loosened her overly tight grip on Sweet Pea's leash and took another step forward into the room.

Tilting her head to the side, she worked on becoming every inch the fine Philadelphia society lady her mother had taught her to be. Both haughty and spoiled. She plastered a smile to her lips as she was introduced to the members of her father's circle—two more officers and their wives.

She tried to put names and faces together. Suddenly Captain Larkin stepped forward to interrupt her concentration. Regan barely held back the sharp remark that sprang to her lips.

"Miss McBain, good evening." His voice was as stiff as he looked, and not a tinge of warmth came through to her.

From near her feet, Sweet Pea growled low in her throat. Regan knew she could always trust her pet to see beneath the surface of a person. She turned her attention to her dog, scooping her up into her arms and avoiding the officer's outstretched hand.

"Why, good evening, Lieutenant," she said in a deceptively sweet voice.

She heard a sound like choked laughter from one of the women.

His smile wavered, and he stiffened up straighter, if that was possible. "It's Captain, ma'am."

"Regan . . ." The reprimand was clear in her father's voice, but she chose to ignore it.

"I never can tell one rank from another." Regan flicked her hand as if brushing away a pesky insect. She wrinkled her nose in obvious distaste. "It is so uncivilized out here in the territories. Not at all like at home."

She spared his uniform a disparaging glance before she added, "At home we always dress for dinner." She brushed at a speck of dust on her skirt.

"Regan."

She turned at her father's voice to find him standing next to her

"Why, good evening, Father," she said coolly.

Her father leveled a censuring look at her before he spoke. "I'll have one of my men tie your dog outside."

Regan tightened her hold on her pet. "That won't be necessary. I never go anywhere without Sweet Pea. She was a birthday gift from Mama."

A birthday her father had neglected to acknowledge with even a letter. She let the unspoken reprimand hang between them.

Turning her back on her father, she placed Sweet Pea on the floor, then walked to a chair and sat down. The little dog sprang into her lap immediately, and Regan slipped a protective arm around her.

Under her plan, Sweet Pea would give her an excuse to leave early, and she desperately needed the moral support her pet offered to stand up to her father's increasing disapproval. She worked hard to keep up her pretense of bored indifference.

The meal was a disaster. Her father's looks progressed from displeasure to near outrage as Regan toyed with the food, feeding most of it to her pet instead. What little Regan ate tasted delicious, but her plan didn't include any outward enjoyment of the meal. Those seated around the table remained unusually quiet.

At last the meal ended. She barely held back her sigh of relief. As her father stood to his feet and caught her elbow, her heart dropped to her toes. Had she overdone her too-bored act?

"Father, I would like to go riding in the morning." She flashed him a smile for show. "Would you allow me the use of a horse? Please?"

In the next breath, Captain Larkin appeared at her side. She could tell he never passed up an opportunity, and she'd just handed him one.

"Colonel, your daughter will need an escort on her ride. I would like to volunteer. With your permission, sir?"

"Of course." Her father smiled warmly at his captain.

Regan bit the side of her cheek. Her father never had smiled at her that way. Not once in her life.

"I'd be happy to escort her during her stay, if it meets your approval, sir?"

Her father nodded and clapped the other man on the back. "Perhaps we can announce an upcoming wedding soon," he said in a low voice.

Regan stomped her foot, but no one heard her or paid her anger any attention. Both men acted as if the marriage was already an accepted fact. She held back her anger; now was not the time, since no one outside the three of them had heard her father's remark.

Why, the captain hadn't even been considerate enough to

ask her. Obviously her father's approval was all he cared about.

Regan crossed her arms and narrowed her eyes on the officer. She had a surprise or two in store for him and his plans.

"It's settled. Miss McBain, I'll escort you on your ride in the morning," he announced, turning his attention back to her.

Regan barely stopped herself from stomping both her feet in fury. Her narrowed eyes were the only outward sign of her anger. No man ordered her about. Much less this too-formal status climber.

How could her papa ever think this was the type of man she would want as a husband? She shuddered at the thought. While the captain was pleasant enough to look at and had manners to meet even her mama's approval, he left her cold.

She didn't think much of his presumptuous attitude regarding her opinions either. She didn't mean a whit to him. Except as the means to a promotion from her father.

"Regan?" her papa prompted.

"Yes, Father?" she taunted with a smile.

"The captain is waiting for your answer." His tone of voice left no doubt as to what answer he demanded from her.

"I'm sorry, I didn't hear him ask me."

"Regan."

Her burst of defiance evaporated at the tone in her father's voice. Well, she'd use this event to put the next step of her plan into action, but at least she'd agree to his escort on her terms.

"Captain, I'll see you at nine o'clock. I do hate to rise too dreadfully early, don't you?" She paused to toss a curl over her shoulder, then quickly added, "Sweet Pea and I should be up and readied then."

Surely that would discourage him. She could just imagine

the officer's reaction to her little dog along on their proposed outing. Waiting for his reaction, she wasn't disappointed.

She caught the pressure of his lips into a line. Ah, yes, next he would refuse and show his true colors to her father.

But he was too practiced and well mannered to rise to her bait. Instead, he returned her smile and stepped closer to her.

"Surely you can't intend to take that ... dog ... with you." His thinly veiled attempt to disguise his dislike failed miserably.

Regan straightened her spine and faced him with only a bare hint of a smile. "But of course. She's gone with me on rides numerous times. I wouldn't dream of leaving her behind."

She held her breath, waiting for his refusal.

"Then I will see you at nine, Miss McBain." Captain Larkin stepped forward and caught her right hand in his. Raising it, he brushed his lips over her knuckles.

She felt absolutely nothing but irritation at herself. It was going to take more than Sweet Pea's presence to discourage this prospective suitor.

Oh, stars and heavens. It was going to be a long morning indeed.

"Colonel, I'd like permission to escort your daughter to her quarters?"

Captain Larkin turned his attention to her father, not even giving her the chance to answer for herself. Regan fumed in silent anger. Why, she'd like permission to throttle the both of them.

"Permission granted," her father announced with a wide smile.

Regan gritted her teeth. There was absolutely no way she intended to stay out the month. Absolutely not. And as for the captain's attentions, she intended to leave no doubt as to their acceptance by her.

"Father, I am quite capable of finding my own way to my room—"

"Regan."

The commanding tone of his voice stopped her in mid-sentence.

"You will not go anywhere, on or off this post, without an escort. Is that understood?"

Regan swallowed down her instant refusal. Nothing would be gained by arguing with him now. Besides, she didn't intend to remain there long enough for it to matter anyway.

"Clearly." She swallowed down her rebellion. "Good night, Papa." Her voice softened with affection.

She leaned forward on tiptoe and brushed a kiss across his leathery cheek. Her father quickly wiped a hand over the place, and she kept her smile fixed on her lips with a great deal of effort.

"Captain, are you ready?" Without waiting for a reply, she turned away, and tugging on Sweet Pea's leash, walked to the door.

Captain Larkin barely reached the door in time to open it for her, not that she cared a whit. Once again her father had rejected her affection for him. Would she never learn?

"Miss McBain, would you care for a stroll around the grounds?" he asked.

"Whatever you wish, Captain," she answered without any enthusiasm. Perhaps it would be better to walk off some of her anger and hurt. She had no hope of a restful night's sleep now.

Captain Larkin took her arm and led her across the parade ground. "Please call me David. I sincerely hope we'll become *friends*."

She just bet he did. Had her father assured him a promotion if he married her and took her off his hands?

"May I call you Regan?" he persisted.

"Fine," she snapped at him.

Why couldn't he shut up and let her take in some of the peace and quiet of the night? Shifting clouds cast the adobe buildings into shadows, but the air was as clear and dry as if it were fresh that minute. There was an almost peace about the vast expanse of land surrounding the fort situated on a plateau.

She stared out at the unknown land and occasional hill stretching away from the outpost and sighed. She knew she was taking her foul temper out on him, but she didn't much care. He was clearly in league with her father. He deserved to experience her temper; perhaps it would dissuade him.

"You did say you were going to show me the fort, didn't you?" she reminded.

The stiffening of his body was almost imperceptible, but she felt it in his hand on her arm. She bit the corner of her cheek to hold in her smile. So, the captain didn't like being questioned or pushed. A fact she'd make good use of, she thought to herself.

"This way, Regan." He nearly jerked her arm in his abrupt turn, then released her.

He led the way without offering her his arm again, which suited her fine. She scooped Sweet Pea up into her arms and followed several deliberate steps behind. He pointed out the storehouses, corrals, and post trader's store, and she sighed in boredom.

"It's relatively safe tonight." He tossed the words back over his shoulder as he passed the hospital.

Regan sniffed at his poor attempt to frighten her. It would take more than that to scare her into his cold, calculating arms.

"The savages seem quiet for now," he added.

"Savages?" she asked, baiting him.

"Apaches." He didn't even attempt to keep the hatred from his voice. "They should be run out of the Territory."

"Captain, the Indians are people—"

The coldness of the look he turned on her stopped her defense.

"I should have expected such sentiments from an Easterner. But not from the commander's daughter."

Regan tensed at the insult, and Sweet Pea growled at him. She patted the dog's head to quiet her. "I express my own opinions, not my father's."

"Not a flattering habit, Regan."

She bent forward and sat Sweet Pea on the flat ground. Straightening, she faced him. "I'm not here to flatter you, Captain."

As if on cue, the little pup walked to the captain's feet and stared up at him.

He grimaced. "Shoo."

Sweet Pea continued to stare at him while she squatted over his boots and watered them thoroughly.

Regan couldn't hold back her laughter. Trust Sweet Pea to—

Captain Larkin swung his foot out to kick the dog, but she dodged to the side. Regan rushed to stand between him and her pet, then scooped the pup up into her arms.

"If you ever attempt that again, you will wish the Apaches had gotten you before I'm finished with you, Captain."

As they stood glaring at each other, an arrow thudded into the ground beside the officer. He jumped back, almost behind Regan. The clouds shifted and the stream of bright moonlight revealed a lone rider in buckskins on a bay horse.

She sucked in her breath. It couldn't be.

She stared in fascination. The man and animal moved as one. She'd never seen such perfection, except at the rail station today when . . .

As if sensing her fascination, the rider whirled his mount around. The dark hair flowing free, the buckskin pants, the arrogant posture, brought the sudden realization to her. It was him.

Branded Wolf.

She stared at him, nearly held spellbound. What was he doing here?

He swept his hat from his head with an insolent flourish and waved it in the air. Then he spun his horse around and galloped off into the night.

Regan didn't realize she'd gasped, until Captain Larkin caught her arm. He jerked her toward him.

"Damn savages," he snarled. "I'll take you to your quarters."

"It's a little late for heroics, isn't it?"

Sweet Pea took as much offense to his action as Regan did. The little dog sunk her sharp teeth into his hand.

Captain Larkin jerked away, tripped, and nearly toppled over backward.

Regan smothered her laughter. He'd gotten no more than he deserved. No man laid a hand on her without her permission. Turning her back on him, she walked to her quarters.

If he showed up for tomorrow morning's ride, she'd reinforce the fact that his attentions were most unwelcome. Before the end of the morning, the man would have no doubt of her feelings.

Regan lay on the lumpy mattress and wished for the softness of her bed back in Philadelphia. She had to talk her father out of his demand that she stay the month out.

She simply couldn't—

The soft thud of horse hooves jolted her out of her thoughts. She scrambled out of bed and ran to the window. Drawing back the curtain, she peered out. A shadowed cluster of men rode past her window and out into the night. Her father's tall figure wasn't among the group of riders. She jumped back away from the pane of glass.

At her feet, Sweet Pea growled low in her throat. Swallowing down the fear that rose, Regan scooped up her pet and climbed back into the bed.

Something strange was going on at the fort. She knew it as sure as she breathed. Even she knew patrols didn't normally go out in the dead of night. Not unless something was wrong.

Fear for her father caused her to bite her lip until she tasted the stinging copper taste of blood. Was he in danger?

Perhaps she would agree to his demand she stay the month after all. Someone needed to look after him. Not that he'd appreciate it one bit. But she intended to see he stayed safe and alive, whether he wanted her concern or not.

Branded Wolf streaked the war paint across his cheek. Tonight he prepared for war. And for final vengeance.

Tonight he stood as the lone Apache warrior, trained by his father and his uncle. He would avenge their deaths. The white half of him had been buried deep within for this night. The trap was ready and waiting. He'd left an easy trail for them to follow, then he'd ringed his camp with small rocks. Now the only thing left to do was to wait.

He tossed his buckskin shirt across the saddle on the ground. His horse, Wind Dancer, shifted uneasily and pawed the ground.

"Easy," Branded Wolf whispered his reassurance. He'd left his mount ground-tied in case they needed to ride quickly.

One last glance around assured all was readied.

He lay on the ground, one hand under his head and the other hand on his Colt .45, waiting. The metal was smooth beneath his fingers and reassuring.

They would come. He was certain of it.

He'd ensured the white-eyes knew of his presence with his display outside the fort. A rare smile tipped his lips. The arrow had sent the cowardly bluecoat scurrying, but the woman had faced him with courage and arrogance. The same arrogance she'd shown on the train earlier. What did the beauty have to do with the bluecoat? Did she belong to him?

He pushed her out of his thoughts. Tonight was the night he'd waited for. By then the killers knew he'd camped outside the fort. The men would be unable to resist the bait he'd laid out for them—himself.

Around him, the air was heavy as if it, too, knew what was to come, and it also waited for his vengeance. He breathed in silence.

High above him hung a dark, now-moonless sky. He gazed up at it. The velvety blackness seemed to envelop him, making him one with the sky. Unfortunately, it would aid his would-be-killers more than him.

Suddenly, he felt the air around him go still and quiet. Too quiet.

The white-eyes had come.

He could sense their presence. Could feel them in the unearthly quiet where now not even an animal stirred in the darkness. He forced himself to lie still, allowing the men easy entry to his trap.

A rock rolled noisily under a careless footstep, and the waiting was over. Now the white-eyes knew their element of surprise was stolen away. Branded Wolf rolled to his feet, ready to spring his own trap. But he'd made a deadly mistake.

Too many shadows rushed his camp. More than two times the number of men he'd expected. Or prepared for.

His trap had netted too large a catch to hold. He'd be overrun and outgunned.

Gunfire erupted, bullets thudding into the dirt around him and ricocheting off the rocks. He dove for his horse, returning the gunfire. He heard the cry of a wounded man and smiled.

The next instant a slug slammed into his shoulder, nearly taking him to the ground. His gun slipped from his grip. Pain seared his flesh, and he clenched his jaw shut against the instinctive outcry. He would never call out in pain to the white-eyes.

And he wouldn't let them take him alive. Neither was he ready to die. Not yet.

Reaching deep within for the last burst of strength, he grabbed hold of his horse's dark mane and swung himself onto his mount's back. He lay low over the bay's back, using his own knees to give the silent command.

The horse leapt forward, racing like the wind he'd been named for. Wind Dancer ran with the endurance and speed of a well-trained Apache warhorse. Bullets zinged through the darkness, and Branded Wolf prayed for Wind Dancer's safety. The horse had been a gift from his father, now all that remained of his memory.

One last bullet fired too low skimmed across the horse's front leg. The horse stumbled, nearly taking them both to the ground, then Wind Dancer stayed true to his name and gathered the strength to race onward.

Shouts and the sound of scrambling men echoed through the dark night. Thankfully, his mount had the speed and the cover of darkness to assist his flight into the night. They rode hard.

At last spent, Wind Dancer slowed to a walk and then stopped. Branded Wolf knew the horse was near exhaustion; he'd given nearly all he had to give. He could have pressed for more, but he wouldn't.

He wouldn't destroy Wind Dancer to save himself. Smoothing a hand over his mount's neck in silent thanks, he slid to the ground. As he reached out to check the animal's leg, a wash of dizziness hit him hard.

Branded Wolf staggered and tried to right himself. He

pressed his fist against the wound in his shoulder, and the warmth of blood spread through his fingers.

He had to stop the bleeding. He had to bind the wound. But first he had to care for Wind Dancer.

He stepped forward toward the proud horse and crumpled to the ground.

A black void sucked him down. Down . . . down into utter darkness.

Chapter Three

The next morning Regan looked around the bright, sunny fort. Across the parade ground, Captain Larkin stood waiting for her beside two saddled horses. Hoping for rain to cancel her ride with the captain had been an effort in futility.

He waved to her, and she nearly grimaced. He looked like he'd wait until a certain place froze over, not that it was likely in the heat shimmering over the dry ground beneath her feet.

"Oh, stars and heavens," she muttered under her breath. "Why couldn't he have changed his mind?"

After all, he'd proved cowardly enough last night when the handsome Apache had paid a visit. She let her mind wander to him. She wondered what was behind his strange visit. He had looked magnificent on his horse. And he'd had the effrontery to acknowledge her with a wave of his hat. She should be insulted, but instead she felt strangely flattered.

A playful tug on the ribboned leash from Sweet Pea

brought Regan back to the matter at hand—her upcoming ride with her father's chosen, Captain Larkin.

With a groan she caught up a handful of her skirt and took slow, dainty steps across the parade ground. Sweet Pea pranced along beside her, the blue ribbon leash tied around her neck bobbing with her steps. Two small bows held the dog's white hair back out of her ebony eyes.

Matching blue bows were artfully pinned among Regan's sun-touched curls. She'd tried her best to look out of place and appear every inch the Philadelphia society lady. The yards of blue muslin making up her flounced skirt swayed with each step she took, and sunlight shimmered off the sapphire-blue satin sash tied around her waist.

She'd been certain also to wear her two fanciest petticoats. A bit overdone and not exactly fashionable, but it served her purpose of looking overdressed while also ensuring to make riding a horse for any time an impossible feat.

It would most assuredly guarantee a short ride with the captain.

As she felt a trickle of perspiration she almost wished for a riding habit in place of the layers of petticoats, but she hadn't packed one. Not that she'd have worn a sensible riding habit anyway. The purpose of her morning's ride was to reinforce her unsuitability to her father's proposed choice of husband.

At the moment the prospective suitor stood not more than ten feet from her, holding the reins of a sorrel and a small white mare. Regan barely bit back the grimace of distaste for both the man and the docile-looking mount she knew he'd chosen for her.

Back home in Philadelphia she rode a spirited black. She didn't have the patience or the temperament for this placid white mare. Not only that, the mare's gentleness would make the ride slow and plodding and would scarcely aid her plan in the slightest.

She might as well be wearing a comfortable riding habit, but she'd never dreamed she'd be in need of a riding habit for a visit to her dying father.

Her dear, dying father.

The deceiver.

Anger darkened her eyes, and she snapped open her parasol. Sweet Pea growled at the sudden movement, then set into a barking fit.

Both the mare and the sorrel reared, jerking Captain Larkin off balance. He tightened his hold on the reins, but it was too late. The terrified horses bolted, dragging him along in their wake. Sweet Pea dashed after them, ready for a game of chase. The ribboned leash was yanked from Regan's hand before she could prevent it.

Chaos erupted in the fort. One soldier chased after the menagerie of horses, officer, and small white barking dog. A sergeant waved his arms to turn the runaway animals. Her father rushed out, yelling orders in a booming voice.

Regan stood with one hand over her mouth, trying to hold back her laughter. Things couldn't be going better. Surely the captain would give up his intention of marriage now. She twirled the parasol while she watched the fun.

At last someone stopped the runaway horses and assisted Captain Larkin to his feet. With the game over, Sweet Pea trotted obediently back to Regan's side. As her father strode forward, the dog ducked under her mistress's skirts.

Regan decided to speak first. "I don't suppose the captain will want to go riding now." Her lips twitched no matter how hard she tried to stop them.

"Why in the hell did you have to bring that dog?" her father asked. He grabbed the lacy blue parasol from her hand and snapped it closed.

Regan raised her chin in the gesture of defiance she knew irritated him. "I told you before, I don't go anywhere without her." She snatched her delicate parasol out of his hold.

"Why didn't you leave the dog in Philadelphia?" he shouted.

"Why didn't you leave me in Philadelphia?" she yelled back.

In an instant her father's anger deflated and he looked at her with a deep sadness in his eyes. "Because I hoped out here you'd amount to something and show some substance."

Regan stepped back as if he'd slapped her. She turned her back on her father before he could witness the pain his words brought. A lump tightened her throat, threatening to choke her next breath.

Why couldn't her papa love her? What was wrong with her that she didn't merit his love, or even his concern? Maybe if she were prettier . . . maybe if she tried harder . . .

Behind her, her father cleared his throat and strode away from her without uttering another word, much less an apology for his hurtful remark. She could feel his disappointment in the thud of his solid footsteps on the hard, dry ground.

Spotting Captain Larkin approach with a slight limp and a small rip in the knee of his pants, she grabbed at the distraction he offered. She refused to retreat to her room and suffer a lecture from her father.

"David, do you still want to take me riding?" She sent him her best smile.

He responded, preening under her attention. "Of course. I wouldn't let something like a runaway horse stop me."

Regan kept her smile in place and her words to herself. At the moment she had to get away from her father. She preferred even the ambitious officer's company to that of her father. Closing the distance between them, she slipped her hand over the captain's arm. "Shall we be on our way?"

Sweet Pea peeked her nose out from Regan's skirt, then ducked back. She trotted at her mistress's heels out of sight of the angry men. They approached the spot where a sergeant stood holding the reins of both horses. She noted his lips twitched uncontrollably, and she could feel Sweet Pea peeking out from her skirt.

As Captain Larkin held out his hand to assist Regan onto the mare, the little dog leapt out from under her skirts and nipped at his ankle.

"Sweet Pea, no." Regan bent down and scooped the dog into her arms.

Turning, she faced the captain with a smile. "I don't know why she doesn't like you, David. Perhaps you can become friends on the ride."

She noticed that he looked as if he'd like to strike someone, so she handed him her parasol to occupy his thoughts and keep his hands off her pet.

Regan turned her face away barely in time to hide a most unladylike grin. Sweet Pea and the captain were no more likely to become friends than she and the captain.

He cleared his throat. "Surely you'd prefer to leave the . . . dog with—"

"No, I wouldn't." She tightened her hold on Sweet Pea. If she left her pet in this dreadful place, who knew what might happen to her.

The captain's eyes narrowed and his jaw tightened beneath her blatant refusal of his wishes.

"If you don't feel up to our ride, I'll understand," she taunted him deliberately.

"You'll find me quite up to this."

"Very well, then, shall we be on our way?"

Regan handed her pet to the surprised sergeant and climbed up onto the sidesaddle without waiting for assistance. She didn't wish to feel the captain's hands on her in any manner. Before the men could react, she reached down and plucked her dog from the sergeant's arms.

"Enjoy your ride, ma'am," the sergeant said with a wide smile.

"Thank you." She nudged the docile mare and rode away from the men.

There was nothing for Captain Larkin to do but follow her. She could practically feel his anger at her insolence in the stiff way he sat his horse.

He attempted to punish her with his silence, but Regan actually preferred not having to make forced small talk. Her enjoyment of the ride was short-lived, as it turned out to be tedious and boring. She had no appreciation for the assortment of cacti, yuccas, and dust that surrounded them. Her layers of petticoats bunched beneath her, and it felt as if she were riding on a rock. She was hot and uncomfortable.

When he finally drew to a halt beside a water hole, Regan felt nothing but relief. At last she could dismount and shake out her skirts. It seemed as if they'd been plodding along forever on the horses.

She allowed the captain to assist her down, then she released Sweet Pea from her ribboned leash to run and explore. She knew her pet wouldn't stray far. Sweet Pea preferred the comfort of a lap or a satin pillow to the outdoors.

"Regan, leave the dog be and let's take a stroll." Captain Larkin took her hand in his.

Regan sighed. She knew what was coming and dreaded it. He'd feign interest in her and likely propose marriage, all to please her father. Oh, how she truly hated to hurt his feelings, but—

Unexpectedly, he pulled her against him and pressed his wet mouth over hers. He tasted like last night's leftover dinner, and Regan nearly wretched. She shoved him, but he only tightened his hold.

Regan pushed harder against his chest, but he didn't budge. A small frisson of fear inched up her back, along with his sweaty palms. She quenched her fear and let her anger have full rein.

She shoved against him with all her might. He'd soon learn she wasn't someone to toy with. His hold loosened slightly, but before she could act, he tightened his arms around her again. He ground his hips against her.

Swinging her foot back, she kicked out as hard as she could through the weight of her petticoats, but missed. Her foot skimmed bare air. The brief thought crossed her mind that if she didn't succeed soon, she might not be wearing those petticoats much longer if the captain had his way.

Fear gave her added strength, and she kicked again. This time her foot connected with his shin. He swore against her mouth, then increased the punishing pressure of his lips on hers.

Using all her strength, she pushed away. She succeeded in freeing one arm, but it was enough. Anger gave her the added strength, and she doubled her free hand into a fist and swung. She connected solidly with his cheek.

Captain Larkin staggered back a step. Regan took full advantage of the opportunity provided. She caught up her petticoats with both hands, yanking them out of her way. Then she took a deep breath and kicked out again, high and hard.

Her foot hit him square between his legs, and he doubled over, then crumpled to the ground. His yelp of pain brought only satisfaction to her. As he rolled to his side, holding himself, she didn't feel the tiniest bit of pity for him.

To add insult to injury, Sweet Pea came bounding over from her investigation of a nearby mesquite and lunged at the fallen man. She promptly sank her sharp little teeth into his backside.

Regan was certain his yell could be heard for miles around. She didn't care to be there when he recovered enough to get to his feet. Spying the horses, she called Sweet Pea, scooped her up into her arms, and ran to the mounts.

She glanced from the placid mare with her sidesaddle to

the strong, faster sorrel and promptly made her decision. She'd take the faster mount and leave the white mare for the captain. A giggle slipped out at the image of the officer perched sidesaddle on the small mare.

A groan from the man on the ground made her hurry. Hooking her dog under one arm, Regan hiked up her petticoats and reached for the saddle. The horse took one wide-eyed look at the bundle of fluffy petticoats billowing around and shied to the side.

Regan barely caught herself in time to avoid tumbling to the ground. Shifting her hold on her dog, she dragged her petticoat and skirt to one side and murmured assurances to the horse.

She would get up on the animal. She wasn't about to leave the faster horse behind. But she knew she'd better do it soon, before the captain recovered sufficiently.

A mixed curse and groan from the ground behind her gave her all the impetus she needed. She'd kill the captain before she submitted to him.

Catching hold of the pommel with her free hand, she lifted her foot and after two tries set it in the stirrup. As the horse pranced to one side, she held on to the pommel of the saddle, not caring a whit how much ankle her fancy gown revealed. Hanging on tight, she flung herself up. She hung suspended for the space of a terrified breath, then landed in the saddle with a *thump*.

The horse took off at a wild gallop, and Regan held on for dear life. Sweet Pea whimpered in her lap, but she ignored her. She had to focus her full concentration on staying in the saddle. Her petticoats flapped around her legs, stinging her calves.

She bit her lip and ignored the impulse to straighten her skirts. She had more important things to attend to, such as escaping from the captain and his not so gentlemanly intentions.

When she informed her father of what happened, Captain Larkin would be sorry. She'd see to it.

Captain Larkin sucked in a breath and nearly yelled aloud at the pain. He didn't know what pained him worse—his back side or his front.

His thoughts of Regan were far from charitable just then. When he caught up with her, he'd teach her the lesson she so richly deserved, and then he'd feed her dog to the coyotes.

Staggering to his feet, he remained bent over until his breathing evened. Then he stood upright and turned to the horses. At the sight of the lone mare, he swore until his throat hurt.

He continued swearing all the way to the horse. The woman would pay dearly for both her act of defense and his humiliation. It took three tries for him to climb aboard the lady's sidesaddle. When at last he succeeded, the saddle struck him solidly in his injured groin.

The mare trotted with a bouncing gait that pained his every breath. When he caught up with Regan McBain . . .

It took less than a quarter hour of trailing her, falling farther and farther behind, for him to realize he'd never catch up with her. Then a more important realization struck him. The fool woman was riding *away* from the fort into the desert.

And straight into Apache territory.

He gave her plight only a moment of regret. She'd either perish in the desert or be captured by the hated Apaches. She deserved whatever disgusting thing the savages would do to her.

Another thought quickly replaced his revenge. What would he tell her father?

Thinking on it a moment, a thin smile settled on his lips. He'd tell the colonel the truth. They were attacked by a band of Apache, and he'd been injured in the fight. He'd embellish the tale of his valiant defense of the colonel's only daughter. However, regrettably, the savages had taken Miss McBain, ripping her from his protective arms. Oh, yes, he'd use this to his advantage. Maybe now the colonel would attack the Indians like he'd been encouraging him to do.

Captain Larkin slowed his horse to a halt. He stared off into the distance for a moment, and his smile widened to a grin.

"Good riddance, Miss McBain," he called out, then turned his mount back toward the fort.

The desert sun beat down mercilessly on Branded Wolf where he lay sprawled on the unforgiving ground. At last the heat from the blazing sun penetrated the velvet blackness that had enveloped him for countless hours. He stirred, and a shaft of pain brought him fully to consciousness, then took his breath away.

He laid his head back down on the hard, sandy ground and sucked in the dry air through clenched teeth. His shoulder felt as if an arrow had seared it and remained within the skin.

As he searched his mind, memory of his baited trap and the ambush that followed returned in short bursts, accompanied by both the pain of his bullet wound and of his failure. He licked his cracked, parched lips and pushed himself up to a sitting position.

Have to get out of the sun, he thought, but his mind refused to take the order. He ran his tongue over his lips again. His body begged for water. Glancing up at the round, glaring sun halfway across the sky, he knew it was well into the morning, nearing the most intense heat of midday.

He had to find shade. Or he'd die. And so might Wind Dancer.

Knowing this, he found the strength to stand, then nearly

crumpled back to the hard, unforgiving desert ground with his first step. He staggered, then righted himself. He must have lost a lot of blood. A look back down at the red-stained sand confirmed this. His lifeblood discolored the sand.

Tentatively, he examined his wound. The blood had dried in the sun and caked his skin. He would leave it for now and attend to it once he reached shade.

Sucking in his breath, he let out a soft whistle. From nearby he heard the answering nicker of Wind Dancer. He closed his eyes in silent thanks. His proud horse still lived.

The bay trotted to him with an uneven gait. Blood caked the animal's foreleg, and for an instant Branded Wolf felt the horse's pain. He reached out and brushed his hand down his horse's neck, then, leaning against him, he checked the animal's foreleg.

Thankfully, the bullet had only grazed the horse. Branded Wolf knew Wind Dancer was in better shape than himself. But it was up to him to save his horse and himself.

"We will make it, Wind Dancer. We'll make it," he vowed, straightening up and patting the proud animal's neck.

Squinting against the sun, he searched the surrounding area. In the distance he spotted the life-saving shadow of an outcropping of rocks. Shade.

He led his beloved horse toward their salvation with slow, beleaguered steps. If they took it easy, they would make it. At least he prayed they would.

Regan slowed her horse to a walk and, shading her eyes with one hand, studied the area around her. Absolute desolateness greeted her.

Heat shimmered in waves from the sand, giving the ground an ethereal appearance. The landscape was unbroken all the way to the horizon save for a scattering of cholla and prickly pear cactus.

Shouldn't she have reached the fort by then?

She lifted her damp hair away from her neck. Her thick curls hung limply in the heat. Letting the hair drop back to her neck, she waved her hand back and forth in front of her face to generate a breeze. It didn't do a whit of good.

Oh, stars and heavens, it was hot.

She closed her eyes halfway and looked up at the bright sun. It blazed down on her. She was perspiring, tired, and thirsty.

And lost.

She sniffed and wiped her nose with her hand. She knew it was unladylike, but she didn't care. It was too hot to care about anything but getting back to the fort.

It was all that stupid Captain Larkin's fault. If he hadn't attacked her, she wouldn't have run off and ended up *here.* What she wanted to do was stomp her feet and scream out her frustration.

She looked around her at the prickly-looking cactus and dry ground. Exactly where was *here?* And where on earth was the fort?

Where was she?

She glanced back over her shoulder. No sight of Captain Larkin. She'd lost him.

Sweet Pea whimpered in her lap. When Regan bent her head to reassure her with a pat, the little dog gave her a dry kiss.

"I'm sorry, Sweetie. I'm afraid I not only lost the dreadful captain, I lost us as well."

Nudging her horse into an easy walk, she pressed on without a single idea of where she was going. But anywhere was better than the middle of the desert.

It was all her deceitful father's fault. If he hadn't lied to her and brought her out there under false pretenses . . .

She gnawed on her lower lip. Would her papa be looking

for her? Or would he simply consider himself well rid of her and the troubles she brought?

Not that she'd blame him. She had been pretty terrible since her arrival. But he'd made her so angry.

She brushed a hand across her eyes, then raised her chin in resolute determination. This wilderness wouldn't get the best of her. Under the sun's heat she felt sweat trickle between her breasts. She suddenly recalled that the captain had lashed her parasol to his saddle. Drawing back on the reins, she pulled the horse to a stop.

Attempting to shove her petticoats to one side, she searched for the parasol. Feeling around beneath the weight of her petticoats, her fingertips brushed the wood handle of the parasol. With a sigh of relief she unhooked it and flicked it open.

Sweet Pea growled in response to the sudden movement and accompanying whoosh of air.

"Oh, shush, Sweetie. It will make us cooler."

As if it could get any hotter, she thought. Under the layers of petticoats she was miserable. She unfastened the top two buttons of her bodice and fanned herself with the fabric. At least no one was around to see her.

It was hot. Why, she was positively sweating. Her mama would be furious if she could see her. A small laugh escaped Regan's lips. Her mama wasn't likely to ever see her again, unless she found the fort.

Where in hell was the fort!

Frustrated, she pulled the reins tight. The hopelessness of her situation struck her. She was probably going to die in the terrible wilderness that she hated so much.

As the disparaging thought pressed her, she stiffened in the saddle. Smoothing her hand over the dog's ruffled fur, Regan drew in a deep breath. She wasn't giving up. Not by a long shot.

She adjusted her parasol to block the sun's rays and

nudged the horse onward. That was better than sitting in the sun, waiting for death. Regan pressed on without glancing back.

At last she couldn't go on any farther without a rest. As she drew her horse to a stop, she shaded her eyes, and a movement in the distance caught her gaze.

She blinked and looked again. A horse?

She was saved!

Regan kicked her heels into the horse's side and urged him on with words of assurance. Surely it was a troop of cavalry sent out to search for her. She'd been found at last.

As she drew nearer, she stared in shock. The troop of cavalry consisted of one horse. One lone, riderless horse.

She swallowed, her throat suddenly dry.

The horse stood with neither a rider nor a saddle. The animal's head was down in defeat and obviously in pain. As Regan stared, the horse turned his head and nickered softly. Her soft heart went out to the injured animal.

Unable to turn away from any hurt animal, Regan swung down from the saddle. Her legs nearly gave out from under her when she took a step, and she steadied herself against the side of the sorrel for a moment.

Holding Sweet Pea close, Regan eased her way toward the injured horse. Murmuring words of reassurance, she held out a hand to the animal. Her special touch with animals didn't fail her. The horse didn't shy away or bolt, but instead softly nuzzled her palm.

Regan set Sweet Pea down on the ground. Instantly, the dog trotted over to a scraggly bush and stretched out in the meager patch of shade. Assured her pet was safe, she turned her attention to the injured horse. It took only a glance to find the wound on the foreleg.

She retrieved the canteen from the captain's saddle and returned to the injured animal. Gently, she washed away the caked blood with her kerchief, then tied it around the wound.

How could an owner leave such a beautiful creature alone and in pain?

Anger rose up in her. She would dearly love to give the owner a piece of her mind.

A bird whistled nearby, and the horse nickered in return. Regan marveled at the horse's reaction. Then came the sound of a human call from a nearby outcropping of rocks. Still angry over the abandonment of the injured animal, Regan crossed to the rocks without thinking of the consequences.

On the other side of the rocks she spotted a man sitting in the shade. Her temper soared. Why, he had heartlessly left his horse injured and standing in the sun, while he rested in the cool shade. Everything in her rose to the animal's defense.

Regan stepped forward, hands planted on her hips. The man's head was lowered, resting on his chest.

"How heartless can you be?" she accused him. "How could you leave your—"

He suddenly stood to his feet in a quick movement, and her voice left her. The next instant, with a lightning-fast move, he reached out and grabbed her.

Regan tilted her head back and looked up into a familiar pair of startling blue eyes.

"You," she whispered.

Chapter Four

Branded Wolf blinked against the glare of the sun. He wavered unsteadily and tightened his hold on whatever was keeping him upright.

He stared down at the woman before him. He'd been lying out in the desert heat too long. Or lost too much blood. He had to be delirious. Or dead. His mind was being visited by people from his past.

Before him stood the white woman from the train, more beautiful than that day, now clothed in a pale gown of softest blue. She faced him, standing proud and defiant, with a light of recognition in her green eyes.

Surely she was a vision. Today her eyes were far from the cool color of a soothing green meadow he remembered. Instead, they flashed with the anger of a storm-tossed sky in the midst of a thunderstorm. His vision was very angry with him.

What had he done to anger her?

Squinting, he struggled to remember. Scattered pieces of

memory brushed his mind like grits of sand blown along
by the hot wind.

The woman . . . a little dog . . . the white-eyes' scorn . . .

He struggled to clear his mind. On the train he'd given
her back her dog unharmed, if one could call that little piece
of fur a dog. He fought the grayness clouding his mind. Had
he kissed her then? No, he hadn't kissed her tempting lips—
only thought about it.

He blinked, but the vision standing before him remained.
Damp tendrils of hair clung to her cheeks, enticing him to
brush them away. Her fair cheeks now held the pink of sun-
touched skin. He couldn't resist the temptation offered him.
He lifted one hand from her shoulder, and a wave of dizziness
hit him with enough force to make him stagger beneath it.

Unsteady, he grabbed hold of the vision again, this time
to keep himself upright. Then he realized she felt real beneath
his hands. Her bones were small under the blue material
covering her smooth skin. Yes, she felt real.

Too real for a vision brought on by the heat of the sun.

Branded Wolf stared down at the woman in confusion.
What was she doing here?

Regan stared up into the blue eyes she remembered so
well. He was the half-breed Apache from the train. The
conductor had called him Branded Wolf.

He was different today. More the savage Apache than
he'd appeared on the train. The only thing about him to
remind her that he was part white was his blue eyes. And
even they held an intenseness that she'd never seen in a
white man's eyes before.

She could sense a fierceness about him that almost frightened her, but instead, it held her enthralled and unable to
move. She stared, fascinated. A hum of excitement coursed
through her body as if she stood on the edge of a very high
cliff with an approaching storm.

He remained silent, then shifted his stance. A look akin

to pain crossed his face, and that's when she first noticed the streaks of paint across his high cheekbones. The color stood out starkly against his sun-darkened skin. An oddly colored red was smeared haphazardly across one cheek and ran along his chin and down the side of his throat.

Regan swallowed. Once. Twice. Fear overcame her strange excitement. Even she recognized blood when she saw it.

Her stomach churned, and she swallowed deeply to calm it. She never could stand the sight of blood. Fear began to gnaw at her. She was alone in the desert with a man—no, with a savage Apache—who had done heaven knew what. She attempted to breathe evenly and not show any sign of outward fear.

Why would he have blood smeared across his face? And whose blood was it?

Fear overcame her fascination. She tried to swallow past the lump in her throat, but she couldn't. While on the stagecoach she'd heard stories about the fearsome and brutal Apache. Those few scattered stories she'd heard of the Indians' violence returned to her mind full force, rocking her already shaky confidence.

She'd heard they tortured their captives. And she was most assuredly his captive now.

The thought struck her, giving her the urge to fight for her freedom. She had to escape. She couldn't be any Indian's captive, especially not one of the feared Apache.

Branded Wolf sensed her fear, could almost smell it in his nostrils. The widening of her eyes gave him warning in time to avoid her sudden attack. He shifted his weight to the side, and the first blow of her foot struck only air, her heavy petticoats hampering her movements.

For an instant he wondered at this. He'd never seen a woman dressed like her for a ride in the desert.

No, she didn't belong in this land of his people. She was

all ruffles and lace with her fancy gown, petticoats sticking out from under her hem, and skin too fair for the desert heat. From the corner of his eye he spotted a blue parasol lying near a white muff. What kind of fool woman would bring a fur muff to use in the spring? And in the desert?

He'd laugh if he had the strength to waste. But keeping hold of the now-struggling white woman and avoiding the blows of her feet was taking all his warrior's strength.

He knew he should set her free . . .

He wanted to set her free . . .

But he couldn't.

She'd head straight back to the soldiers to tell them where to find him, and she'd run into the band of men masquerading as Apache. If that happened, she'd get them both killed.

If she didn't succeed in killing him herself first, he thought as he tried to sidestep her next kick. This time her foot connected with his shin. He bit back a muffled groan. She packed a wallop for such a little thing.

Using all his weakening strength, he dragged her closer to halt her attack. He had no wish to harm her, only to keep her from fleeing. At her soft whimper he eased his harsh hold as much as he dared.

Looking down into her face, he saw the mixture of fear and anger there. Her cheeks were flushed with her efforts, and her eyes shone her fury. She trembled ever so slightly beneath his hands, but the stiffening of her spine told him she was fighting her fear, refusing to give it any power over her.

He'd never seen such a courageous white woman before. She stirred his blood in spite of his injuries. He gazed at the pulse beating in her throat; it fluttered like the wings of a frightened butterfly. His hands gentled on her arms.

Regan stilled and stared into his eyes for the space of a heartbeat. He had the most incredible deep blue eyes she'd ever seen. As she gazed up at him, she saw his eyes darken with a hunger that most assuredly didn't come from his belly.

She knew that look.

The hunger seemed palpable between them, almost reaching out and touching her with a heat all its own. At the growing warmth in his gaze, she recalled her previous experience with the captain.

Captain Larkin had practically the same look back at the water just before he'd forced himself on her. Not again, she vowed. She hadn't subjected herself to the captain's desires, and she wasn't about to submit now either. She realized Branded Wolf's tight hold had lessened. It was all the opening she needed.

Before he could sense her intention, she struck out with both fists against his chest, sending him stumbling backward. He sucked in his breath, wincing against the pain that followed.

Suddenly, she jerked free and spun away from him. Grabbing up her skirts with both hands, she raced toward the spot where her white muff lay discarded. He had to stop her. He shoved himself away from the rocks and forced his body to move with as much speed as he could gather.

Before she could flee more than a few paces, he caught up with her. He spun her around and pulled her to him. She slammed into his chest, nearly knocking him down.

She struggled against him, kicking and trying to elbow him. The battle threw him off balance, and he felt his feet go out from underneath him. His bulk sent them both tumbling to the ground. She landed atop him with a jolt that took his breath.

They both lay still for the space of a long breath. Her soft curves pressed into him, reminding his body that he was a man. A warrior trained to take what he wanted. And right then he wanted her.

Branded Wolf never imagined the fiery white woman

would feel so good in his arms. At first he'd intended only to stop her from fleeing and giving away his position to those who wanted him dead. Even then they could still be out there waiting for him ... waiting to finish the job they started when they ambushed him and left him for dead.

Damn, but she felt good in his arms. She was soft and womanly. And when her hair brushed against his cheek, he noticed that she smelled of flowers. He closed his eyes and inhaled deeply, unable to stop himself.

It was as if his act released her from whatever had held her still. She pushed her small fists against his chest and wiggled against him. Her movements caused him to suck in his breath sharply. If she knew what her movements were doing to him ...

She reared back suddenly and drew up her right knee. Once again her petticoats hampered her movements, thankfully cushioning her blow.

Branded Wolf clamped his arms around her, drawing her closer. Too close to do him any damage except to his senses.

Or so he thought. Unexpectedly, her elbow jabbed his ribs, sinking in sharply. Damn.

As he struggled to subdue her without harming her, the fancy lady's white fur muff he'd spotted lying on the ground came to life in the form of a fur ball of yapping defense. It launched itself at his legs.

A feeling like sharp cholla cactus spines sank into his ankle. He let loose a yell.

The woman kicked and pushed and wiggled until he thought she'd actually free herself. Using all his remaining strength, he rolled to his uninjured side. If he could get her beneath his weight, he could hold her. If not ...

The next instant he heard a shrill bark at his ear. It echoed through his head. Then once again sharp cactus spines caught at his ankle. And pulled.

Pulled? He raised his head slightly to glance at his legs.

A white ball of fur had attached itself to his left leg and was furiously tugging at the leg of his buckskin pants.

"What the—" he began to say, but never got to finish.

The woman took full advantage of his momentary distraction. She jabbed her elbow into his injured side. Pain seared through his body, and he thought he called out, but he wasn't sure.

The darkness threatened him again. He fought it but lost the battle. The darkness returned to claim him, taking him down in its fierce hold.

Regan felt the Apache's firm grip grow slack and didn't question it. Instead, she rolled to her feet, shoving her petticoats out of her way. She caught up her skirt to free her legs, and bolted. In the dry heat she ran out of breath much too soon. Daring to glance over her shoulder, she saw that instead of coming after her, Branded Wolf lay still.

Deathly still.

Sweet Pea released his pants leg to race over to join her mistress. Once there, she growled low in her throat, then trotted back to where he lay. Cocking her head, she studied him a minute.

Regan watched the act with nervous awareness. Would he sit up? Come after her? She sucked in several breaths of air.

Sweet Pea lunged and caught his pants leg again. He didn't respond. She tugged, then sat back on her haunches and waited. When he didn't move, she whined and looked at Regan in puzzlement.

Regan studied his still form for another full minute. Surely he was playacting? Wasn't he?

He didn't move. In fact, she couldn't tell if his chest even rose and fell with breath. She gnawed on her lower lip, wondering.

Had she hurt him? Surely not!

Why would a healthy man up and collapse?

The answer was easy. He wouldn't. Not unless he was faking, or wasn't as healthy as she first thought.

Regan leaned forward, then took a tentative step closer. She studied his face. The war paint stood out in stark definition, following the line of his cheekbones. She noticed that the skin around the bright color held a strange pallor. She released her lower lip from between her teeth and swallowed.

She took another hesitant step toward where he lay, half expecting him to rise up and grab for her. Nothing happened. She glanced around, and her gaze settled on the strange discoloration against the rock. Blood? She was sure of it. And it was the same rock he'd been leaning against when she found him.

She stared at the bloodstained rock. Then she looked from the rock back to the man on the ground. He'd been wounded.

Unable to leave anyone hurt and in need, she debated as to whether to help him or flee on the horse while she could. Her soft heart warred with her selfish desire for her freedom. She looked back at the Apache lying crumpled on the ground.

He wasn't moving.

She should escape while she had the chance. Before he awoke. Before . . .

She turned away and took a hesitant step forward toward her horse, then stopped. He could die out here alone.

He could kill her if he awoke and caught her again. But something inside her told her he wouldn't hurt her. She stood still, waiting. This indecision plaguing her was insanity.

She should leave him where he lay. She should take the chance she'd been given and run. She should . . .

"Oh, stars and heavens!"

As she stood there, his horse nickered. Her decision was made. She'd stay and nurse the injured man. She couldn't abandon both an injured man and his injured horse, could she?

Regan caught up her skirt and turned back around. Muttering under her breath with every step, she stomped back straight toward the injured Apache.

Sweet Pea followed in her wake, prancing beside her as if this were all a grand adventure.

Captain David Larkin swallowed down the bitter taste of fear in his throat as he withstood Colonel McBain's scrutiny. It was as if his commander were looking into his very soul and not liking what he found there.

"You left my daughter in the desert?" Colonel McBain nearly shouted the question.

Captain Larkin tried not to flinch. If he showed the slightest hesitation by action or words, the commander would know he was lying.

"No, sir. I told you the Apaches attacked us." He stared at the toes of his boots. "They took her and the horse. I wasn't given a choice."

"But you left her there—"

"No, sir. I fought for her, but there were too many of them. Damned Apaches." He spat out the last word as if it were something rotten.

"Why did they let you go?"

Larkin tried to look embarrassed. "I was knocked down. Unconscious. They thought I was dead."

Colonel McBain placed his hands behind his back and rocked forward. "Explain to me how you could return without her?"

This time Larkin nearly flinched at the anger behind the question. "I had no choice, sir. When I came to, they were already gone. I rode back here to tell you. Surely, you—"

He fell silent and shifted underneath his commander's anger.

"I'm waiting." The two words were an order.

Larkin was silent a moment before answering. He had to

word this right. His future hung in the balance. Maybe his damn life as well. If the colonel learned the truth of what happened on that ride . . .

Suffice it to say, his career would be ruined. And he might end up spending his days in the stockade. Damn, what a position. And all because Miss High-and-Mighty McBain thought she was too good for him.

She wouldn't be too good for the redskin Apaches. The lot of them would have her, and none too pleasantly either, he'd bet. He bit his cheek to hold in the smile of sudden glee.

He straightened under the colonel's glare. He had nothing to worry about if he kept his head. There was no way the colonel would ever find out the truth about that ride. No, he was certain the haughty Miss McBain was dead by then. Or wished she were.

"Colonel, I know how you feel—"

"Don't presume to know that."

"Sir, she's your daughter, but"—Larkin paused and sighed deeply for effect—"but she was going to be my *wife.*"

Larkin bowed his head and dragged his hand down his face. "That's why we'd stopped. We'd dismounted, walked away from our horses." He put one hand over his mouth and took a long breath, then continued as if forced to utter painful words. "It's all my fault."

"That is exactly how I see it." Colonel McBain remained standing, stiff and untouched.

Damn, he'd have to put more emotion into this for sure, or he was going to end up locked in the stockade before nightfall. An idea dawned on him. If he could shift the blame, perhaps he'd get out of this and retain the colonel's trust. It was no secret that the colonel had no use for his daughter's fancy eastern ways and spoiled impertinence.

"Normally, I knew better than to ride so far from the

fort. But Regan . . ." Larkin paused to close his eyes and sigh.

When he opened his eyes, the colonel had stepped closer to him.

"She what?"

"I was taken with her. Still am," he quickly corrected himself in case the colonel took offense.

"What's that got to do with this?" the older man blustered.

"She kept insisting on riding farther. I wanted only to please her." Larkin threw back his head and released a groan. "I should have turned back right then and there. I should have demanded, but I didn't want to anger her. She doesn't take well to orders. I meant to turn back, but then . . ." He let the words trail off as if it hurt too much to say more.

"Then what?" Colonel McBain ordered, his voice sharp with what sounded like concern.

Larkin hesitated, wondering if he'd gone too far. Surely that hadn't been true concern he'd heard in the commander's question. The man obviously didn't care for his daughter, did he?

"What?" the colonel repeated, obvious concern edging his voice.

Larkin knew he had to continue. It was too late to turn back. He couldn't even consider telling the truth now. Not if the colonel cared the slightest for his daughter.

"Sir." He cleared his throat to dislodge a sudden lump of fear. He *had* to make the colonel believe him. "She challenged me to a race, and when I refused, she took off. Seeing her gallop across that treacherous desert." He shuddered ever so slightly. "But I'd . . . I'd made her angry."

Well, that part was true. She had been furious when she took his horse.

Colonel McBain's face hardened. "Why does she insist on letting her temper—"

"Sir," Larkin cut in with a pretense of defense. "Surely you can't blame her. It's me—" He paused and waited to see if his act of shifting blame in the colonel's mind to his daughter had worked.

"No." The colonel shook his head. "She's as headstrong as her mother." He sighed and closed his eyes for a moment, then stiffened his back. "I'll lead a company of men out immediately."

Was that concern again? Larkin sincerely hoped not, but it seemed he may have misconstrued the commander's relationship with his daughter. He swallowed the knot forming in his throat. Now it was more important than ever that the colonel never learn the truth.

"Sir, I'd proposed marriage. Finding her is my responsibility now." He raised his chin in a gesture of calculated defiance. "I'll lead the men myself. I won't rest until I find her."

"Thank you." Colonel McBain slumped his shoulders. "But I—"

"Sir, pardon my insolence, but you should remain here in case she returns on her own."

Not very damn likely. Larkin smirked to himself. He intended to insure she didn't return. If she were still alive.

Colonel McBain sighed and turned to stare out the window. "Bring her back to me."

The softly spoken words sounded more like a plea than an order. Larkin felt the start of trepidation snake up his back. He'd better see this to an end or else not return to the post.

"Captain." Colonel McBain didn't turn around. "Godspeed and good luck."

He continued to stare out the window. His daughter was somewhere out there, scared and alone. He prayed she was alone. Surely the young captain would find Regan. He brushed a hand over his mouth, for once not caring if his mustache was mussed.

"Captain, take a couple of the Indian scouts with you. Perhaps they'd be able to find her faster."

Captain Larkin nodded and, turning on his heel, strode out the door. He'd pick his men most carefully.

Colonel McBain rubbed his hand over his face. He swallowed unevenly. The captain and the men would find her, he attempted to assure himself, but it was hollow reassurance.

He didn't want to think about the alternative. They had to find her, and quickly.

Time would run out soon for his daughter. Regan didn't have the slightest idea how to survive out here. Maybe he'd been wrong in bringing her here. Her sharp words that morning about leaving her in Philadelphia returned to haunt him.

He'd done this only for her. He wanted to give her some foundation, some substance. He didn't want her to turn out like Elise, a woman who didn't have what it took to stand by her man.

His throat tightened at the memory of his lovely wife. He hadn't seen her in years, but she'd never been far from his thoughts.

His wife was on her way there. He knew it deep in his very bones.

How much time did he have until Elise McBain arrived at the fort? He paled at the thought of her fury when she learned what had happened. Within hours of her arrival, the entire fort would know of his failures. And there wasn't a single thing he could do to stop it.

Things couldn't get much worse.

His daughter was missing, and his estranged wife was on her way to the fort. Heaven help him when Elise McBain arrived.

All hell would break loose.

He couldn't tell her that Regan was missing. Lost in the desert and probably a prisoner of the Apaches. He closed his eyes. Maybe dead.

All he'd tried to do was find her a husband. Get her settled. Now look at how she had repaid him for his efforts. She'd rode off and gotten herself lost.

Where was his daughter?

Regan pushed her hair out of her eyes, and a blue bow fluttered to the ground. Her hair fell free, curls streaming down her back and into her eyes again. Gritting her teeth, she caught her hair back with one hand and grabbed her skirts with the other. Those petticoats were becoming more than an inconvenience. Sweat trickled down between her breasts again, and the satin sash chafed her waist. She rubbed her hand over her eyes.

She had to get Branded Wolf to some kind of shelter out of the sun. Even she knew that much.

Looking down at him, she studied the problem. He was big. And it was going to take every ounce of her strength to move him. Nibbling her lower lip, she glanced around the area, and her gaze rested on the outcropping of rocks where she'd encountered him.

Shade . . . shelter.

She eyed the distance between where she stood and the rocks. There was nothing to do but drag him. It was probably good that he was unconscious, because this would hurt like the very dickens if he were awake.

Bending down, she placed her hands under his shoulders. The heat of his skin startled her, and she almost pulled her hands back. His skin was firmly muscled beneath her fingertips.

She'd never touched a man's bare skin before. It felt slick

and smooth beneath her hands. And it caused her palms to tingle in the oddest manner. Without thinking what she was doing, she ran her fingertips across his muscled shoulder and over his broad chest.

Realizing what she'd just done, Regan gulped and pulled her trembling hand back. If he awoke to find her touching him, stroking his skin, she'd just die.

Chapter Five

Regan forced herself to slide her hand beneath Branded Wolf's shoulder again. She attempted to ignore the pleasurable feel of his damp bare skin against hers. She had to get him over to the rocks.

She kept muttering this to herself, pushing aside the thought of the smoothness of his firm muscles against her hands.

Gritting her teeth, she slid her hands lower and lifted him as gently as she could. She took a step back and pulled. He moved barely an inch.

Stars and heavens, the man was heavy!

She looked down at the stretched-out length of his body. He was tall and leanly muscled, and it didn't look as if he had an ounce of fat to his frame. Why, the top of her head would scarcely reach his shoulder. If he held her in his arms, why, he would surely . . .

Regan let out her breath in a heated rush and sucked in fresh air. She blamed the desert heat for her unladylike thoughts. She'd never in all her days entertained such thoughts about a man until then. But she'd never met a man like this one before, a little voice whispered.

Stomping her foot, she closed her mind against such thinking. She was stranded in the desert, for heaven's sake. How ever had she ended up in this predicament?

Here she was, lost in the desert, with an injured Apache and his horse. She was hot, sweating, and thirsty. Not to mention dusty. If her friends back in Philadelphia could see her now. Well, the thought didn't even bear thinking about— her friends weren't there to see her.

Or help her.

In fact, there wasn't another soul to help her. If she was going to survive this, she'd have to do so on her own. A sobering thought most assuredly.

With this in mind she redoubled her efforts to drag Branded Wolf to the rocks. Tensing her back, she pulled as hard as she could. His body moved several inches this time, and she nearly dropped her hold on him in relief. It was working.

She bent to her task again. Taking another deep breath, she tugged, then stopped to breathe in and out again. Then she pulled again.

After several attempts she got him to the shelter of the rocks at last. Once there, she eased his head and shoulders down, then sank down beside him to rest a moment, not giving a whit if she was sitting on the dirty ground with nothing to protect her gown. She wiped her sweating hands down her skirt.

Around them the heat shimmered in waves. She looked about the area, suddenly remembering her pet.

"Sweet Pea," she called out. Once. Twice.

The little dog landed in her lap a second later, burying her head in the folds of Regan's gown with a soft whine.

She knew just how the dog felt. She wanted to bury her head and cry too.

This was all the fault of that dreadful Captain Larkin. Why, she hoped he was still lying on the ground in pain for what he'd done to her. While he might be an officer, he certainly was no gentleman. She raised her chin and sniffed in disdain.

Neither is the man beside you, a little voice nagged at her.

Regan nibbled on her lip and stared down at the Apache. He seemingly slept peacefully, but she knew the sound sleep was caused by his injury. A horrible thought came to mind— had she killed him with her efforts to drag him to shade?

She rested her hand on his cheek and thankfully felt the warmth of his breath on her thumb. He'd survived her dragging him across the ground, but she still had to see to his injury. How badly injured was he?

Swallowing down the nervousness in her stomach that told her she couldn't do this, she gripped her courage in both hands. She'd seen her mama tend to the cook's injury once, and she'd also watched her help a maid who'd been cut. As long as she didn't let herself faint away at the sight and smell of blood, she'd be fine. Just fine, she assured herself.

With shaking hands she rolled Branded Wolf to his side, then gasped at what she saw. Blood and dirt caked an area just below his shoulder blade. The wound oozed blood, obviously from her dragging him by the shoulders. Her stomach lurched, but she forced herself to think of something beside the coppery smell of the blood.

Water. She needed water to clean the wound.

Standing on legs that were suddenly unsteady, Regan forced herself to walk to the horses and retrieve one of the captain's two canteens. A movement to her side caught her attention, and she jumped, then laughed in relief. She watched with a wan smile as Sweet Pea tugged the parasol, growling at it the entire time.

It gave her an idea. The parasol would provide additional shade. As soon as she tended to Branded Wolf, she'd set up the parasol somehow.

One of the horses nickered, and Regan clasped her hands over her mouth. She'd forgotten the poor things. The captain's horse needed to be unsaddled and watered. And she imagined the other horse needed water as well.

"Oh, stars and heavens," she muttered. "Be patient, boys," she assured the animals. "As soon as I finish playing nurse and doctor, I'll be back for you."

Guilt rushed over her. She hated to leave the horses, but the wounded Apache was in more serious condition just then. He could die without care. Pulling her skirts to one side, she turned back to him.

She could do this, she told herself over and over. She could.

Holding tight to the canteen, she crossed to where Branded Wolf lay unmoving. She couldn't stand the thought of him sleeping on the dirty ground. Surely it wouldn't be good for him.

Without another thought she raised her skirt and drew off one of the petticoats, then spread the white-ruffled material out on the ground for a blanket. As gently as she could she rolled Branded Wolf onto it on his stomach. Her own stomach churned in revolt at the wound in his back. She swallowed down the bile and caught up the canteen.

Kneeling beside him, she ripped off a strip of the last petticoat remaining beneath her skirt and dampened it with the water in the canteen. She wiped the blue cloth across his wound and had to pause to close her eyes once when she found the exit wound in his side.

Telling herself it had to be done, she set to cleaning and bandaging him as best she could. She only hoped she'd remembered enough from watching her mama. Finished at last, she eased him over onto his back and leaned her head against the rocks. She'd done it, she thought with pride, and without losing the contents of her stomach.

As she looked at the strips of pale blue petticoat wrapped around his chest and over his shoulder, her lips twitched. She wondered what an Apache warrior would think of being bound up in a lady's petticoat.

Sweet Pea whimpered softly, the parasol now held between her paws. She paused to pant a moment and seemed to be smiling at Regan in pride at her accomplishment of dragging the parasol all the way to the rocks. Seeing the parasol reminded Regan of her earlier idea. If she could prop the opened parasol up with the saddle, it would give them additional shade. She'd tend to that as soon as she finished with the horses.

Everything in her rebelled at the idea of leaving the animals another minute without water or care.

Thankfully, early on in her riding lessons in Philadelphia she'd insisted on learning how to care for her mount. Armed with that knowledge, she made short work of unsaddling the captain's horse and caring for both horses. She smiled at the sudden picture of the captain riding the white mare sidesaddle. That would teach him to toy with her.

Swiping her hair out of her eyes, she dragged the one saddle and blanket across the ground with both hands. She marveled a moment at the thought of Branded Wolf riding bareback. It was something she'd never been allowed to attempt.

Back at his side, she propped the saddle up against the rocks. The smelly horse blanket was dispatched of farther away and downwind. Then she dropped onto the ground and wiped her forehead.

A growl from Sweet Pea drew a smile. She hadn't budged from her spot guarding the parasol, which now looked a little worse for wear to Regan. She reached for the frilly parasol, but Sweet Pea grabbed it up in her mouth again. She backed away with her prize, tiny play growls coming from her throat.

Regan reached out again, and Sweet Pea jumped back, dragging the parasol with her. The handle showed it had lost the war with tiny teeth. The little dog wasn't going to take kindly to losing the new toy she'd worked so hard to claim as hers.

Regan lunged for the parasol and caught the edge of it. Sweet Pea tugged, and Regan heard the distinct sound of fabric ripping. She winced at it.

If she didn't get it away from her pet soon, there wouldn't be enough left to provide shade. A growl from the stubborn pup warned her just before the pup shook the parasol as hard as she could with a series of muffled woofs and low growls. Now the dilemma was how to get the blasted thing away from Sweet Pea without destroying it.

Regan ordered, cajoled, and finally caught the recalcitrant pup up in her arms when her patience ran out. Muttering dire threats she had no intention of carrying out, she pried the parasol loose from the tiny puppy teeth, flipped it fully open, and wedged it firmly upright with the saddle.

That accomplished, she sat down beside Branded Wolf. His darkened skin, almost the color of copper, contrasted sharply with the white of her petticoat beneath him. A lock of dark hair dangled across his forehead, and she gave in to the temptation to brush it back. The hair was silky beneath her fingers. She studied him, taking in each of his features, from the faint scar at his temple to his strong jaw and back to his painted cheekbones. She shivered.

The streaks of paint had to go. Her hands trembled as she dampened another strip of her petticoat. She washed his face, easing the damp cloth across his forehead and along his cheeks. He didn't stir under her awkward ministrations.

Noting his chapped lips, she dampened the edge of the washcloth again and smoothed it over his lips as gently as she could. Carefully, she trickled water past his lips.

His eyelids fluttered open, and then he was staring up into her own eyes. Regan's breath caught somewhere on its way to her throat and stuck there. He blinked and closed his eyes, then opened them eyes again, almost as if the action were an effort.

He raised one hand and pushed his fingers into the curls beside her cheek. He closed his fist around the hair and several strands wound around his fingers. Regan felt her own breath rush out between her lips. Her heart raced in her breast faster than ever in her life. She couldn't move if she had to and wasn't even considering doing so.

With the lightest of touches Branded Wolf tugged on the curls wrapped around his hand, slowly drawing her down to him. He didn't stop until Regan's face was only an inch above his. She didn't fight him.

Rising up slightly on his other elbow, he pressed his lips against hers and felt her soft gasp of surprise on his lips. He tasted her sweetness, then, smiling, he slid back down and into the darkness of sleep once again. His hand fell limp at his side, releasing her.

Regan stared at the unconscious man. Had she imagined the kiss?

She ran her fingertips over her lips and could still feel the pleasant moistness from their kiss. No, she hadn't imagined it.

She glanced around, uncertainty making her swallow hard. Everything remained exactly as it was before the kiss. The saddle and blanket still rested on the ground; the parasol still blocked the sun. The only thing different was her.

She focused on the dusty horse blanket. The blanket might come in handy if what she'd heard about cold desert nights was true.

Regan stopped at the thought of nightfall and gulped. She wouldn't allow herself to think of the coming night. Of sleeping with the Apache.

She forced herself to think of her father. Was he looking for her? Or did he even care that she was lost? She tried to picture her father's face, but the only one she could see was Branded Wolf.

The man was riding fast and hard. Straight for the fort.

Colonel McBain shielded his eyes from the sun and studied the man's approach. Disappointment caught at his breath. The rider was coming from town. He wouldn't be bringing news of Regan.

With a deeply instilled sense of dread he watched the lone rider approach. It always seemed to him that a lone rider spelled trouble.

The man drew his horse to a stop and dismounted with a huff. He was obviously in a hurry. He appeared to spot the commander immediately, and headed straight for Colonel McBain.

"You the colonel?" the man asked, slapping his hat on his thigh.

A cloud of dust rose up from the contact, and he stifled his instinctive cough. "Yes, I'm Colonel McBain." He stiffened to attention out of habit.

Without another word the man reached into his breast pocket and withdrew a folded piece of paper. He extended it.

Colonel McBain took the paper and hesitated a moment The parchment was of the finest and held the monogram M. It couldn't be.

The growing sense of dread settled deep in the pit of his stomach even before he unfolded the missive. Then he read the flowing script, and his stomach sank even further, if possible.

Elise.

He'd known it was from his wife even before he'd recognized her writing. Before he'd seen the monogram she always used in any correspondence to him. However, something in him had still hoped he was wrong, hoped the note was from someone else. Anyone else.

He swallowed, his mouth suddenly dry.

He read the words, then cleared his throat and reread the words, although he didn't need to do so. They were burned into his mind.

> *Dearest Carson,*
>   *Am on my way. Have my daughter ready when I arrive. We'll talk then.*
>
>   *Ever,*
>   *Elise Wentworth McBain*

He knew his face paled. She just had to taunt him by throwing in her maiden name, didn't she? He closed his eyes and swallowed his irritation. Of more concern was her coming arrival.

How long did he have?

"Yup, the lady was sure right as rain." The rider slapped his hat on his thigh again and chortled. "Said you'd be real surprised. Yup."

Colonel McBain fixed the man with a hard stare. He didn't share the man's good humor, far from it. The word *surprise* denoted something pleasant. This event was far from it.

"You spoke to Mrs. McBain?" the colonel asked, realizing the importance of the rider's words. His own voice was uneven, almost ragged.

"Yessiree. She asked me to ride straight here and deliver

that there message to the colonel.'' He smiled widely. ''Paid me right well too if'n I could beat the covered coach here.''

''Coach?'' His voice croaked on the word, causing the rider to chuckle.

Elise was coming on the two-horse covered coach that delivered mail and passengers from Tucson. Now. He squeezed his eyes shut, then sighed and opened them again.

''Yup. That be her coming out there.'' The man looked back over his shoulder and waved in the direction he'd come from.

Colonel McBain followed the man's gaze. On the horizon rose a cloud of dust. The coach. His stomach sank to the vicinity of his boots.

He smoothed his mustache. Once. Twice.

Thankfully, distance was deceiving out in the desert. The coach was much farther away than it looked. He needed as much time as possible to prepare himself mentally for his wife's arrival.

He swallowed. Hell, there wasn't that much time left on earth.

Just how was he to inform his wife that he'd lost their daughter?

He stood, stiffening unconsciously to attention, and watched the cloud of dust that signaled the distant approach of his wife from back east. He wished he could gather up a company of men and ride out—in the opposite direction.

He silently shook his head in refusal. His riding out now would raise too many questions, cause too much speculation at this fort. The arrival of his *wife* was going to bring enough havoc without adding to the disruption beforehand.

Elise Wentworth McBain would create enough disruption to rock the entire post. When she found out about Regan . . .

He wished he could devise a story to tell her, but she'd see right through any lies he told. He'd never been any good at lying, and she'd caught him at it more than once. In fact, one time too many, after which she refused to believe him. He thought back to that night so long ago; he never should have lied about going into town. Elise McBain had always been able to spot a lie at any distance, especially one from him.

Smoothing his mustache into place, he stood like a condemned man awaiting a bullet from a firing squad. It would be far less painful than what was to come, he was certain of that. Focused on his wife's arrival, he didn't even hear the rider chortle again, then mount up and ride out.

All he could hear was his wife's anger.

Branded Wolf regained consciousness to the sight of blue above his head. He didn't know when he'd seen a prettier sky, or one that looked so close. He blinked and the sky came into clear focus.

It was blue lace fanned out above him, and it belonged to a lady's parasol. The realization jolted him. His next observation jerked him fully awake. A beautiful woman was curled up beside him asleep.

He didn't know which surprised him more.

As he stared at her, she opened her eyes. Their gazes locked, then she jerked upright as if she'd been burned. Was she afraid she'd be soiled by an Indian's touch, he thought to himself. He'd seen white women cross to the other side of a street to avoid him. He'd felt their scorn and knew it well. It had been part of the reason he'd abandoned his white heritage and his mother's relatives. In his heart he was Apache.

He stiffened with pride and nearly gasped at the pain that rippled through his body in waves. He clamped his mouth shut on any outcry.

"You ... you're awake." The woman spoke in a low, hesitant voice.

He turned his gaze back to her.

"You must be thirsty." With this, she jumped up and hurried to where a canteen lay propped against the base of the rocks.

Branded Wolf opened his mouth to call her back, but no sound came out. He swallowed at the barren dryness in his mouth that robbed him of speech.

He blinked again, his eyes feeling strangely heavy. He was tired, so tired.

A scattered memory tugged at his consciousness. Ambush. He needed to escape. Had to ride. He levered himself up to a sitting position. It took almost all his strength. With the last of his strength he shoved himself to his feet. He wavered, weakness shaming him as a warrior.

He had to . . .

Regan heard a muffled sound and turned around in time to see Branded Wolf stagger. She dropped the canteen and reached his side just as he collapsed.

She caught him in her arms, nearly falling under his weight. Holding him tight to her, she tried to ease his body back to the ground. The force of a fall could start his wound bleeding again if she wasn't careful, she was certain of it.

His weight bore down on her, and she took a step back. The fabric of the petticoat slipped beneath her feet, and she struggled to remain upright. She feared it was a losing battle.

By some miracle she regained her footing. Using all her strength, she began to ease the man's body down. He slid against her inch by inch. Her breathing quickened, and she knew it had nothing to do with the exertion.

Sweet Pea chose that moment to wake up from her nap and bound to her feet. She dashed to Regan's side with instinctive protectiveness and gave a sharp bark.

Regan jerked at the unexpected sound and lost her balance. She struggled to right herself and keep hold of the man in her arms at the same time. His body shifted in her grip, and for an instant she thought he'd fall to the hard ground.

The next thing she knew, her feet tangled in the petticoat and she went down. She hit the ground with a thud, the force of her landing nearly knocking her breathless. But when Branded Wolf landed atop her, he stole her breath away completely.

It took a moment for Regan to regain her senses. She sipped in a tentative breath for her air-starved lungs. Then another. When she could breathe again, she turned her head to check on the man atop her and met his blue-eyed stare.

His eyes darkened, and in that instant she knew he was going to kiss her. Again.

Oh, stars and heavens, she thought.

Chapter Six

Regan stared up at him, waiting.

Her eyelids drifted closed, and she tensed in readiness. Her breath caught in her suddenly dry throat. Still, she waited.

Dazed, she opened her eyes to see his close in the second before he fell back atop her. She drew in a breath and blinked.

He'd fallen asleep again.

Here she'd been, shamelessly waiting for him to kiss her, and he'd fallen asleep. Why, she'd never been so insulted in her entire life.

She resisted the childish impulse to shove him away from her. He was injured, she reasoned. He couldn't help himself.

Besides, she hadn't wanted him to kiss her anyway. No, absolutely not.

Liar.

She sniffed and eased Branded Wolf's body to the side. Then she scrambled out from under his weight. Once again he was lying on her petticoat as if none of this had ever happened. She stared at the darkness of his body against her intimate clothing, and a tiny thrill ran along her veins.

She was merely pleased that he was alive. That's all it was, she told herself. Nothing more.

Liar, the little voice whispered again.

She wished she knew how to silence it.

Stomping to the rocks, she sank to the ground and leaned her back against the rocks. What she wouldn't give for a nice, soft pillow. Sweet Pea bounded up and settled into her lap. Regan petted her silky fur and stared off into the distance of the wide desert. Her stomach growled, a reminder of a missed meal.

Now what? Could things get any worse?

As if in answer, a sudden gust of wind blew across her face, stinging her cheeks with dust. She batted away the dust from her eyes. Another breeze blew more of the sandy dirt at her. She brushed off her arms, then watched in amazement at the transformation taking place before her very eyes.

Around her the dust begin to swirl, gathering more and more up in its wake. It stung her hands as clouds of dust blew around her. She waved her hand back and forth in front of her mouth and spit out the dry, sandy grit. She coughed once, twice. The desert dust nearly choked her, and she knew it couldn't be doing Branded Wolf much good either.

Once again Sweet Pea buried her head in Regan's thick skirts and let out a loud whimper. It gave Regan an idea. If it worked to shelter Sweet Pea, why wouldn't it work for all of them?

She scooped up her pet, set her on the ground, then ordered her to stay. For once the little pup obeyed, most assuredly afraid to do anything else.

Rising to her feet, Regan braced her back against the rock and tugged off her last ruffled petticoat. Thank goodness it was so generous with its multilayers of ruffles. There was still plenty left after she'd bandaged his wounds.

Trying to think of anything but the building wind, she sank back to the ground and wrapped the muslin about herself, Branded Wolf, and Sweet Pea. The dust seemed to settle, and they were shielded from the wind and swirling dust in their little cocoon.

As the wind continued to blow, Regan leaned forward with an instinct to protect and pressed close against Branded Wolf's hard body. His muscles were firm and ungiving against her softer curves, quite different from what she'd expected to feel. Being pressed against a man while she wore no petticoat was a very different feeling indeed.

Against the howl of the wind Regan huddled closer to Branded Wolf. She wasn't certain if she was offering comfort and protection or seeking it from him.

A while later the material stopped billowing around them, and Regan dared to peek out from the folds of the petticoat. The wind had died down. Thankfully, it had been a short storm, merely sweeping the area all about them clean and clear. Why, she couldn't even see the marks in the ground she'd left dragging Branded Wolf over to the rocks.

She gingerly stood and shook out the loose petticoat. A layer of dust blew into the air. She felt like she could use a good shaking too, but she'd settle for washing the dust out of her mouth.

She swore she'd swallowed nearly half the desert dust.

She glanced down at where Branded Wolf lay so still. She imagined he'd welcome a drink of water about then too. Well, not exactly welcome, she amended, since he was asleep. She sighed in dejection.

He'd better appreciate all she'd done for him once he finally woke up.

He'd just better appreciate it, she thought.

Why, he likely as not owed her his life.

Now, there was a thought to work on. If she nursed him back to health, he would most assuredly owe her. He'd have to help her return to the fort.

As her spirits lifted, she shook out her skirt and picked up the canteen. Yes, Branded Wolf would definitely owe her. And the first thing she'd ask for was an escort back to her father's fort.

She stared off in the distance, wondering which way that fort lay. What she wouldn't give to be back on the stagecoach now.

The coach rumbled into the fort with a cloud of dust. Colonel McBain stood waiting, every one of his senses at attention, his heart stopped.

He didn't have long to wait. The horses eased to a stop, the coach creaked, and the door was flung open from inside.

He watched with his tongue nearly tied up in his throat as a dainty turn of ankle slid out from the door. He'd recognize that ankle anywhere.

The woman who stepped from the coach with the dignity of a queen was as beautiful as ever.

Colonel Carson McBain swallowed and felt his heart start up again. She'd always affected him this way, and most likely always would, worse the luck.

He watched, unable to move from stiff attention as she shook the dust of her travels from her expensive traveling gown. It was deep burgundy and brought out the highlights in her auburn hair. She was as beautiful as the day she left him, ten long years ago.

When she raised her chin to look at him, his heart stopped for certain this time. Carefully masked disdain hid any show of other emotion on her face.

But Elise McBain's green eyes spoke volumes. Blame, accusation, and anger.

He lifted a hand to brush his mustache without realizing it. She knew, he thought in desperation. Somehow she already knew about Regan.

Elise stared at her husband and ordered her heart to stop pounding so. You'd think she actually cared about him the way her body was carrying on so at the sight of him standing there tall and proud. Not very likely. Not after what he'd done.

She felt the anger build up just like in the old days. He could fire her anger faster than any other person on earth. And her body as well, she remembered with a hint of fondness.

Tossing her head, she threw off the memories. If she gave in to them then, she'd either choke the pompousness out of him or kiss him senseless. She wasn't certain which would cause more harm.

She attempted to calm her unsettled emotional state. She hadn't expected to feel this, no, most certainly not this mixture of feelings. She absolutely refused to put a name to the one emotion that was troubling her the most.

She didn't say his name. She wasn't sure if she could get it out without her voice giving away her unsettled state. Instead, she merely inclined her head in a gesture that more than hinted at a haughty nature.

Carson McBain stiffened up straighter. He thought his back would snap if he even breathed. Smoothing a finger across his mustache, he stepped closer.

"Elise, you're looking lovely." He forced the casual words out.

"And you're looking quite well yourself," she replied in a soft voice.

He almost had to strain to catch her words. Damn, the woman could whisper loud enough to be heard several feet away if she wanted to, or make him grovel to hang on to her every word.

Suddenly, Elise's gaze settled on his face. She stared hard at him with a knowing look, and he found himself flushing under her steady perusal.

"In fact, you're looking particularly well for a sick man. A sick, *dying* man."

This time he had no trouble in hearing her words. No trouble at all. "I knew I was right," she said triumphantly. "Your letter was a lie. You weren't ill."

"Now, dear—"

"You old reprobate!" she shouted loud enough for the entire camp to hear.

He cleared his throat. "Perhaps we should go to my quarters—"

"Over my dead body," she snapped back.

He almost flinched, but instead he rubbed his mustache with his index finger. If he didn't rise to her baiting him, she'd settle down soon enough. Elise had always been like a high-strung mare. She just needed some gentle handling.

If he made a single mistake in his handling of the situation—he shuddered at the thought—all hell would break loose.

Why, Regan would probably be able to hear her mother's yelling and follow it back.

At the reminder of his lost daughter, he did flinch.

The movement didn't escape Elise's keen eyes. She smiled at him, but the gesture held a certain devious quality to it, as it always had in the past. And as always before, it shook him all the way to his boots.

"Ah, Elise." He cleared his throat again.

"Yes?" she answered, seemingly enjoying his discomfort.

"Perhaps you'd like something to drink—"

She snapped her head up at this, and he nearly groaned at his poor choice of words. The woman never forgot a single fault.

"Why, Carson, that's not my forte. It's yours, if I recall correctly." She rolled the drawstrings of her reticule back and forth between her fingers.

"I was asking about a lemonade," he snapped back, shouting at her.

"Really? There's no reason to raise your voice, is there?"

He couldn't be around her for more than ten minutes without doing just that. The woman could aggravate him faster than a—

"Where's Regan?" Elise suddenly inquired, looking around them.

His anger evaporated like a drop of water on a stone in the middle of summer. What could he tell her?

Elise's half-smile faded, and she narrowed her eyes on him. "Is Regan ill?"

"No," he assured her. At least, he didn't think she'd taken sick.

No, their daughter wasn't ill—just missing and possibly dead. But he couldn't very well blurt that out, could he?

"Carson," Elise demanded, no quarter in her voice.

He stared at the toe of one of his boots. It was dusty, and he could spot a scuff on it.

"Regan did arrive, didn't she?"

"Yes, she arrived just fine," he said. "And thoroughly spoiled," he couldn't resist adding.

"She's your daughter," Elise fired back.

"She should have been my son."

Elise flinched at the cruel reminder.

He fell silent.

"Where the blazes is Regan?" she demanded.

He crossed the fingers of one hand in a subconscious gesture. "She's gone riding."

"Riding?"

"Yes. With a respectable young officer who is quite taken with her. While we wait for them to return, why don't I show you to your quarters," he offered quickly, hoping for a reprieve.

He'd settle for anything. He desperately needed to put together a story for her.

Elise studied him for a full minute, then spoke. "Very well. I'll stay with Regan in *her* quarters."

"Yes, dear." He closed his eyes a second.

He'd rather be facing a band of charging Apache than his wife just then.

How long could he stall her?

Perhaps a story of an elopement would deter his wife from the truth at least long enough to provide his troops the time to find his daughter.

He stared out past his wife at the wide expanse of land leading away from the fort.

Regan, where the hell are you?

Regan snapped her head up. For a brief moment it seemed as if—

An embarrassing growl from her stomach interrupted all such fanciful thoughts. A lady's stomach never made noises. But hers was loudly attesting to the fact that she was hungry.

If it wasn't for that dreadful Captain Larkin, she'd be sitting down to a wonderful dinner just then. She hoped he starved to death right where she left him.

The thought brought another right on its heels. Had he perhaps packed any food for their outing? It sent her scrambling to her feet with a swish of her skirts.

She rushed over to where she'd dropped his saddlebags and horse blanket, and sure enough in his saddlebags she found a cloth bag of food. Eagerly, she pulled out a biscuit.

"Oh, stars and heavens, Sweet Pea," she called out. "We're saved."

The little dog responded with a sharp bark and waved her front paws in the air, begging for a bite.

Laughing, Regan shared the biscuit with her pet.

Branded Wolf heard the sounds as if they came from far off. Blinking his eyes open, he stared at the woman, and memory returned. She'd tended his wound and cared for him.

His woman, he thought suddenly. Then he shook off the foolishness.

"This serves him right." Regan spoke around the biscuit in her mouth. "I hope he's the one hungry now."

He was hungry, Branded Wolf thought. But why was the white-eyes wishing it on him?

"I hope he starves," Regan announced with a wave of her hand.

He was likely to if she kept waving food at him, Branded Wolf thought. His stomach rumbled, drawing her attention.

"Oh." She stared at him a moment, then hurried to his side, swiping her hand across her mouth. "You're awake again."

He didn't know what he was supposed to answer to her strange remark. The little white pup bounded up and sniffed at his leg. He wished he could draw the knife in his boot but kept still, waiting.

"Sweet Pea, leave him alone," the woman ordered. "Come here."

The pup raked the air with her front paws, and he watched in amazement when the white-eyes gave her a bite of food. Watching her feed the dog was nearly torture. His stomach rumbled again.

He saw her eyes widen. "You must be hungry too. Huh?"

He kept his silence. He wouldn't give the white-eyes reason to taunt him.

With a lightning-fast turn she spun away from him. What did she plan next? he wondered. Ladylike steps carried her to where a horse blanket and saddlebags lay. In spite of his determination not to amuse her, he watched as she withdrew something from the bag and turned back to him.

"Do you feel like eating?" She held out a biscuit to him.

He narrowed his eyes, waiting for her to pull it back. He'd seen white-eyes at the reservation play the same kind of game.

"Please try?" She broke off a tiny piece and held it up to his mouth.

Against his will his lips opened.

"There." She eased the bread between his lips, her fingers brushing his lower lip.

He nearly pulled back from the combination of surprise and the touch of her soft fingers against his lips. Instead, he chewed the food.

"I bet you're thirsty too," she observed, and caught up a canteen.

He eyed her with suspicion, but she held the canteen against his mouth for him to drink. He did so deeply.

She continued to feed him the remainder of the biscuit bite by bite. He couldn't figure out what her game was, especially after her words about starving him.

When she leaned forward and patted his lips with a strip of blue cloth, he nearly hit his head on the ground pulling away.

"Oh, no." She snapped her hand back. "I won't hurt you."

Her voice was gentle and soft, like one the People used to tame a wild horse.

"My name's Regan," she offered, "Regan McBain." She cocked her head and waited for his response.

He held his own counsel.

When he didn't answer, she rushed on as if suddenly nervous. "I know your name's Branded Wolf—"

He jerked his head to stare hard into her eyes. How had she—

"The conductor told me on the train." As if realizing a mistake, she rushed to add, "Not that I asked him. He offered the information all on his own. He was pretty angry with me at the time though, because of Sweet Pea. She didn't mean any harm. She was just bored with traveling, this being her first long trip and all."

Blazes, but the woman could talk. An Apache maiden would never go on so.

"I offered to pay for his pants and all, but he just shrugged me off."

What had he missed? He didn't have the slightest notion what she was talking about.

"Oh, that reminds me"—she glanced down and paused for a second, then rushed on—"did she hurt your hat?"

He watched as her lips twitched slightly.

"That day on the train when she bit it," she added in explanation.

At his continued silence her cheeks turned a becoming shade of rose. Like a desert sunset, he thought. She was pretty—for a white-eyes.

She glanced down at her hands and seemed to study them. "I . . . I know you're half Indian."

Her cheeks seemed to deepen in color, and he stiffened at her words.

She kept her gaze focused on her fingers as she threaded them together. "I want you to know that . . . that it doesn't bother me like it did the horrible woman on the train. I thought she behaved dreadfully."

She looked up at him for a moment, and her gaze touched him as briefly as a butterfly's wings. He sucked in his breath but forced himself to keep his face expressionless.

"Well, I just wanted you to know that. And when you're well, you can take me back to the fort," she announced to him. Her chin tilted slightly in defiance. "It's the least you can do for my caring for you." Her face reddened, and she rushed to correct herself. "I mean tending you."

With this she fell silent and stared at him.

Suddenly, she threw up her hands. The little dog gave a sharp yap that hurt his ears. "Oh, dear," she bemoaned. She turned away and muttered, "Apachas."

"Apache," Branded Wolf corrected her pronunciation automatically.

"God bless you," she said politely. Her words were very slow and distinct, not like when she'd chattered on before.

He stared at her in disbelief.

She sighed, then spoke slowly in a loud voice. "You sneezed." She paused to gesture with her hand, first pointing to him then to her nose. She waved her hand to her chest. "I said, God bless you."

He blinked and kept silent. Why did the white-eyes feel the need to speak so slowly, as if explaining something to a small child but in a near shout? Did the woman think he was deaf, or—

Realization hit him along with the insult. She thought he didn't speak English. She assumed he was a "savage." He didn't see any reason to enlighten her otherwise.

At least not yet.

Chapter Seven

Regan woke the next morning, snuggled up against a hard, unyielding pillow. Not at all the way her pillow usually felt, she thought. This one was lumpy. She'd have to insist Mama buy a new one for her.

That problem settled, she opened her eyes and stretched leisurely. Turning her head, she came face-to-face with a pair of intense blue eyes.

Branded Wolf.

Recognition came immediately, and along with it a strange sense of safety. She blinked her eyes at his closeness.

With a yelp of surprise Regan jumped to her feet.

How?

What?

The last thing she remembered was the feeling of exhaustion that had settled down on her after Branded Wolf had insisted on moving the makeshift bed away from the rocks. She hadn't any idea why he'd gestured and insisted so, but she'd gone along with him.

She recalled lying down on the far edge of the petticoat on the hard ground. How had she ended up pressed against him?

It was all his fault. Surely he'd pulled her to him during the night while she slept. He'd . . . he'd taken liberties with her. There couldn't be any other explanation.

Could there?

Of course not. She tossed her head at the very thought.

It wasn't as if she'd purposely snuggled up close to him. How improper. Why, she would never! She eyed him suspiciously.

He returned a decidedly smug smile. He looked so self-satisfied lying on the petticoat, as if this were all her fault. Her temper began to soar, then a faint inkling of memory of her waking up cold tickled at the back of her mind.

Regan frowned and nibbled her lower lip. Of course, she'd been cold last night; she thought it over. She'd slept in the desert, for heaven's sake. She crossed her arms over her chest.

And stayed quite warm, a little voice prodded the recesses of her memory.

She recalled a strong, warm arm holding her close to a hard, firm body. While firmly muscled, that male body had shifted, fitting her curves perfectly. A strange sensation such as she'd never experienced before in her life flooded over her at the night's memories.

Her eyes widened. Oh, no.

She hadn't.

Glancing down at the petticoat spread over the ground, she knew she had indeed rolled over and snuggled up against Branded Wolf's long, warm body. She remembered it clearly now. Mortified, she raised her head barely enough to meet his eyes.

He returned her gaze evenly.

His knowing smile and even, white teeth made him look devilishly handsome to her. And so dangerous to her heart.

Regan whirled away. She couldn't face him. She absolutely couldn't. What would he think of her? Why, her behavior had been absolutely scandalous even if she had been half asleep. There had been no excuse for her lack of deportment.

And it most assuredly wouldn't happen again, she told herself hurriedly.

Branded Wolf watched the play of emotions across her face. No one had been more surprised than he to wake up with a beautiful woman's arms around him. She'd been wrapped so close to him that he knew the slightest move from him would wake her. So he'd remained still, like a warrior on a hunt, and he'd studied her in the amber light of the rising sun.

She possessed high cheekbones that would make an Indian maiden proud to call her own. But her skin was creamy and fair. Already it had turned pink. The freckles across her nose stood out, tempting, begging to be kissed. The stubborn tilt of her chin had vanished like a mist while she slept. Her lips had softened in sleep, becoming even more inviting, and nearly tempted him beyond endurance.

He'd resisted the urge to take her right then and make her his.

Only the certainty that she was unaware what she was doing stopped him. White women did not lay with half-breeds. It was a cold, hard fact of life in his world.

One look at her beautiful face, now awake and in the full light of day, and he knew it was true. Embarrassment heated her fair skin, obvious for anyone to see. He could almost feel the shame radiating from her.

A curse pulled at his lips, asking to be let free. All this shame on her face, and nothing had happened between them. He hadn't laid a hand on her white skin. He could imagine her reaction if he had given in to the urges screaming at him when he'd held her warm body close last night.

In spite of his thoughts, he couldn't seem to look away from the woman. He watched as she shook out her skirt, and wondered if she was shaking off his touch.

"Stars and heavens, I swear I've had enough dust to last a lifetime," she muttered.

Surprise overtook him at her words. She was grumbling about the *dust*. Not him.

Some vague sense of unease told him this woman, this Regan, would be a constant amazement to him. Wasn't he even now wearing strips of her intimate clothing around his wound?

"I don't know what we are going to eat for breakfast," she continued, her voice soft and melodic to his ears.

He still couldn't believe she wasn't screaming her head off, berating him for daring to touch her. Not that he thought for a moment she'd actually welcome his touch if he were to stand up and take her into his arms.

"The biscuits were a pleasant surprise, weren't they?" She glanced over her shoulder at him and shrugged. "But we ate the last of them last night, I think."

Her cheeks flushed a darker shade of pink, and she busied herself looking at her hands all of a sudden. Branded Wolf almost smiled at her hesitancy, almost, but not quite.

"I . . . I'll check the . . . the saddlebags and see if there is anything else left in them." Keeping her face averted, she crossed to the saddlebags and pulled out a cloth sack.

While she was busied at her task, Branded Wolf stood, dragged the petticoat back to the shade of the rocks, and lay back down. During the heat of the day there weren't any snakes to be concerned about, he knew. But he hadn't been able to explain that last night to Regan without words.

As she rummaged in the bag, he heard her mumbling almost beneath her breath. "Practically empty except for a flask of whiskey. The least thing David could have done is left me some decent food. The low-down, good-for-nothing . . .''

Her voice dropped lower, and he couldn't hear the rest. A frown drew his eyebrows closer together. He propped one arm behind his head and watched her movements.

Who was David?

"Ah, here we go." Regan's triumphant shout caused the little dog lying beside the saddle to spring to life and set to barking.

Branded Wolf resisted the urge to cover his ears against the shrill sound. His headache had returned. If he got his hands on that dog, he'd—

As if knowing his thoughts, the little pup bounded up to him, plumed tail wagging so much, her little body shook along with it. The dog barked right in his face, then had the nerve to lick his chin.

Taken aback by the act, Branded Wolf nearly yelled. The pup trotted away to sniff a yucca as if it didn't have a care in the world.

One more lick and the dog wouldn't have another thing in life to worry about, he swore to himself.

The indignity of it. To be given dog kisses from a little handful of fur too small to even count as a real dog.

Branded Wolf closed his eyes against the shame. At least no one else had seen it happen. If he could get to his feet, he'd—

"I'm sorry," a soft voice whispered to him.

He snapped his eyes open to find Regan bending over him. She laid her hand lightly across his cheek. Her thumb rested on his chin. He watched as she worried her lower lip.

"When Sweet Pea takes to someone, she just naturally gives kisses." Regan shrugged one shoulder, and her fingers brushed his cheek with the slight movement.

He lay still, unwilling to move for the moment. Her hand

felt nice, soft and gentle, like the silken touch of a butterfly against his bare skin. He envisioned her pressed against him, her fair skin a sharp contrast to his bronze, darker skin.

Suddenly, he shook his head, dislodging her hand from his face. She jerked back, and once again her cheeks colored.

"I . . . I'm . . . sorry. I didn't mean to be so forward."

She was apologizing for touching him?

Unexpectedly, her face broke into a smile. "You should count yourself lucky with Sweet Pea. Why, she didn't take to David at all. She bit him."

She grinned as if laughing at a private joke, then added with a hint of glee, "You don't want to know where."

He was left to wonder once again who David was. And what was he to this woman?

Calling the little dog back to her side, she set up the blue lacy parasol to block the sun and returned to searching the saddlebags. Minutes later she pulled out a wrapped parcel with a shout.

"More biscuits." She turned to wave them at him. "Here we go. I'll feed you some."

He didn't know whether to groan or smile.

By midmorning, Regan was hot and bored. She couldn't go for a ride, and had no one to talk to except for Branded Wolf and Sweet Pea, neither of which could answer her.

Oh, stars and heavens, she bemoaned her fate. She was stranded in the desert with a man who couldn't even communicate with her.

She pulled out the last of the biscuits, which were now looking much worse for wear, and divided them among the three of them. Her hands trembled this time when she fed Branded Wolf a bite.

His firm lips were so foreign to her fingers. She kept imagining how his lips would feel kissing her. His long, dark hair brushed her wrist once, and a skittering of sensations followed in its wake. She'd never before in her life wondered what a man's hair would feel like against her bare skin . . . against her neck . . . her breasts. But she did now. She swallowed and searched for something—anything—to distract herself.

"Branded Wolf." She tried his name on her tongue, nearly stumbling over it in her nervousness.

She paused to cock her head and stare at him a moment.

He met her stare with one of his own that left her shaken all the way to her slippers. In fact, it absolutely curled her toes.

"That's entirely too big a mouthful to constantly say all the time. I'll call you Brand," she announced with a tilt of her stubborn chin.

The hell she would. He started to tell her so and barely stopped himself in time. If he said the words, she'd know he could speak English, and he wasn't ready for that just yet. However, he didn't know how much longer he could keep his silence.

"I wonder how you ever got that as a name?" she wondered aloud.

He didn't tell her his father and uncle had called him Wolf after the lonely hunter. And the People of his tribe had added Branded because his blue eyes branded him as half white. It wasn't something he shared with anyone, particularly with a white-eyes.

He found himself not thinking of her in the same way he thought of other white-eyes he'd met in his time as a bounty hunter. She was different somehow. She had the fire and passion of an Apache.

And the soft, fair skin of a white, his mind told him. She had silken skin that tempted a man almost beyond endurance. He swore she had the power to pain him more than any bullet.

She turned to him and pursed her lips. A pain shot through his gut. He wanted to taste her lips again, to see if they were as sweet and tender as he remembered, or if it had been a fever that had heated his blood before at the brief touch of his lips on hers.

"It's probably time to look at your wound again and clean it, since I found the whiskey." She wrinkled her nose in distaste. "I have to give you proper warning, I'm not too good a nurse."

Gritting her teeth, she leaned over and began to unwind the torn strips of blue petticoat. The same color blue as the gown she wore, he noticed for the first time. Branded Wolf thought she was unwinding his resolve as well.

Soon he would have to start moving around, getting his full strength back, although a part of him wanted to keep Regan's hands tending him for some time to come.

He had to see to Wind Dancer soon. Surely this woman, this Regan, hadn't known how to care for his horse the right way. He studied her, watching her gentle, hesitant movements. As he stared, her hands began to tremble ever so lightly.

She raised her skirt slightly and tore off a fresh strip of blue petticoat. Branded Wolf had trouble swallowing for a moment.

"I hope I'm doing this properly," she grumbled, folding the material, and her hands shook worse. "But it's not as if you could tell me anyway. So why in heaven am I wasting my breath talking to you!" she snapped at him for no reason, and caught up the flask.

Leaning forward, she poured the liquor over his wound, and his entire shoulder erupted into flames of pain. He almost yelled. Damn, the woman was likely going to kill him with her nursing. Maybe he should have taken her warning seriously.

When she began rewrapping the makeshift bandage

around his chest, a warning of a different kind tore at him. Her small hands rubbed along his skin, smoothing out the cloth. She left a trail of fire in her wake, a fire that threatened to consume them both if he so much as breathed in her scent.

She must have felt him stiffen beneath her ministrations, because she scooted away from him suddenly. He noticed that her hands trembled again, their movement matching his own. Yes, he knew he should take her warning very seriously.

At last she busied herself with her dog and let him regain some of his peace. But he knew her every breath, her every movement throughout the day.

Over her many objections, Brand—as she'd taken to calling him—began walking around to strengthen his muscles. He also needed the diversion from watching her, hearing her stir about, smelling her scent. It was becoming harder and harder to keep from touching her. Only the scorn he knew he'd see in her face kept him from doing so.

Surprisingly, he found Wind Dancer doing well under Regan's care. He wondered where a fancy eastern woman such as she had learned to care for a horse. It was only one piece to the growing puzzle about her.

He made a poultice and wrapped it about his horse's leg, noting it was nearly healed. How had she gotten the horse to allow her touch? Wind Dancer allowed no one near him.

He also noticed the bandage on his mount's leg was a fancy lady's kerchief. Regan's. It seemed both he and his horse were to bear her colors. As the day wore on, he continued to observe her every move.

By late afternoon she was grumbling about being hungry again, and, he had to admit, his own stomach was none too full.

Regan checked the saddlebags again. He watched as she

poked and prodded, then dumped the contents onto the ground with a huff. She threw up her hands.

"Just as I figured. No more biscuits. Thanks a lot, David." She propped her hands on her hips. "I hope you starve. In the blistering hot sun. All alone," she muttered, heaping additional insults on the man's manhood as well.

Branded Wolf found himself glad he was not this David, especially if Regan ever caught up with him.

Gradually she ran out of insults for the unwary man and gingerly picked up a small bundle of strips of meat. She raised it to her nose, sniffed, then wrinkled her nose in disgust. "Yuck."

Branded Wolf frowned at her reaction. Hadn't the woman ever seen jerky before? His mouth practically watered at the sight of it.

Regan's reaction was quite different. She held the darkened strips at arm's length with a frown. Beside her, Sweet Pea wagged her tail furiously, then sat back on her haunches and pawed the air.

Staring at the pup, Regan laughed aloud. "So you want a bite, do you?"

The pup yipped her agreement.

At this Regan twisted a corner of the jerky, tugged, then pulled off a small bite. She held it out, and Sweet Pea nearly nipped her fingers in her hurry to devour the new treat.

Regan watched in amazement as the dog licked her mouth noisily and begged for more, her little white paws beating the air.

"I guess if it's that good, I'll try it myself," Regan mumbled, and set to working a small piece loose.

Gingerly, she put the small taste in her mouth and bit down on it. She yelped and grimaced in distaste. "Why, this stuff is as tough as shoe leather."

She spit the bite out, and Sweet Pea rushed over to pounce on it with a growl of delight.

"I'd say you were welcome to the whole bunch of it, but it's the only thing left for us to eat," Regan nearly wailed her distress.

With a frown she tore off another tiny morsel. Closing her eyes tightly, she popped the piece in her mouth. Without opening her eyes she bit down on the thin piece of darkened meat with a wrinkle of her nose. Tentatively, she chewed. And chewed. And chewed.

Then she swallowed. Twice.

"Heavens."

She opened her eyes and blinked several times. It truly didn't taste so bad, that was if one got past the chewing it took to eat it. Perhaps all the dry, toughened meat needed was some tenderizing. She'd seen Mama's cook do that to a cut of meat once, and listened to a lengthy explanation along with it. She glanced around and located a small rock.

She stood, then crossed over and picked up the rock and carried it and the strips of meat to a larger rock. She began to pound the meat with the smaller rock until her arm ached.

When she turned back to Branded Wolf with the jerky strips dangling between her fingers like thin strings, it was all he could do not to laugh. Instead, he chewed the jerky she handed him and kept his humor to himself. Something told him she would not appreciate his laughter at that moment.

Later that night, all humor left him as Regan lay down on the petticoat nearby in the growing dark. He knew it would be a long time before he slept.

He remained awake long after Regan quit moving about on the ground, trying to get comfortable. At last she settled down and gradually fell sleep. He watched the slight rise and fall of her breasts. As the air about them cooled to a chill, he smiled as she rolled closer, snuggling against his warmth.

Finally in the stillness and peace of the desert, Branded

Wolf fell asleep with Regan curled against him, and the sound of her pup snoring, furry chin resting heavily on his foot.

Elise Wentworth McBain paced the hard floor of the small bedroom at the fort. Her footsteps disturbed a fine layer of dust. Regan would hate the dust, she was certain of it.

Whirling about, she took two steps and stopped. She studied the room. Something was wrong.

She could feel it.

Regan?

She should have stopped her from coming out here. She knew the effect the letter from Carson would have on her softhearted daughter. She should have known she'd take off. As headstrong as her daughter was, she couldn't have done anything else. And the girl fancied that there was affection between her father and her.

Regan couldn't be more wrong. Her heart went out to her daughter.

The old fool had been so set on producing a son that he'd never appreciated the beautiful daughter they'd been given.

And for that Elise couldn't forgive him. Watching her daughter hurt because of his callous behavior, she nearly hated him for it.

What would it take for him to see reason? Regan had always worshipped her father, and Elise hadn't had it in her heart to tell her the truth about him.

Now look where that dishonesty had gotten them. In the middle of the dreadful wilderness where she'd sworn she'd never set a foot again. She shuddered with old memories.

What had she been thinking to let Regan even consider the idea of coming out here to this wild territory?

She blamed her temporary lapse on the receipt of Carson's letter. The thought of him sick and dying had shaken her to her core. Even she, knowing him as she did, had believed his words for a short while. A very short while.

But, oh, no, he'd proven true to character, as always. The lying old fool.

His deviousness had brought Regan running to him, running away from home in the middle of the night to this desolate wilderness, and straight into trouble. She knew it for a fact in her heart.

That same heart questioned if perhaps she hadn't allowed this to happen ... hadn't perhaps *wanted* to see Carson again.

No, absolutely not!

The only thing she wanted to see him for now was to find out where Regan was. And see him she would. She tapped her foot on the floor with her growing temper. He wouldn't sidestep her this time. She'd learned a few things in her time as an officer's wife, and a lot of things from living without a man in Philadelphia.

He wouldn't put her off again with delays. This time she'd get to the bottom of his stalling, and she'd get answers from him.

And take her daughter and head straight back to Philadelphia, where they both belonged!

With the light of anger in her eyes she headed out door. Colonel Carson McBain was in for one blazing campaign, and he didn't even know it. Oh, but he would soon, she vowed.

She strode across the parade ground and entered his quarters with a perfunctory knock to warn him before the door slammed against the wall with the force of her determination.

"Where is she, Carson?"

He looked up from the papers he'd been studying, and she could swear she saw him blanch.

"Ah, Elise. How was your rest?"

"As if you cared." Her voice rose.

He swallowed and smoothed his mustache with an unsteady hand. "I trust you found everything satisfactory."

Elise walked to the desk with firm steps. Keeping him pinned with her eyes, she rounded the scarred wooden desk and walked closer. Too close. She stopped within inches of his face.

"The truth." She planted her hands on her hips and leaned closer. "Where is Regan?"

Each of her carefully enunciated words spelled his doom.

"Hasn't she returned from her ride?" He tried the lie, but it hung on his tongue. He watched as her eyes narrowed with the knowledge.

"Cut to the chase. The truth."

He sighed deeply, knowing the time for stalling was long past. His wife would settle for nothing but the truth this time. And she'd make life hell until she got it. He swallowed. Once she knew the truth, things would only worsen.

He opened his mouth and blurted out, "She didn't come back from her ride."

"This afternoon?"

"Yesterday," he admitted solemnly.

Elise stared at him for several seconds, then whispered, "What happened?"

"Darling, she's lost."

He stood to his feet just in time to catch his wife as she fainted.

The faint gold of sunrise pricked the desert sky. The stars retreated back into their hiding places to make room for the day to appear.

Branded Wolf scarcely breathed. He didn't wish to disturb the sleeping woman in his arms. Her hair trailed across his chest, shimmering darkly against the bandages in the pale rays of early daybreak.

She felt right in his arms.

Branded Wolf stared out at the slowly awakening desert. Soon the pale pink of dawn would begin, then recede beneath the blazing sunlight to come. The heat would follow hard on its heels like a young brave chasing after the buffalo. He was thankful summer had not yet arrived.

He looked up into the blue of the parasol directly overhead. A torn edge of matching blue lace trailed off one corner. A smile tugged at his lips. Only a white-eyes would devise such a thing.

He gazed back out at the land he loved. His heart caught in his chest. The land of the People. But they would lose this; they would lose everything if the men caught him here.

Both he and the woman lying in his arms would die.

Time was running out for him here.

With a stealthy grace born of years of training, he slid his arm out from under Regan's sleeping body curled up next to him. She never stirred. He eased his foot away from the snoring pup without even raising a hair of the pup's fur.

Bracing his hands on the ground, he stood and breathed in the fresh air of the coming dawn. Then he turned away from the sleeping woman. His footsteps were soundless on the desert sands.

He had no choice. His course had been set for him when the white-eyes killed his family. He would do what he had to do to stay alive, to protect his People from blame. And to extract his revenge.

With soundless steps that never hesitated, he walked across the desert ground.

He did what he had to do. And he knew she'd hate him for it.

Chapter Eight

With a warrior's stealth he slipped the reins off the cavalry horse and gently ran his hand over the animal's nose to keep it quiet. Even in the near dark he could see it was a beautiful animal, one any Apache would be proud to have stolen from the bluecoats.

He regretted what he had to do.

Stepping back, he swung the edge of a rein on the sorrel's rump, sending it galloping away across the desert. He knew the animal would head for a water hole to the east, then with certainty it would make its way eventually back to the fort.

First, the shod horse would leave a trail to confuse even the best scouts. By the time anyone successfully tracked them here, he and the white-eyes woman would be far away.

At the sound of the horse's hooves hitting the ground, Regan awoke with a start. Without hesitation she scrambled to her feet and raced to where Branded Wolf stood watching the sorrel disappear.

"No!" Regan began to run after the horse.

She hadn't gotten more than three steps, when she was yanked back against a hard-muscled chest. A man's bare chest.

Her breath rushed out in a soft whoosh, and she ignored any feelings except anger. He'd sent her horse away. Well, not exactly *her* horse, but she'd ridden the animal there. And it did belong to the cavalry, and her father was head of the post. How dare Brand up and shoo *her* horse away? Added to this, he had the nerve to prevent her from chasing after the animal.

In the next instant she sucked in another deep breath and kicked backward with all her strength. Her heel connected with his leg. She couldn't help the wince she felt at the contact.

Branded Wolf muttered an oath below his breath in Apache. When she kicked the next time, he dodged and then had to catch her to stop her from landing in the dirt at his feet. She stilled in his arms. It seemed to take the fight out of her.

When he released his hold on her, she spun around at him. He barely ducked her outstretched fist in time. It had been aimed squarely at his jaw.

"You let my horse go!" She stomped one foot in the sandy dirt.

He met her angry gaze with a determined one of his own. If he kept her attention long enough, the horse would be too far away to do anything about it.

"Why did you do that?" she shouted.

Anger and puzzlement clashed on her pretty face. The puzzlement he could remove with the explanation that the shod cavalry horse was too easy to track. However, that answer would fire her anger even more. So he remained silent.

Better to keep his own counsel than to tell her that without her horse she would be unable to escape from him. Better than to explain that Wind Dancer would never let her ride without him seated with her.

No, he retained his silence. And listened.

Regan shouted and swore at him. He raised his brows once at her choice of words. He wondered briefly where she'd learned such words.

His patience nearing its end, he took one step toward her, and then watched her suck in her breath. Her eyes widened and she fell silent.

Regan stared up at him, her head tilted back to meet his gaze. Why did he have to tower over her? It gave her a distinct disadvantage. His eyes darkened, and she knew her own breath stopped somewhere on its way to her lungs.

He took another slow, deliberate step toward her, his eyes never leaving hers. Regan swallowed, unable to move a limb beneath his powerful gaze. She wouldn't run even if she could do so.

Suddenly, he whirled away from her and strode away. His footsteps were silent on the ground. She opened her mouth, then snapped it shut again. She didn't know if she was relieved or insulted. But she had a tiny suspicion it was the latter. That admission fueled her anger.

As if dismissing her, he didn't stop walking until he reached the outcropping of rocks. Leaning against them, he flexed his stiff muscles. And waited.

He didn't have long to do so. The thud of angry footsteps sounded behind him. They sounded more like someone stomping than a ladylike tread. He resisted the urge that told him to whirl around and take a battle stance. It was certain a battle was coming—in the person of Regan McBain.

He was right.

She caught his arm and yanked him around. Hands on hips, she faced him, her breasts rising and falling with the fury of her drawing breath.

"Why did you do that?" she yelled.

When he remained silent, she stomped one little foot and glared at him.

"Horse." She pawed the ground with her foot. "Mine!" She pointed her finger at her chest.

Once again she was speaking slowly, like to a small child, and very loudly. Did she think shouting would make someone understand better?

She motioned with her hands, pantomiming riding a horse. Then she shouted, "Mine."

Branded Wolf felt his lips twitch. It took all his resolve not to laugh. Only apprehension of a full temper showing from her stopped him.

That would come later, when he let her know that they were riding out, leaving the desert behind for the safety of the mountains. He resisted the instinct that told him to travel to Cochise's mountain stronghold. The army wouldn't send out as many men after himself and the one woman as they had after the great Cochise many years past. The chief's former stronghold would provide safety, solitude, and a good place to rest.

He nearly shook his head in answer to the thoughts. It was too far away. He refused to flee the area where the killers prowled. If he did so, it would be the same as turning his back on his People, his dead family, his revenge.

He couldn't do it. Not even to keep Regan safe.

Guilt pricked at him like a spiny cactus needle as he looked down into her beautiful face. He would keep her safe, he vowed.

But he would have his revenge.

He was in no doubt of her fury to come when she realized his intention was not to return her to the fort as she'd demanded, but to take her farther away, much farther away. Only the windstorm had allowed them to remain there in the desert flatland as long as they had. It swept clear any tracks she had made on her way to him.

And he intended that they didn't find any further trace of her.

However, soon they would run out of water and food. He knew where both were plentiful, and yet within striking range of the men he sought.

Suddenly, Regan threw up her hands in disgust. She whirled around and stomped away from him. Her act drew his full attention on her again. Her hips swayed temptingly with her steps. He recalled how her sleep-mussed hair had given her the look of a woman who'd been made love to. But he hadn't touched her that long night. He knew her scorn if he ever did. It would make her anger look like nothing.

"Sweet Pea," she called out, but kept walking away from him.

The little dog trotted after her, prancing for all the world to see. He wondered for a moment where the pup got the boundless energy. The little dog had heart, he thought to himself. If only the thing weren't so aggravating.

He shook his head and watched Regan's steps. They were firm and with purpose. She was planning something, he was sure of it.

Regan didn't stop so much as even to look back until she reached where Wind Dancer stood. She patted the horse, then shoved her skirt out of the way.

Before he could make a move to stop her, she grabbed hold of the horse's mane and swung herself upward onto the animal's bare back. She tossed him a smug smile in the instant before Wind Dancer reared.

Slowly, Regan slid backward to land on her backside in the dirt with a thud and a yelp.

She scrambled to her feet and whirled on Branded Wolf

as he approached. "Get away from me. Just get away from me."

She dusted off her skirt and glared at the horse, then at him. Her eyes narrowed in growing comprehension. "You knew he'd do that, didn't you?"

When he remained silent, she scooped her dog up into her arms and turned her back on him. "What am I wasting my breath talking to you for? You don't even speak English." With this, she flounced to the shade of the parasol, the pup held close to her chest.

Branded Wolf remained with the horse for then. He knew enough to stay clear of her for a little while. He'd seen her temper flare more than once this day and had no desire to see it again any too soon.

Regan fumed all the way to the parasol. He'd known. And he let her humiliate herself anyway. And get thrown from his horse. She rubbed her backside gingerly and wished belatedly for the padding offered by the two petticoats.

It was all his fault.

"Oh, stars and heavens, Sweet Pea," Regan grumbled. "Why does Brand have to be so blasted handsome that he makes my toes curl?"

She kicked at a small rock in frustration. It wasn't as if the Apache could understand her or anything.

"And why does he have to be so tall and make me feel safe, hmm?" she asked the dog. "And with such a wide chest?"

She rubbed her nose in the dog's fur and sighed loudly.

"And it's such a comfortable chest too. Is it no wonder I wake up to find myself snuggled up against him?" She shook her head and quickly added, "Not that I do it on purpose. I'm just cold." She paused, then rushed on. "I can resist him anytime I want to. And don't you dare tell me differently."

She thought she heard a strangled cough from behind her and nearly jumped out of her skin.

Regan frowned and glanced over her shoulder to find Brand's eyes fixed firmly on her. She swallowed in sudden nervousness.

He'd heard what she'd been saying.

But he couldn't understand a word she said, she assured herself.

Although life would be easier if he did. If he understood English, she wouldn't have to keep making those foolish hand gestures to try to help him comprehend her questions. It really was quite frustrating. The least thing he could have done was let her know his stupid horse wouldn't let her ride him.

She let her breath out in a whoosh of anger. He staged that on purpose. Oh, he'd pay for that. She'd see to it, somehow, some way.

She didn't know who she was madder at right then, the man or the horse she'd cared for and tended. The horse had betrayed her friendship. She'd never been thrown from a mount in her life. And she didn't intend to be again.

She'd just have to set out to win over his horse. Then *he'd* be the one stranded when *she* rode off. A smug sense of satisfaction came over her. She'd show him.

And could she win over the man? a little voice prodded her.

She tossed her head in denial. The thought didn't bear thinking about. She had other plans for Brand, entirely different plans.

At least she hadn't wakened that morning to find herself snuggled up to the Apache. She raised her head with an indignant sniff. All it had taken was mind over matter.

She could resist his handsome charm if she set her mind to it. And she'd make him pay for that morning's indignity.

Why, before the day was out, he'd be sorry he embarrassed her.

Thoughtfully, she stroked Sweet Pea's fur and set to devising a plan.

Branded Wolf watched Regan as she gently petted the dog. At that moment he would give anything to trade places with the pup. Listening to her reveal her feelings to the dog when she thought he couldn't understand her had heated his blood.

A smile pulled at his lips, and he fought to hold it at bay. So she liked his looks—and his chest? He held similar feelings about her body. In truth, he wanted her badly.

Perhaps tonight he would . . .

He shoved the temptation away. If he attempted to take her, she'd fight him—a half-breed—all the way. No, he had to keep her with him and keep her from escaping and either leading the bluecoats to him or getting them both killed. With her fine eastern ways, she'd run for her life if he laid an improper hand on her.

He watched her as she stroked the dog's fur over and over again. A devious smile tilted her lips. An uneasy feeling settled deep in his chest. The woman was up to something. He'd seen that look on the warriors' faces before they planned an attack.

Shaking off the foolish feeling, he derided himself. There was no way to compare the beautiful white-eyes with her shapely body to a warrior and his strength. No, he had nothing to worry about.

He watched her with a hooded gaze. Soon she would come asking for his help. Soon.

Wind Dancer allowed no one too near him but Branded Wolf. It had always been that way.

Regan would be unable to control the horse or to manage in the desert without help, his help. He'd have to make sure she understood this.

A white-eyes such as she with her fancy gown and eastern ways could not make it in the desert. She wouldn't know what to do. Yes, soon she would come to him asking for his help. Then he would speak to her.

And not until then.

Colonel Carson McBain stared down at the woman in his arms. He swung her limp body up into his embrace. Long-forgotten emotions coursed through him.

He carried her into the next room and gently laid her on the horsehair sofa. When he stepped back, he noticed with irritation that his hands were trembling. He, an old campaigner, an Indian fighter, and his hands trembled like a woman's. And all because his wife had lapsed into a harmless swoon. He was a fool.

He would have laughed in scorn if he could find a morsel of laughter within him.

Easing himself down onto the edge of the sofa, he gazed down at his wife. His wife.

He knew he should call one of the other officers' wives to tend to her. Or he should call for the doctor to bring the smelling salts he kept in his cabinet, but he gave in to the selfish desire to have her all to himself just for a little while.

He gently brushed a tendril of hair away from her cheek. Amazingly, her skin was as soft as he remembered it being. He smoothed down his mustache in a burst of nervousness that until recently had been entirely out of character for him. Now he seemed to be performing that gesture on a quite frequent basis.

It didn't take an overly intelligent man to know why. He still cared for her.

There had never been anyone for him but Elise. There had been other women willing to take her place through the years, but he never could bring himself to take them up on their offers. He wondered if it had been the same way for her. But she'd never believed him after that night.

He realized with sudden clarity that he'd given her his heart years before, and she still held it in the palm of her hand.

What was he going to do about her?

He didn't know. How did a man go about winning back the heart of a woman he'd lost?

At that moment Elise's eyelids fluttered open, and he swallowed. However, the lump in his throat remained, and grew as she gazed up into his eyes.

"Carson?"

He had to lean closer to make out her soft, trembling words. "Yes, dear?"

Elise stared into his eyes a moment longer, then pushed herself out of his arms. Her softness hardened before his gaze.

"Carson, if you don't find her and bring her back safe, I'll never forgive you."

With this, she turned away from him and walked out the door as if he'd never held her in his arms at all.

The morning wore on in silence. It bore hard on Branded Wolf. He'd never minded silence before, but for some unknown reason this was different. He found his gaze going again and again to Regan.

He seemed unable to keep her out of his mind. And it was beginning to take an effort to keep from taking her into his arms. When she'd walked by and her skirt ruffle had brushed his foot, he'd nearly leapt up and caught her into his arms.

However much he disliked it, he was finding himself beginning to desire a kiss from Regan's sweet lips. It didn't take much to imagine her reaction if a half-breed attempted to take liberties with her. To his disgust, the scorn he was certain would come from her was becoming of greater importance to him. She was a mixture of the spoiled society women he hated and a softhearted woman-child he was hard pressed to resist.

He would wait until afternoon, then he would gather up their things for their ride out. Something told him a raiding party would be easier than what he had planned. Tomorrow they would reach the mountains.

He watched Regan's graceful movements as she wandered around the area. He bit back his smile when she tried to make friends with Wind Dancer, only to be rebuffed with a flick of the animal's tail.

Regan stomped away from the horse, mumbling complaints under her breath. He thought he caught something about himself and the horse being related, at least their backsides.

In a fine temper, she kicked up dust in her wake as she walked past him without even a pause. Nose in the air, she continued on by and grabbed up the parasol from behind him. Crossing to the rocks, she kicked aside a small cluster and stuck the parasol handle inside the opening.

Fluffing out her skirts, she sat on the bare ground as if she were seating herself on the finest furniture in a fancy room. The little pup bounded onto her lap and promptly lay down. A chuckle worked its way up from Branded Wolf's chest but froze at a movement.

He sprang to his feet in a quick, soundless move. Fear like he'd never felt in his life ate at him.

"Regan," he said softly.

Her head snapped up at the sound of her name on Branded Wolf's lips. He'd said her name. She smiled at him in encouragement. He was learning some English.

Her smile faded at the harsh, almost deadly look on his

face. She forced herself to answer him past the lump in her throat. "Yes?"

"Stay still."

She opened her mouth, but at a rapid slice of his hand she fell silent, her words forgotten. A twinge of fear crept up her neck. He looked so—

"Do exactly as I say," he ordered in a low tone. "Stay there."

He took one menacing step toward her. Regan swallowed, her eyes widening on him. Had she pushed too far today? He looked so different . . . so . . . savage.

She didn't think she could move if her life depended on it at that moment. She tightened her fingers into Sweet Pea's fur. The desert air seemed to still around her; utter silence covered them. Time slowed and the air must have chilled, for her arms broke out in goose bumps.

Her full attention on Branded Wolf, she watched as he dropped his hand to his leg and withdrew a knife quicker than she could blink her eyes. The knife gleamed long and deadly in the sunlight.

An unreasonable fear rose up within her. She tried to move, but her limbs were leaden and refused the orders of her mind. One horrible thought kept running through her mind.

He was going to scalp her.

The next instant he threw the knife. She screamed and then collapsed in a dead faint.

Chapter Nine

Regan came to slowly with Sweet Pea licking her chin, and Branded Wolf bent low over her. The memory of the moment when he'd thrown the knife engulfed her again. He had—

She stared up at him to meet concern in the depths of his blue eyes. Why would he be concerned now?

She pushed herself up into a sitting position and caught Sweet Pea close to her chest.

"You . . . threw a . . . knife at me." Her accusation was spoken almost too low to hear.

Branded Wolf bent closer, and she shrank from him. She tightened her hold on her pet until the dog squirmed in her arms.

Her eyes asked the question why even before she voiced the words themselves.

"You tried to kill me?"

His expression darkened, but not before Regan caught a glimpse of the look of pain that flickered in his eyes. He abruptly stood up and pointed to where his knife protruded from the body of a long, deadly looking snake. Even in the shade of the rock she could see the glimmer of the rattles on its tail.

A rattlesnake.

She stared transfixed at the writhing body of the snake. It continued to twitch and undulate.

"Is . . . it . . . de-dead?" she whispered.

The thing was horrible. She gulped and shivered, looking at it. It was long and slithery and just horrible.

"Yes, it's dead. It can't hurt you now."

She continued to stare, unable to tear her gaze away from the creature. She tried to swallow past the knot in her throat, and instead it grew.

"Regan, look at me." Branded Wolf's voice was low and commanding.

She tried to look away from the dreadful snake, but she couldn't do it no matter how hard she tried.

"Regan." He squatted down beside her.

When she didn't turn, he reached out and cupped her chin in his palm. Gently, he forced her face away from the sight of the dead snake. Her eyes met his.

Regan shuddered and closed her eyes. Once again a mental image of Brand throwing the knife filled her mind. He hadn't been going to scalp her. He'd saved her from the deadly snake.

A shudder racked her body and she stiffened with the pride that had been ingrained in her. She wouldn't give in to tears. He was the one hurting, not her. Humiliation at her cruel accusations filled her. He'd saved her life and she'd accused him of trying to kill her.

Embarrassment colored her pale cheeks. How could she have behaved that terribly when he'd saved her life? And he'd—

He'd spoken. Clearly.

The realization swept away all other feelings inside her. *He'd warned her in English. In English, no less!*

"You talked. In English." She stated the words in a tight voice.

Branded Wolf merely nodded.

"You speak English."

Anger sent her to her feet in a rush of movement. She backed away from him, her arms wrapped around the dog. She glared at him, her anger growing with each silent second that stretched between them.

Why, he'd been able to talk all along. And he hadn't done so. Even worse, he'd understood every single word she said to him.

Damn him.

"You speak English!" Regan shouted.

Her eyes narrowed on him, and he could see the thoughts and memories of their days together as they crossed her mind.

He knew the instant she had all the pieces put together. Her eyes darkened to the color of an emerald stone, and she set the dog at her feet. The pup scooted back away from the snake until she peeked out from behind Regan's skirts.

"You . . ." Regan sputtered. "You could speak English all along."

He wisely remained silent. She hadn't even thanked him for saving her life.

She curled her shaking hands into fists and planted them on her hips. For a brief moment he thought she was going to take a swing at him, and he tensed to take the blow.

"You tricked me." She leaned forward, shouting the words at him.

Then she straightened, and in her fury she was beautiful. Every bit an equal to any warrior, he thought to himself. Desire stirred in him, surprising him with its intensity.

"You low-down, lying, conniving man," she yelled at him. "No good, rotten, sneaky."

With each insult she advanced an angry step forward. Her speech gathered speed along with her anger.

"You good-for-nothing liar."

She didn't stop shouting until she stood toe-to-toe with him.

"You . . . why, you're no better than . . . than my father!"

She snapped her lips together and glared at him as if that had been the highest insult she could give him. He waited, but she remained silently fuming. Apparently, she had finished.

He stared back at her, and a surprising realization hit him. She'd insulted him, called him names, and yelled at him. However, she hadn't uttered one word about his mixed blood or his Indian heritage.

With a haughty shake of her head obviously meant to simply dismiss him, she turned her back on him. He watched her in amazement. She had insulted him, thrown off his saving her life as if it were nothing, and then dismissed him.

In spite of all this, or perhaps because of it, he wanted her. Yes, he wanted her with a burning that he refused to acknowledge. But he didn't wish to desire her at all, much less with this intensity.

Angry at both himself and at her, he reached out and caught her shoulder. She gave a yelp of indignation. Angered even more at her reaction, he spun her back around to face him.

"You are an ungrateful white-eyes," he stated.

Regan's mouth gaped. No one had ever talked back to her before. Not once in her entire life.

If he thought for one minute that she was going to tolerate this . . . this insolence from him, well, he had another surprise coming.

Raising her chin in defiance, she raked him with her glare.

"Take your hands off me." Her voice nearly shook with her fury.

When he didn't instantly do as she ordered, she slapped his hands away and stepped back. Angry green eyes met an equally angry blue gaze.

"Ungrateful?" she yelled at him. "Ungrateful. I'll tell you what ungrateful is." She plopped her hands on her hips again.

Advancing a step, she raised her chin another notch and glared into his face. "I took care of you. I washed you." Her voice rose with each pronouncement. "I bandaged you. I worried about you. And, dammit, I fed you."

At the memory of the tempting feel of her tender fingers against his lips, Branded Wolf felt his blood warm. He recalled the words she'd said to the dog about his body, and a small smile tipped his lips.

She'd liked his wide chest, said something about him curling her toes, if he recalled correctly. His smile widened.

"Don't you dare laugh at me!"

Regan glared her anger. Why, she'd been nursing him and doing all kinds of disgusting housekeeping duties in the wilderness, and all the while he'd been laughing at her behind her back—in English no less.

That was the final indignation for her. As her temper soared, it got the better of her. She swung at him, her hand skimming his chin as he tipped his head back out of her arm's reach.

Branded Wolf stepped forward, the look in his dark eyes putting an end to any and all of her thoughts. Every single one of them flew from her mind like butterflies scattered by a strong breeze.

He pulled her into his embrace, and she knew she should fight him. She should shove him away. She raised her hands, but instead of pushing him, she rested her palms on his wide chest.

His eyes burned with a passion she'd never witnessed before in her life. It held her mesmerized, fascinated, excited.

Her mind told her to push away; her body stayed still. Her mind told her to tell him no; her lips said absolutely nothing at all.

She could feel the beat of his heart beneath the palm of her hand. His bare, sun-bronzed skin was warm under her fingertips. As she stared up at him, she felt his heartbeat quicken, and she knew hers raced right along with his.

This was insanity, she told herself.

This was what she'd been waiting for, a little voice whispered in the far recesses of her mind.

Branded Wolf's hold on her tightened, and he drew her closer and closer.

Regan took a small step nearer, feeling as if she were stepping into a raging fire.

Pulling her to his chest with one arm, he slid his other hand down lower and pressed her hips to his. Regan gasped aloud at the intimate contact. He took her lips in a hungry kiss that stole her next breath clean away from her.

One thought crossed her mind. *She'd never been kissed like this before.*

He slid his hand from her shoulders up to her head and tightened his hold, his fingers weaving into her curls. Regan breathed against his lips. His lips were firm against hers. Demanding.

She kissed him back, tilting her head in an instinctive act to invite him to deepen the kiss. He took the invitation, slanting his mouth firmly, hard over hers, taking her very breath and mingling it with his. She didn't know where he left off or where she began anymore. And she didn't care.

When she sighed against him, he shifted his mouth over hers, sliding his tongue between her lips. Regan stiffened at the sudden intrusion, but he stroked her lips with his tongue, probing, hinting at something to come, demanding.

His tongue plunged into her mouth, soft and velvet to her. She felt her legs weaken beneath his loving onslaught and the strange unfamiliar emotions he was evoking in her. Sliding her hands upward, she caught hold of his shoulders to steady herself.

It didn't do her any good at all. When he pressed his hand against her backside, pulling her even closer to him, she thought she'd swoon then and there. Her knees nearly buckled.

Branded Wolf took her weight in his arms and gently lowered her to the ground, then rolled atop her. His weight was a pleasant feel to her. She was beyond any complaint. She gripped his shoulders as shudders of delight coursed through her from her lips to her toes. She absolutely knew they were curled in her slippers.

She slipped one hand along his sweat-slickened skin and over his broad-muscled shoulder to the length of his neck. Her fingers curled in the long strands of his silken hair. She moaned against his mouth.

Branded Wolf took the sound to his heart. She tasted sweet, so sweet.

Her soft moans fired his blood hotter than he'd ever thought possible. He felt as if he would burst into flame with her next sound. Her fingertips kneaded his shoulder; her other hand tugged on his hair.

He leaned into the next kiss, each subsequent kiss better than the one before. They blended together.

Suddenly, a sharp, piercing yap jarred his mind. The sound continued, even shriller than before.

Branded Wolf leapt to his feet, whirling around to face the sound. Sweet Pea stood not four feet away. Her fur ruffled out around her neck and she had her front paws planted solidly in front of her. Sharp barks escalated in intensity and volume. Her black eyes were focused on the dead snake.

Slowly, she backed up, one paw at a time, until she bumped into Branded Wolf's leg. She promptly sat down on his foot.

"What's ... what's wrong?" Regan pushed herself to her feet and self-consciously straightened the bodice of her gown. Humiliation rushed over her in waves of shame. She'd been lying on the ground, shamelessly kissing a man. Why, if Sweet Pea hadn't interrupted them—

Regan gulped, and she knew her cheeks colored. What must Brand think of her? She dared a glimpse at his face. It was set in harsh lines of strain. She closed her eyes and gulped.

Her behavior was shameless. It was—

"Regan." He caught her hand in his.

She opened her eyes but refused to face him. She couldn't chance seeing scorn in his blue depths. For that's what society would do; it would scorn her for her forward, wanton behavior.

"Regan, I'm sorry." He dropped her hand. "That shouldn't have happened."

He was sorry for kissing her?

She raised her head with a snap that jolted her neck. His expression was unreadable.

He'd said he was sorry for kissing her. He'd apologized.

A shaft of pain hit her chest, and for an instant she thought her legs would buckle under the intensity of it. No one had ever told her he was sorry for kissing her. No one had ever kissed her the way Brand had just done.

She knew she couldn't let him see her pain. She never let anyone witness her pain; it gave them more power to hurt her. Hadn't she learned that from her father? Oh, she'd learned her lessons well through the years. Brand would never know he hurt her, no matter what.

Her temper came to the fore, salvaging her wounded pride. And perhaps a tiny corner of her heart as well.

He had the nerve to apologize! Well, she'd let him know that it didn't matter in the least little bit. No, not at all.

"What a coincidence." She laughed, but it came out sounding strangely hollow to her own ears. "I thought I was the only one feeling that emotion."

His brows drew together, and she resisted the sudden urge to smooth her hand over his forehead.

"I felt sorry for you when I thought you couldn't speak English—like a civilized man!"

Her cutting words cooled his blood instantly. His own anger riled at the insult she'd thrown down. "I don't want your pity."

"Well, that's good, because you don't have it." She tossed her head.

"You're lucky I don't leave you here."

"You wouldn't dare. You owe me." She tossed her head again in defiance.

He stared down at her a full moment before he spoke again. "I owe the white-eyes nothing. Nothing."

"But I saved your life."

He pointed to the dead snake. "And I yours."

She opened and shut her mouth twice. No words would come out.

This couldn't be right. He had to owe her. He *had* to take her back to the fort.

"Fine." She spat out the word at him. "Then just take me back to Fort Bowie."

"No.

"But . . . but, what do you mean, no?"

"No. Obviously, it is a word you're not used to hearing."

"But you *have* to return me to the fort."

"No."

"Will you quit saying that!" she snapped.

"That is the way it will be. I will not take you to the fort."

"You have to."

He faced her squarely. "I don't have to do anything. But you are coming with me."

"Where?" She eyed him warily.

"There." He pointed off into the distance.

She honestly didn't know if he'd gestured toward the fort or away from it, but she suspected the latter.

"No," she answered back.

"Oh, yes, you're coming with me, Regan. If I have to tie you to my horse."

She opened her mouth to dare him, then thought better of it and remained silent.

"That's good. We will start out at dusk," he announced to her. "We're running low on water, so we'll travel when it cools."

Regan sucked in an angry breath. If she weren't hopelessly lost, she'd escape on her own. And if he thought she'd follow along meekly in his footsteps, well, he had more than one surprise in store for him.

Regan stared off across at the sun. Its brilliant hues of rose, mauve, and gold nearly stole her breath away. The desert shimmered like an opal set in pale gold. For the briefest moment she understood why her father loved this land.

She took a step, and the corner of a rock caught the ball of her foot, clad in her fancy slipper. Muttering a soft curse under her breath, she recalled why her mama hated the place.

She wrinkled her nose in distaste at the dust and grit and shook out her skirt. It was showing worse for the wear. She promptly forgot all about the earlier beauty of the desert sunset.

The beauty held hidden dangers, didn't it? She recalled the rattlesnake with a shiver. Brand had mumbled something

APACHE PRIDE   137

about dinner, but after one look at her face, he'd disposed
of the horrible thing out of sight.

She sighed. Once again, they had feasted, hardly the correct word, on the tough, stringy jerky stuff he seemed to
like. And she hated it.

"It's time."

Regan whirled around at the words from Branded Wolf.
She hadn't even heard him approach.

"Time for what?" She crossed her arms over her chest,
instinctively preparing for battle.

"Time to leave," he stated.

"I don't think so." She tossed back her head.

"I can either leave you here for the rattlesnakes, or tie
you up and throw you over Wind Dancer. Or you can come
agreeably."

At the flash of anger in her eyes, he added, "Maybe
agreeably is asking too much. Let's say you can come on
your own steam, or I'll drag you."

Regan glared at him. This couldn't be the same man who
had kissed her so wonderfully. Who had . . .

She shoved aside the heated memories.

One look at his face told her he'd do exactly as he threatened if she forced him.

"Damn you," she said softly.

He merely raised his eyebrows. "Well, what's it to be?"

As much as a part of her wanted to push him, she didn't.
She caught up her skirt in one hand and raised her chin.
"All right, I'm coming."

Abruptly, she turned her back on him and patted her
thighs.

"Sweet Pea, here, Sweetie," she called out.

The little pup came bounding up to her, white hair bedraggled and dirty. Regan ignored the dusty hair and caught the
dog up into her arms. Then she turned back around and
began walking toward Brand.

"All right. We're ready," she announced.

He narrowed his eyes on her. "What do you think you're doing with that dog?"

"I'm holding her. What's it look like I'm doing?" The words slipped out before she could stop them.

Gritting his teeth, he swung up onto Wind Dancer's back. "Put the dog down and give me your hand."

"What for?"

He blew his breath out between his teeth. "So I can lift you up onto the horse. Now, put the dog down."

She shook her head, then added, "No."

Then she surprised him by holding out one hand.

"Regan."

She waved her hand at him. "I'm ready."

"Put the dog down." He wasn't going to say it again.

Instead, she tightened her other hand on the dog. "Sweet Pea rides when I do."

"What!" His thundered shout caused Wind Dancer to sidestep. He calmed the horse with a command from his knees.

She was playing a joke on him, wasn't she? The white-eyes couldn't be serious.

Regan smiled up at him, a look of pure innocence on her pretty face. "It's really quite simple. I'll explain it to you."

"I wish you would," he muttered below his breath.

She waved her hand at him. "You lift me up in front of you. I carry Sweet Pea up—"

"No."

"And she rides in my lap." Regan continued on as if he hadn't even spoken.

"No," he thundered out the denial.

Wind Dancer sidestepped, then backed up. Branded Wolf nudged him forward again.

"Put the—"

Regan tilted her head back and met his glare. "Are we

riding or not? Because I'm getting tired of standing here in the sun. If you can't make up your mind, I'll go sit in the shade until you do.''

She turned as if to walk away from him.

''Regan!''

She looked back over her shoulder. ''Yes? Have you made a decision?''

''Get on the horse,'' he gritted out the order.

''Sweet Pea is really quite a good rider. You'll see,'' she assured him, turning around and extending her free hand to him.

Right then Branded Wolf had the sudden urge to strangle her or to make love to her, he wasn't sure which. Now the white-eyes had him unable to make up his mind.

She slipped her hand in his and looked up into his eyes without blinking. He met her stare and released his breath between his clenched teeth.

An Apache warrior, riding a trained warhorse along with a white-eyes and her dog. He resisted the urge to shake his head in disbelief.

He'd be damned lucky if the horse didn't throw all of them.

Chapter Ten

Regan tried to hold herself stiffly away from the tempting comfort of Branded Wolf's broad chest. Every time a shift in the horse's gait caused her to brush against him, memories of the kisses they'd shared engulfed her.

The heat . . . the strength of the muscles beneath her hands . . . the too-pleasurable feel of his lips on hers. Heat skimmed each and every place he'd touched her.

Stars and heavens, it was hot. She knew she was perspiring. How she wished she dare raise her hand to fan herself, even for a moment.

She dare not.

Each step the horse took jostled her. She knew from her previous riding experience that her stiff posture caused the discomfort, but she couldn't give in and let her body slide back against his.

Embarrassment heated her cheeks, and she longed to fan herself to cool the blush. What she wouldn't give for a nice, pretty fan, maybe one made of feathers. She closed her eyes and tried to conjure up memories of a cool evening. Moments later, she could almost imagine herself fanning her face and neck, enjoying a cold lemonade, and listening to the strains of a waltz.

A sudden misstep from the horse jolted Regan back to the reality of the desert. She grabbed hold of the horse's mane to steady herself, nearly upsetting both herself and Sweet Pea. That's what she got for letting her mind wander so.

She shoved aside her fanciful wishes. She'd better concentrate on remaining on the moving horse. It was all she could do to sit up straight, keep a hand on Sweet Pea in her lap, and ensure that she didn't brush back against Branded Wolf any more than was absolutely necessary to stay upright on the horse.

Suddenly, Branded Wolf said something in Apache and pulled her against him.

"Relax," he ordered, this time in English.

The thought crossed her mind that the instruction had sounded so much prettier when he'd said it in the other language.

"It's too long a ride to go in anger," he added in a low voice.

A part of Regan responded to his half-apology, and she smiled in spite of her earlier anger at him. She'd be gracious and accept his repentance. It's what her mama would expect. Using his order and subsequent apology as an excuse, she allowed herself to relax, leaning back against him.

Oh, heavens, it felt good, she thought.

"It is more comfortable this way," she observed aloud with all the dignity she could muster, what with the heat of his chest radiating through her gown.

"Yes."

Branded Wolf bit back his next comment. *Comfortable* was a long way from the word he would choose to use.

Torture would be a better way of describing the sensations she was evoking in his lower body. He shifted on the horse.

With each step Wind Dancer took, Branded Wolf became increasingly *uncomfortable*. The horse's easy gait brought Regan's soft backside into closer and closer contact, settling her firmly between his thighs. It was sweet torture.

He tried to remind himself that he had no use for the white-eyes, men or women, but it did little or no good. His body responded to her closeness, ignoring the commands of his mind.

Without thinking, he slid one hand from the reins to lay it across Regan's stomach. He heard her soft gasp, and he half expected her to slap his hand away. But she did nothing. Instead, it seemed to him that she settled a little closer against his chest. He smiled, then the dog laid her paw on his hand.

Branded Wolf merely shook his head in derision. An Apache warrior, saddled with a woman and her little bit of a dog. He felt like laughing, but a strange sense of responsibility rose up in him.

The woman and her dog were his to care for no matter what came.

The ride was long, and eventually, he felt her grow heavy in his arms with sleep. Surprisingly, she hadn't complained as he'd expected from a woman of her kind. Much about her surprised him.

The trust she'd shown by falling asleep in his arms touched him. He held her close, shifting his body so that her head rested below his shoulder. At a slight movement he tightened his fingers into the pup's fur to keep it atop her lap.

Regan didn't even notice when he reined the horse in and stopped to make camp for the night. Tomorrow they would be out of the desert and into the mountains that had once belonged to his people. The days would be cooler, and the nights peaceful. He longed for the peace of the place his people called Land of the Standing-Up Rocks.

He gazed at the clear sky above them, where the stars glimmered in the dark canopy of twilight. Easily, he slid off Wind Dancer's back without a sound, then caught Regan's sleeping form in his arms. The pup shifted and snuggled his hand as he carried them both to a resting place for the night.

After he'd settled Regan on the tattered petticoat, he paused to brush a curl from her cheek. He rested his fingers against her soft skin for a moment.

"Sleep well, little one," he whispered. Unable to resist, he pressed a light kiss on her forehead.

She turned her cheek into his palm, nuzzling him like a horse its master.

Branded Wolf stood to his feet in a surge of movement. He needed a walk. A long one.

He welcomed the desert solitude. As he stood staring out at the vastness, he let the desert work its magic on his soul.

Over an hour later, Branded Wolf lay on the petticoat, still awake. Almost the moment he lay down beside her, Regan curled into his arms, snuggling against him. Her deep, even breathing stirred at his neck. It heated his blood more than any desert sun ever could do.

"An Apache warrior, a woman, and a dog," he muttered below his breath.

Neither Regan nor the pup stirred a muscle at his grumbled comment.

He gazed down at her. She slept peacefully, the sleep of the exhausted. He let her be. But for him, he knew sleep would be a long time in coming this night.

Regan woke the next day to find Branded Wolf watching her. She shifted uneasily under his scrutiny. It seemed this was beginning to become a regular morning ritual.

Today she wasn't in the mood for such a thing. She ached in places she didn't know she could ache. And she was hungry.

She tried to ignore the truth behind her foul mood. Once again her body had betrayed her in sleep. She was ashamed at finding herself snuggled up to him, much less with him staring at her and smiling. *Smiling.* How dare he laugh at her need for warmth. As if she'd be snuggled up to him for anything else!

Embarrassment flooded her cheeks. She was appalled at her unseemly behavior. Her mama would be so ashamed of her, to find her *sleeping* with a man before marriage. Not that they'd done anything, but she'd still *slept* with him.

Not that anything about their being together was regular in any way. He'd put her to bed last night, for heaven's sake. She didn't even want to think about what her mama would say to that.

Regan could feel Brand's gaze on her. It compelled her to look up at him, to face him. This time there was no laughter in his eyes, but something else.

She swallowed, nervous all of a sudden. Jumping to her feet, she made some excuse and hurried off to put a short distance between them. Last night something had changed between them. She couldn't explain exactly what it was, but something was different. She could feel it.

And it made her downright jumpy.

To make matters worse, she could have sworn she heard Branded Wolf's deep chuckle behind her as she walked away.

Elise McBain gave one short knock, then walked into her husband's office. She was cool, poised, and half scared to death, but she'd never let him see it.

"Good morning." Her voice held precisely the right amount of coolness.

He stood to meet her. "My dear, I hope you're feeling better."

In a few steps he rounded the desk and held out his hands. She dismissed his gesture with a flick of her gloved hands.

"How can I feel better with my daughter still missing somewhere out there?"

He smoothed his mustache with his fingers, at a loss as to what to do with his outstretched but empty hands.

"Carson, what are you doing to bring Regan back?"

"I assure you—"

She waved a hand, effectively cutting him off. "Save the speeches for your men. I want the truth."

"Darling—"

Elise stamped her foot, shaking the inkwell on his desk with the vehemence of her action.

"Don't call me that."

"I—"

"What are you doing? Precisely what are you doing to find my daughter?"

He sighed deeply. "Our daughter," he added.

She merely raised her brows at him.

"I have a patrol of men out searching for her."

"And?"

He sighed again, and his voice sank with defeat when he spoke. "We haven't found anything yet."

"And why not?" she demanded, her voice rising in near despair.

He couldn't lie to her. Not now. Not knowing he still cared for her.

Stepping forward, he drew her into his arms.

"I don't know, Elise," he stated, his voice wavering. "I don't know."

For the first time in years, she willingly leaned against him.

Regan thought the day's ride would never end.

The desert had stretched on and on for what seemed like forever. Then suddenly, she'd noticed a discernible rise in the desert floor. They were climbing. Even the air seemed cooler, the sun less intense. Closing her eyes, she'd dozed, Branded Wolf's chest strong and sure at her back.

At long last Branded Wolf reined the horse to a stop in a wooded area. After dismounting, he picked up Sweet Pea and set the dog on the ground. Then he turned and lifted Regan down. As she stood, her legs turned rubbery, and she nearly slid to the ground.

Branded Wolf tightened his hold on her waist, steadying her.

"Can you stand now?" he asked.

"I think so."

Smiling, he eased his hands from her waist until she was standing on her own. She took a tentative step and took in the strange-looking rock formations towering above, almost like giants staring down on them. She tore her gaze away and sighed at the sparse grass underfoot and the sprinkling of Indian paintbrush and prickly poppy wildflowers.

"Trees. And grass," she murmured.

She wanted to take off her slippers and wiggle her toes in it, even though it was scraggly and thin. No more sand and desert grit.

"Look." Branded Wolf pointed to one side.

In the distance, she wasn't certain if it was east or west, she saw a glimmer of what looked like water.

"Is it—"

"Water."

"Real water?"

"A seasonal mountain stream," he assured her. "Nestled between two rocks."

"Ah." She sighed and smiled.

"With a pool below, for bathing," he added.

Regan tilted her head back, and her face broke into a wide smile. "Thank heavens!"

This time she knew she heard him chuckle. The deep, rich sound sent something skittering along her nerve endings.

"Come. There's something else I want to show you." Branded Wolf took her by the hand and gently dragged her along behind him.

Regan followed willingly, curiosity eating at her. He was different here. Less restrained. More . . . savage . . . or more uncivilized perhaps?

Sweet Pea bounded up to them with a soft "woof," then left Regan's side to trot along at his heels.

Branded Wolf narrowly missed tripping over the pup when she weaved in front of his feet. He sidestepped the dog and kept walking.

Just what he'd always wanted, he thought in disgust, a little fluff of a dog following him around everywhere he walked. However, he found himself slowing his pace so both the pup and Regan could keep up without having to struggle.

After a few minutes, he reached his destination and stopped. Regan nearly plowed into his back. She looked around his shoulder at the clearing and her mouth dropped open.

"What is . . . that?" she asked, trepidation obvious in her halting words.

"A wickiup." He stepped aside to give her a better view.

Regan licked her lips and stared at the unusual structure. If one could call it that, she thought.

"What is it for?"

"Shelter. It's where we'll sleep."

"In there?" She wrinkled her nose in distaste.

She was certain it housed an abundance of bugs and *things*. And she bet it even smelled.

Without realizing what she did, she stepped back, shaking her head.

Branded Wolf tensed. "I know it isn't fancy—"

"Hardly."

"But it will be comfortable."

"I doubt that."

He straightened up taller, distancing himself from her. All laughter left him.

"It is more than good enough for an Apache woman," he snapped, a part of him responding to her obvious scorn and snobbery. The one he'd built years ago had been good enough for Soaring Dove. She'd exclaimed over it in pleasure, not contempt.

"I am not an Apache." Regan tossed her head.

"Never doubt that I remember that."

He turned on his heel and strode away, disappearing into the odd structure.

Regan watched him go, and a twinge of guilt assailed her. She had been rather awful to him, but the—what had he called it—the wickiup looked so uncivilized.

As she stood there, he exited the wickiup, carrying something in his hand.

"Brand." She hesitated.

His head snapped up, and his gaze bore into hers. "What?"

"Ah, how did you know that would be here?" She pointed at the structure.

"Because I built it over a year ago."

"Oh." She stared from the wickiup to him thoughtfully.

He tightened his hands on something. "I'll set a snare. With any luck, tonight we'll be eating roasted rabbit." He walked away from her.

Regan's stomach rumbled. She never thought she'd admit to actually looking forward to food cooked outside, much less rabbit. But she could hardly wait.

Branded Wolf was true to his word. They feasted on substantial food that night, with Regan even licking her fingers at the end.

Her stomach pleasantly full for the first time in what seemed like forever to her, she could barely keep her eyes open. She covered her mouth with her hand to hide a yawn. By the fourth yawn she gave up any attempt to disguise her action.

As her head nodded forward, she felt Branded Wolf's strong arms around her.

"Umm, nice," she murmured.

"Nice," he answered in a voice that sounded strangely rough to her ears.

It didn't sound to her like he agreed with her remark at all. She licked her lips and smiled. She'd explain it to him in just a minute.

She heard his heart beating against her ear and frowned. What was his heart doing there? she wondered. Then she was being lowered to the ground, except it wasn't hard at all. It was soft and smelled like the holidays. Pine or something, she thought, trying to place the pleasant scent.

Stifling her next yawn, she gave in to sleep.

Branded Wolf squatted beside her. Her deep, even breaths told him she slept soundly. Shutting his eyes, he leaned his head back.

This wasn't at all the way he'd planned on this night ending.

Pushing himself to his feet, he returned to the small campfire. The moment he sat down, the little white pup clambered up into his lap. As he watched in amazement, the pup circled twice, then plopped in the middle of his lap and rested her chin on his knee.

The pup he didn't want was curled in his lap, while the woman he wanted was sound asleep away from him.

Branded Wolf shook his head. Now he understood why wolves howled at the moon.

Branded Wolf stared into the fire until the small blaze had burned down to dying embers. The moon rose high above the pine trees. He stroked the pup sleeping peacefully in his lap. Still, the peace of sleep eluded him.

The night sounds of the mountain hideaway had lulled around him, broken only by an occasional snore from the pup. He knew they were safe there, protected by the canyon walls, but still he could not sleep.

A strange restlessness overtook his thoughts.

He longed for the past, the companionship of his tribe, his family.

But it was all gone, stripped away from him by the white-eyes and their greed.

The pup stirred in his lap. She gave a soft yip in her sleep, and her paws twitched. Chasing rabbits, he'd bet.

He shook his head. This city dog had likely never seen a rabbit except for the small pieces of meat eaten tonight. The pup whined, and he found himself stroking the soft fur and murmuring in reassurance.

Branded Wolf almost groaned aloud. Now Regan even had him pampering her spoiled dog.

Surging to his feet, he carried the sleeping pup to the wickiup. He gently laid the dog down inside, then stretched out on the boughs beside Regan. The night air didn't have the chill of the desert cold, and he wondered if she would seek out his warmth this night as she'd done every night before.

In silent answer to his query, she rolled onto her side,

snuggling into the curve of his arm. He tightened his arm around her, pulling her closer.

She sighed softly in her sleep, and his stomach coiled into a knot at the sound. It was so like the tempting noises she'd made when he kissed her. It seemed like more than a year ago.

Closing his eyes, he willed his body to relax, to seek the rest and peace usually offered by sleep.

Gradually, bit by bit, muscle by muscle, the tenseness left him. Beside him, Regan slept peacefully, curled into his embrace. At his feet, the pup slept with her chin atop his foot again.

Branded Wolf fell into a restless sleep. Sometime later, past and present merged together.

He heard the cries of terror. Flinging out his arm, he reached for his war lance as an Apache war cry split the night.

Chapter Eleven

Jerked awake, her heart in her throat, Regan lay unmoving, trying to locate the sound. Shivers raced up and down her spine.

Fighting against her own scream lodged in her throat, she struggled to sit up, but something held her down. The only light came from the moon shining through the opening in the wickiup. Fear engulfed her, and she fought back against the unknown danger.

She pushed against the barrier of a firmly muscled arm, frantically trying to free herself.

Suddenly, the outcry came again. It sent her pulses racing, but this time it also tugged at her heart. The sound carried such pain with it.

She clasped her hands around the weight holding her down, then realized it was Brand's arm across her. For an instant, she stilled her struggles. His arm lay where it was, resting atop her. All was quiet around them.

At the sound of a low, guttural groan, she turned her head to search his face. The sound had come from him.

Regan nearly held her breath, waiting.

The painful moan came again. It reached out to touch her, pulling at her heart. Everything within her had a sudden desire to offer comfort.

He was in pain.

She had to do something.

"Brand?" she whispered, shifting to roll her body toward him.

He didn't answer.

"Is it your wound?" she asked, once again her voice barely above a whisper.

Tentatively, she laid her hand on his shoulder. His body jerked beneath her touch. She pulled her hand back, then leaned closer.

His breathing was ragged, uneven. Labored. He called out again, and Regan felt his pain. She couldn't stand him going through this.

"Brand," she called softly.

He didn't hear her. He was caught up in his own private hell. He could hear cries, and smoke stung his nostrils. In the distance, he could see three plumes of smoke rising into the sky.

"No," he cried out, thrashing his arms.

He tried to race back to the tiny village of his family and his bride-to-be. His chest burned with the thundering in his ears. He pushed himself faster. Faster.

He had to save them. He had to . . .

As he topped the small rise, blind rage swept over him in waves as he saw the carnage that had once been his village. The three wickiups of his father, his uncle and aunt, and Soaring Dove burned, flames shooting high into the sky.

"No!"

He raced down the hill, his rifle and bow lost in the ruins

of his father's burning wickiup. Desperately, he searched for his loved ones. Four bodies lay in the dirt. The stench of death carried across the distance separating them.

He could see five white-eyes, two dressed in the blue coats of the cavalry, standing in the midst of the destruction. Laughing.

The blue of the soldiers' jackets mocked him, reminding him of his own blue-eyed heritage. Hatred built up in him, blocking out everything else.

He took a step forward, his whole being focused in that instant on the man standing over Soaring Dove's broken body. The soldier turned to face him, a glint of laughter in his cold eyes, and Soaring Dove's blood on his hands.

"Don't worry, Injun. She wasn't that good." The soldier reached out and wiped his hands on what was left of her deerskin dress.

Branded Wolf reacted in rage. Drawing his knife from his moccasin, he threw it straight at the soldier. At the same instant, the soldier raised and fired his Colt.

Hot lead struck Branded Wolf in the chest, and he reeled backward. Hatred in his eyes, he took one step forward, ignoring the pain.

He saw the white-eyes jerk the knife from his shoulder and toss it to the dirt. He ground the heel of his boot onto the bloodstained blade. With a laugh, he wiped his jaw where the knife had skimmed on its path to his shoulder, then spat into the dirt.

Branded Wolf felt the moment's satisfaction in knowing that the soldier would carry his scar from the blade for the rest of his life.

The soldier rubbed his jawline, then glared his own hatred in the instant before he raised his gun and fired again. The bullet hit Branded Wolf in the shoulder, this time spinning him about, and he collapsed into darkness.

He called out in despair.

"Brand!" Regan called his name again and again. She sat up and leaned over him.

He fought her touch, shoving her hands aside, nearly knocking her to the ground with his arm.

"Brand. Wake up."

She grabbed hold of his uninjured shoulder and shook him as hard as she could, trying to pull him back from whatever horror he was reliving.

His eyes snapped open, and in the light from the moon streaming into the enclosure she could see they were still clouded with the horrible memories he'd been reliving.

"Brand," she called out more gently this time. "You were dreaming."

He shook his head as if trying to focus his thoughts on the person leaning over him. He drew in a ragged breath and reached out.

"Soaring Dove?" His voice gentled.

"Brand." Regan shook his shoulder.

"Noch-ay-del-klinne? Is it you?" he asked in a hoarse voice edged with pain.

"Brand, it's me. Regan." She leaned closer so he could see her clearly.

Branded Wolf closed his eyes and then reopened them. No, it wasn't Noch-ay-del-klinne, the Apache medicine man who had found him those years ago. The shaman had tended his wounds, using his healing arts to keep him alive.

No, it was the beautiful white-eyes, the woman called Regan, leaning over him now.

He sat up, feeling his chest for the blood he was certain he'd find. Nothing. His hand came back clean but shaky.

"You were dreaming," Regan told him.

Her soft voice cut into the last remnants of the horror, bringing him back to her. He'd had the nightmare again. This time more vivid than in over a year. He rubbed his hands over his face.

Getting to his feet, he stepped out into the clear night air. He gulped in several deep breaths, letting it wash over his soul.

Regan watched him as he strode away, his footsteps nearly silent in the night. She followed his progress to the stream where he splashed his face and arms. Turning quietly, she left him alone for a few minutes.

She longed to go to him, but she sensed that he needed some time alone. Whatever he'd been dreaming about had shaken him terribly.

She shut her mind against the sounds of his outcries, the way he'd thrashed and fought her, the engulfing strength of his pain. She blinked back her own tears, knowing they weren't for her, but for the horror he'd suffered.

Brushing off a spot, she sat beside the cold campfire and waited. She wanted to be there for him when he returned. He might need her.

Sweet Pea whimpered at her side, and Regan absently petted her on the head. She scarcely noticed when the pup scampered off.

Branded Wolf spun around at the light touch at his leg. Couldn't the woman leave him in peace?

He looked down in amazement to find the little white pup sitting beside him. He squatted down, and she leaned forward and laid her muzzle on his calf. A soft whimper came from her throat. Dark eyes glimmering in the moon's light, she stared up at him.

"Damn," he muttered in a breath.

The pup continued to stare up at him.

"Go on. Go back to Regan, where you belong," he said to the dog.

Another soft whimper was his answer. The white pup pawed his leg, then dropped her chin down to rest on his calf again.

He reached down to push her away, but instead found

himself petting her soft fur. Her little tongue flicked his thumb.

Sitting back, he lifted the pup into his lap and stared at the towering rocks. Oddly, the little dog gave him some sense of comfort. She snuggled down into his lap, giving his palm several small licks.

Puppy kisses, he thought in derision, then found himself smiling. The little pup was worming its way into his heart as surely as the woman with her tender touch and gentle concern. Now he understood how Wind Dancer had allowed her to tend to him. Regan had a special touch, almost like that of a shaman.

He sighed, more at peace. It was time he returned to her. She would be worried.

Branded Wolf was surprised to see Regan sitting beside the cold ashes of the fire. She'd been waiting for him. The thought touched something deep inside him and warmed a cold corner of his heart.

He walked up to where she sat, then deposited Sweet Pea gently into her lap. "Your dog wandered off," he explained.

"Oh," was all she said in response.

Her soft gaze sought his. He saw the pulse in her throat flutter.

"The fire's long cold. It will be warmer in the wickiup," he stated, drawing her to her feet.

She nibbled on her lower lip, and he knew she fought the questions she must have in her mind.

Suddenly tired, he turned and walked back to the wickiup. She followed behind him. He paused at the entrance, letting her enter first.

As if nervous, she sat primly on the covering. Looking up at him, she patted the spot beside her. He joined her, a part of him needing companionship at that moment. The wickiup seemed to close in about him, and he struggled for breath, trying to keep the old memories at bay.

"Talk to me, Regan." He needed her soft voice to chase away the horrors of his own memories.

"What about?"

She leaned closer to him, and he could see the concern on her face, bathed in the moonlight shining through the opening of the wickiup.

It didn't matter what she talked about, he needed only to hear the melodic sound of her soft voice.

"Tell me how you got here."

"You brought me on Wind Dancer."

He could hear the slight teasing in her voice.

"Before that," he pointed out.

"I came to visit my dying father. Who wasn't. Dying, that is."

At Branded Wolf's confused frown, she grudgingly added, "He's quite healthy."

"He must be worried—"

"Papa doesn't worry about anything. Least of all me," she stated in a matter-of-fact tone. "No, he's quite busy commanding the fort."

The fort commander's daughter.

Branded Wolf closed his eyes and held back his groan. He had to have kidnapped the daughter of the fort commander. He opened his eyes again.

Mentally, he upped the number of troopers who would be sent out to search for her. And him.

"Your father must be tearing up the countryside looking for you."

"I doubt it. You have nothing to worry about there," she assured him, an edge in her low voice. "I have no gun-toting protective papa coming after me."

Her softly spoken answer carried a world of hurt in it. He wondered at the parts she wasn't telling.

"Your mother?"

Regan grinned. "Now, her you need to worry about.

Although I can't picture my society-minded mama bringing a gun with her on the train from Philadelphia.'' She giggled at the image of her slender mother holding a firearm of any kind.

"Your mother is here?"

Regan clamped her lips down on her smile. "I'm certain of it. If not now, then she'll arrive at the fort soon. We will probably be able to hear their shouting from clear out here."

At his frown, she added, "Mama and Papa can't spend ten minutes in each other's company without a declaration of hostilities."

She eyed him an instant. At least she was distracting him from his nightmare. She marveled at how easy it was to talk in the darkness of night.

"Mama will be furious when she learns what happened." Regan sighed, and a small smile tipped her lips. "When she gets her hands on Captain David Larkin—"

She broke into a wide grin.

"The man you were so angry with," he observed, remembering her muttered comments.

Regan's eyes darkened with renewed anger. "The skunk. He thought my papa's approval gave him liberties with me." Crossing her arms over her chest, she sniffed. "Well, he learned differently."

Branded Wolf felt his own anger stirring at another man holding her in his arms. "Regan, what did he do?"

"He . . . he . . . kissed me," she spat out the admission.

Branded Wolf frowned. He himself had done that same thing.

"And . . . he tried to—" She cut off the explanation, too embarrassed to continue.

"Regan? Did he?"

"Certainly not." She planted her hands on her thighs. "I defended my honor. And left him in the dirt on the ground."

Recalling what he did of her skill with her feet and knees,

he didn't need to ask exactly how the cavalry officer had ended up on the ground. He had a pretty good idea from his experience with her himself.

"And that's when Sweet Pea protected me." Her lips twitched with suppressed laughter.

Branded Wolf glanced from Regan's lips to the snoozing pup and had to ask, "How?"

Regan pressed her fingers to her lips to hold back her giggles. "She bit him."

"I guess that would do it." He rubbed his ankle, remembering her needle-sharp teeth.

"Not on his ankle."

He met her look.

"In his backside," she added, and burst into laughter.

He winced.

"I bet they could hear him yelling all the way back to the fort. And I saw to it that he had a very uncomfortable ride back too."

A soft chuckle from him stirred the hair at her neck. Regan swallowed deeply, suddenly nervous in the close confines of the wickiup. When had the structure gotten so small?

"Now your turn." She paused for a breath. "Tell me about your dream."

He tensed beside her.

"It will help," she urged.

She laid a hand on his arm in a touch that reminded him of a butterfly lighting.

"It always helped me to tell my nightmares to Mama."

"I didn't have a mother to talk to." He said the words without thinking.

She frowned up at him. "Everyone has a mother."

"Mine died giving birth to me in the desert, after her family threw her out for carrying a bastard."

Regan gasped. "Why, that's horrible. They—"

"Were white," he spat out the words as if that were explanation enough.

"But how could they be so cruel?"

"That's what happens to white women who lay with Indians."

He'd said the words to warn her, perhaps to frighten her away from him. Every minute spent with her was becoming more difficult to keep his hands off her. He wanted her, and he wasn't sure he could continue to tell himself no. He needed her to tell him.

"Not all people are that way," she said with certainty in her voice.

"You really are an innocent."

His remark stung, and she snapped back at him. "I am not."

He turned his head to look down at her. At his raised brows, she felt her cheeks flush. He knew precisely how innocent she was, she realized, and knew that she was a virgin.

"We're talking about you," she prompted, challenging him to change the subject.

He remained silent, and she rested her hand on his arm again.

"What about your father? Did you . . . know him?" she forced the difficult question out.

A smile creased Branded Wolf's face. "I knew him." The declaration was made with a ring of pride. "He was a great warrior when he met my mother. Foolish though. He later said he fell in love the moment he laid eyes on her."

"She must have been very beautiful."

He shrugged off her remark.

"You have her blue eyes, then?"

"You once wondered how I got my name."

Regan blushed to the roots of her hair at the reminder

that he had clearly understood every word she'd ever said to him when she'd assumed he didn't speak English.

"Um-huh" was all she could get past her lips.

"My father called me Wolf for the solitary hunter, and Branded for the eyes of a white man."

"They're beautiful eyes."

He turned to find her staring up at him. His heart surely gave a lurch in his chest. It took a moment for it to right itself again and begin beating normally once more. Suddenly, he turned his head away from her.

"How do you come to speak English so well?" She blurted out the question, then wished she could take it back. It sounded so . . . so presumptuous.

"My mother's people had a change of heart. Her brother brought the bluecoats to my village and took me." Bitterness welled up inside him with a violence.

"Took you?"

He flung his head back, his dark hair nearly black in the dim light of the moon. "We've talked enough. It's time to go to sleep."

With this he turned away from her and lay down.

Regan longed to reach out to him. For a brief instant, she had a glimpse into the child who'd been hurt so badly. At least when her mother had taken her away to live in Philadelphia, it had been done with love.

Biting her lip, she scooted down onto the Apache bed and willed herself to lie still. She realized Branded Wolf still hadn't told her about his nightmare. Every part of her being wanted to take him into her arms. She'd never in her entire life experienced this desire to give comfort, much less so overwhelmingly. It was all she could do to stay still.

"Regan." Branded Wolf's voice broke the tense silence.

"Yes?" she whispered, almost afraid to speak aloud.

"Your pup is lying on my foot."

"Oh." She didn't know what she'd expected him to say

or hoped he would say to her. But that most assuredly wasn't it.

Leaning up, she lifted Sweet Pea none too gently and laid her farther away from his legs.

Regan lay back down with a soft huff. She didn't know if it was disappointment or irritation or both.

"Regan," Branded Wolf said in a low voice that stroked her skin like a rose petal in a warm bath.

"Yes?" She knew she held her breath, waiting for him to speak again.

"If you're cold, you can come closer."

"I'm fine," she answered, resisting the lure of his offer.

"Regan."

This time his voice felt like a shower of rose petals, fluttering down and touching every part of her.

When she answered, she was nearly breathless. "Um?"

"Come here."

The two simple words were all she needed to roll over into his arms. They'd been spoken half as an order and half as a plea.

She couldn't resist either one.

His arms came around her like bands of steel, then his hold gentled. He drew her closer into his embrace, and she followed.

Willingly.

Breathlessly.

Hopefully.

Chapter Twelve

Branded Wolf's lips came down on hers with a fierce hunger that Regan felt all the way to her toes. She melted against him.

No one had ever made her feel this way. This wanted, this womanly

She slid her hands up along his arms, from his elbows to his shoulders, marveling at the strength she felt beneath her hands as his muscles rippled. He pulled her tighter against the length of him, and she instinctively wiggled to get closer.

She returned his kiss, any shyness gone. This felt so good, so right.

His hands roamed along her back as he traced the outline of her body. He captured the curve of her breast and the flare of her hips.

His kiss changed to one of possession. It deepened until Regan thought she would die from the sensations he brought in her. He slid his tongue between her lips, and she released a sigh of wonder.

This time his tongue plundered her mouth. He tasted the velvetness within. When she moaned softly deep in her throat, he caught the sound and drew it to him. It was as if he breathed each breath with her. It had never been like this for him. He slanted his mouth more fully over hers, wanting to taste more of her.

Any differences between them ceased to exist. Nothing mattered except the touch and feel of each other, the sharing of each breath they drew.

His tongue mated with hers, touching and retreating over and over until she thought she'd faint from the sheer pleasure of it.

She ran her hands up the back of his neck and through his dark hair. It lay long and heavy against her white hands. The feel of the silken strands sliding between her fingers thrilled her. She'd never imagined anything like it before.

In the sure, smooth move of a warrior, he shifted his body, sliding it over hers. At the brush of his hot flesh across her, Regan gasped. She could feel the heat of his skin penetrating the fine material of her gown. Then a touch of cool air skimmed her neck as Branded Wolf released the tiny buttons of her bodice one by one.

Regan counted them in a haze. One. Two. Three. Four.

He spread the muslin material apart and eased her chemise aside, baring her skin to his gaze. Bereft of his kisses, Regan stared up at him. His eyes gleamed with desire. She moistened her lips in an unknown invitation, and he responded by pressing his lips against hers until she cried out in pleasure.

Drawing away, he ran his mouth along her chin and down the slim column of her throat. He sipped at the pulse beat at the hollow of her throat.

Regan gasped in shock at the sensations coursing through her. Waves of heat. Tingles of pleasure. Desire.

She tightened her hands on his neck, and he threw his

head back to stare down into her eyes. She trembled at what she saw there in his dark blue depths.

Lowering his head, he laved the skin above her breasts with his tongue, then dipped into the hollow between her breasts. With agonizing slowness he worked his way to one breast and took it in his mouth.

At the feel of his moist mouth on the bare skin of her nipple, she cried out. Nothing had ever prepared her for this. She'd never dreamed sensation like this existed, or that a man's mere touch could be this way. Heat pooled within her body.

She moaned in a soft whisper of sound and ran her hands down the length of his broad back, exploring the feel of the corded muscles beneath the bandage. It wasn't enough. Confusion edged at the corner of her mind. She wanted more than this, but she didn't know what.

His touch awakened something within her, something she didn't know existed.

She raised one hand to plunge it into the hair trailing over his shoulders, tightening her hand in it, and pulled him closer with her other hand on his broad back. She felt like she'd go insane with the wanting that was threatening to consume her.

Ripples of pleasure started low in her stomach and radiated outward. And the heat. She'd never felt such heat in her entire life.

It threatened to consume her.

Somehow he'd found the wildness hidden deep within her, and it confused her. She hadn't known that streak of wildness lay in her, and it frightened her.

She tensed in his embrace. Confusion swept over her. Part of her urged her to ignore everything else and hold him tight. Instinct told her to flee, that this wildness, whatever it was, could consume her.

She didn't know which to listen to.

Branded Wolf sensed her withdrawal. His chest tightened as if a band of steel had slipped around it, almost too much to allow him to breathe. He fought against the heat of desire and slowly pushed himself away from her. His hands clenched into fists.

Regan stared up at him, a mixture of confusion, desire, and hesitancy on her beautiful face. He swallowed down his own desire, his passion cooled by what he saw in her face.

She'd obviously realized she was about to make love to an Indian, or, worse, a half-breed. He stiffened and pushed himself to his knees. It wasn't the first time he'd encountered this with a white woman.

"Brand, I . . ." She fell silent.

He saw the flush of her cheeks in the moonlight. Was she embarrassed? Shamed?

He wouldn't wait around to see the disdain that was sure to follow. He'd experienced it too many times in the past from white women who'd been fascinated by the Indian's darker skin, then withdrew as they thought themselves too pure to lie with him.

His face a mask of pride, his eyes shuttered, he surged to his feet.

Regan stared up at him, biting her lower lip. His eyes had gone cold, not a trace of the earlier heat she'd seen remained. Nor the desire.

How could she have allowed things to go so far?

As Regan reached out a hand for him, tentatively, he spun away, rejecting her offering.

"Go to sleep, Regan," he said before he walked out of the wickiup.

Branded Wolf strode to the cold campfire. It was suited to his mood. He kicked aside a cold piece of unburned wood. Just like her heart, he thought.

Regan McBain was no different from the society women

friends of his white aunt's back in Boston. He could still recall the disdain they'd shown for his skin and his hated mixed blood. A couple of the woman had flirted with him, but when it came down to more, they'd swept their skirts aside in scorn.

One day, he'd had enough and packed up and returned to his Apache homeland, where he belonged. Since then he'd stayed clear of pure-as-snow white women. Until he'd met Regan. But it seemed he hadn't learned his lesson well enough.

What had made him think Regan would be any different from the other white women?

Regan was no different from those women, no different at all.

The tiny corner of his heart she'd warmed refused to accept this answer no matter how many times he repeated it to himself as he settled down to sleep by the cold campfire.

As the first rays of sunlight filtered through the pine trees, Branded Wolf crushed the clump of grass in his fist. He threw back his head, breathed in deeply, and released a silent moan of disgust.

He wanted to go into the wickiup and wake Regan, with kisses. He wanted her.

Last night with Regan had been unexpected. She'd awakened feelings in him he didn't believe existed anymore. For the first time in his life, he'd nearly lost himself in a woman.

He'd forgotten about being gentle, forgotten about sheathing his innate savagery. He'd kissed her with a warrior's strength and passions. Surely he'd hurt Regan with his lovemaking during the night. Even more than her rejection had hurt him.

In the light of day his conscience took over. He was too rough for her, too savage for a fragile city woman like her.

If he didn't watch himself, he'd crush her like the broken blades of grass in his hands.

Couldn't she see? He was the one she needed protecting from the most.

He should return her to the fort, to her own people. But he couldn't.

He wouldn't. Not now.

But he would protect her from himself.

Elise McBain checked the watch pinned to her bodice and smiled. Ten minutes late.

She knocked on her husband's quarters.

Not late enough to anger him, but just enough to throw him off balance. Carson so hated to be kept waiting. And she'd always so enjoyed this little game of upsetting his careful poise.

The door swung open to reveal a young cavalry officer whom she didn't recall seeing before. It seemed Carson had beat her at her own game. Now she was the one off balance.

"Good afternoon, Mrs. McBain." The officer stepped forward and took her hand in his.

She endured the kiss he placed on her hand, and she sent a questioning glance to her husband as he came toward her. She could tell by the expression on his face there had been no news of Regan.

"Elise, dear. You're looking lovely today." Carson took her arm in his. "I'd like you to meet Captain David Larkin."

"Captain." She inclined her head.

What was Carson up to? This was highly unusual for him.

He led her to a dining table set for three. She took her seat, smoothed out her taffeta skirt, and studied the young man now seated across from her.

"Elise, dear"—Carson McBain cleared his throat before

he continued—"I wanted you to have the chance to become acquainted with Captain Larkin."

She looked from her husband to the young man who had obviously won his favor. She studied his good looks and military bearing.

In a snap she made her decision. She did not like him.

"Why, Carson, planning to foist me off on one of your officers so soon?" she asked, her lips curving into a half smile.

Beside her, Carson sputtered, nearly spilling his drink.

Across from her, David Larkin's eyes narrowed before he bestowed a wide smile on her. The smile was as superficial as he was, she thought to herself.

"Mrs. McBain, I see where Regan gets her sense of humor."

"Oh, really?" She tilted her head in his direction. "But I wasn't joking."

His smile faltered. "Ma'am—" Then he picked up his fork and concentrated on the meal.

She tried to force down the light repast, but a mother's worry wouldn't let her do so. Minutes later, she turned to her husband, putting away any pretense at eating. "What is being done to find Regan?"

"David is leading the search for Regan."

"Then, what is he doing here?" she asked abruptly. "Why isn't he out looking for her? There's plenty of daylight left."

Carson leaned forward and his voice tightened. "Captain Larkin returned only a short while ago from the search. I'm sure he is hungry and tired. It has taken its toll on him as well."

"Oh, and why is that?"

"He's her fiancé."

"What?" Elise shouted out the question.

"That's what I planned on telling you, except you arrived late."

"Ma'am, I had proposed to her on our ride, the day she was lost."

Elise turned to study the young officer with the neat brown hair. She didn't believe him for a moment.

"And what did Regan say in return?"

"Why, yes, of course."

She held him pinned a moment with her eyes. "So, you are the escort who was incapable of protecting her?"

"Elise." Carson raised his voice.

"I tried to, ma'am. And I failed, but I haven't given up hope." Captain Larkin turned to his commander. "We found my horse today."

"*Your* horse?" Elise cut in.

His face turned a dull shade of red under her question. "Yes, the Indians took it along with Regan."

"Why did they take only one horse?" Elise asked pointedly.

"I can't say, Mrs. McBain. Perhaps they didn't think the mare was a good mount."

"Indeed?"

He ignored her question. "The scouts couldn't make much of the tracks. The windstorm the afternoon she disappeared obliterated the Apache tracks. It seems the sorrel must have slipped loose later and been wandering awhile."

"Indeed?" Elise repeated.

Captain Larkin pushed his chair back. "Thank you for lunch, sir." He paused. "Mrs. McBain. If you will excuse me, I'd like to get some rest. I'm heading back out at first light."

"Certainly." Carson stood to see him to the door.

"It was nice meeting you, Mrs. McBain."

Elise inclined her head but didn't respond in kind. She would not be a hypocrite.

After a brief, low conversation at the door, Carson returned to the table.

"I don't like him," Elise stated.

He stared at her, surprise written on his face. "I think he's quite suitable. Now, dear. Once you get to know him—"

"Oh, Carson, what can you have been thinking?" Elise scowled at him. "That young man of yours is completely unsuitable for our Regan."

She tossed down her napkin and rushed out of his quarters. The door slammed behind her.

Once in her own quarters, she slammed her door shut in frustration and leaned back against it. Her husband was an old fool.

No wonder Regan hadn't returned, with Captain Larkin awaiting her. She knew her daughter well enough to know she'd never settle for the young officer.

Captain Larkin was a tad too well mannered, too cool and collected, and she found him boorish herself.

How could Carson have presumed to pick out a husband for their daughter without her knowledge or consent?

She wanted to march right back to his quarters and give him a piece of her mind. She turned back toward the door and stopped with her hand on the knob. A memory of other fights that had started that same way sprang to mind.

Right on their heels followed the memories of their making up afterward. A smile tipped her lips. Now, those were some pleasant memories.

She tightened her hand on the doorknob. A part of her longed for those days. He still was a handsome figure of a man.

"Well, damn," she muttered.

At least one part of her body wanted the old fool back. She had to admit the truth.

But now what?

*   *   *

Regan hoped a long bath in the pool Branded Wolf had pointed out to her would put her in a better mood. He looked as if he hadn't slept much, and she didn't have the heart to take her foul temper out on him.

It was herself she was mad at anyway.

She walked in the direction of the pool, calling for Sweet Pea over her shoulder. Darned if her pet hadn't taken to following Branded Wolf around every chance she got.

"The little traitor," she grumbled.

In truth, she'd like to trade places with the dog and have him stroke her and murmur to her the way she'd caught him doing to her pet earlier today.

"Sweet Pea," she called out sharper than she'd intended.

A woof sounded from behind her, and Regan turned to scoop up her pet.

Sweet Pea bestowed several wet puppy kisses of welcome on her chin, then turned dark, soulful eyes back to the camp where Branded Wolf sat.

Regan sighed. "I know just how you feel," she admitted to the dog in a whisper.

Sweet Pea whined her agreement and licked Regan's hand.

She wondered how Branded Wolf was taking to the little dog's turn of affection. She could imagine his grimace every time Sweet Pea gave kisses. Imagine, an Apache warrior accepting puppy kisses. She had to hold back a giggle.

Turning back toward the pool in better spirits, she covered the distance, softly humming a tune under her breath.

At the pool she fell silent. It was breathtakingly beautiful. The crystal-blue water sat rimmed by bits of grass and yucca, surrounded by towering pines. Pretty white flowers with yellow centers dotted the ground.

Her breath left in a low "oh" of admiration.

It looked like a blue stone set in golden green. Smiling

in anticipation, she set Sweet Pea down. The pup bounded to the water's edge, tail wagging. Regan wasted no time in stripping off her gown. Her petticoat followed, and she draped them over a bush and slowly waded into the pool of blue with only her chemise to cover her.

The water was a near-perfect temperature, warmed by the sun high overhead. She'd expected it to be cold, but forgot these mountains were lower than others she'd seen farther east.

She swirled her arms in the water, making ripples in the smooth surface. A sigh of contentment slipped past her lips, and she nearly laughed aloud at the thought. She, Regan McBain of Philadelphia, was content bathing in a mountain pool without the sweet-smelling soap she was accustomed to. As funny as it sounded, it was quite true.

With a giggle, she called Sweet Pea. The little dog balked at the water's edge. She dipped in one paw, then shook it daintily like a cat and backed away from the pool. After much coaxing, Sweet Pea ventured into the water. Regan couldn't help but laugh as the tiny paws beat the water into waves. The dog splashed like she'd always been in water.

At a sound from the bank, Regan turned to find Branded Wolf watching her. She started to stand but stopped herself. She swallowed, not having the courage to get to her feet and expose herself to him.

Not in broad daylight.

His gaze captured hers, and a sensation like sharp tingles ran from her head to her toes. She curled her toes into the bottom of the pool. And she held her breath, waiting.

She saw his gaze go to the bush where her gown and petticoat hung, then return to her. One strap of her chemise slipped off her shoulder. He was near enough for her to see the muscles in his throat flex when he swallowed deeply.

Desire rose in her, and she looked away from him in

embarrassment. What had happened to her sensibilities since coming to this wilderness? Shame heated her cheeks.

She heard Branded Wolf utter a word in Apache she didn't understand. Then without saying another word, he turned away. She watched him walk slowly back toward camp. She longed for him to turn around, but he didn't. She wanted to call out to him, but she didn't.

Regan watched him until he was out of sight, but she knew he hadn't gone far. In spite of everything, he still offered her his protection. He'd stay near enough to hear if she called out.

For a moment she had a sudden impulse to do just that. Call him back to her. Slide her wet arms around him. Stare up into his fascinating blue eyes. Pull his dark head down and press her lips against his.

Her body began to heat in the smooth water. She knew her cheeks were flushed with heat as well.

Horrified at her wanton tendencies, she quelled the impulse to call out to Branded Wolf. A lady didn't call a man to her.

A lady didn't bathe nearly nude in a mountain pool of water either, she thought with a flush of embarrassment.

And what had happened to her plans for escape? she asked herself.

They had flown away with the birds overhead. She knew she should be ashamed of her acquiescence, but for the life of her, she wasn't.

Instead, she found herself wondering about the coming night in the wickiup.

Would Branded Wolf take her in his arms?

Regan feared she could deny him nothing if he asked. Realization hit her like a cold breeze blowing over the water. She had to admit to the truth. She was more than merely fascinated by his blue eyes and different ways. She was quite possibly falling for the strong yet compassionate man

eneath the handsome exterior who was even beginning to
ake to Sweet Pea.

Regan leaned her head back and closed her eyes as the
ruth rushed over her.

She was falling in love with Branded Wolf.

Chapter Thirteen

Regan stared off to where she knew Branded Wolf waited for her to finish her bath. Disappointment swept over her. She admitted that she'd wanted him to join her.

Desperately so.

Why had he walked away from her?

Blinking back a sudden sharp burning in her eyes, she knew the handsome warrior had walked away with more than he ever knew.

He had spirited away her heart.

A twinge of fear at the strength of the feeling made her stiffen. She'd never backed down in fear before. She wasn't about to start then.

She walked out of the water and slowly dressed. She admitted a desire to stall, but she rejected it just as quickly. It was past time to leave the pool and face the warrior.

Branded Wolf was standing beside the small fire, where she knew he would be waiting for her. She gathered up her courage and approached him. He didn't turn. She walked closer until her skirt brushed his ankle, then she reached out and laid her trembling hand on his arm.

He jerked away as if her touch burned.

She had to clear any misunderstandings between them, starting with last night.

"Brand, I'm sorry about last night." She had to get the words out. They were nearly choking her.

He stiffened and stepped away from her, disgust written across his bitter face. "Now you're apologizing? For us?"

"What do you mean?" She attempted to ignore the coldness behind his words. It frightened her more than she was willing to admit.

"Us."

She stared at him, her silence condemning her in his eyes.

"Was it an experiment so you could go back home to your fancy life and friends and laugh about your high time in the desert with the Injun?"

Regan gasped and her hand flew to her mouth. She mutely shook her head, stunned by his words.

"Tell me," he snapped out the order.

She flinched, then stiffened under his hard-edged regard. Raising her chin, she faced him squarely. "How dare you think that."

"What am I supposed to think?"

"I never once gave you any reason to think that. Not once, do you hear me?" She planted her hands on her hips in a burst of anger.

He cocked a dark eyebrow at her denial. "You didn't?" he challenged.

Regan tossed her head in irritation. "Your being an Apache didn't bother me—"

"Then what did?"

"Your being a fool!" she snapped.

She whirled away from him and ran back toward the pool. Just then she needed its solace. Or she'd . . .

She'd either hit him or kiss him!

Either one would be disastrous.

She paused for a moment to catch her breath. Silence surrounded her, and not even the hummingbird made a sound as it hung suspended in air.

Regan nearly held her breath waiting. Waiting for the sound of footsteps behind her. They didn't come. She noted with a sense of disappointment that he hadn't bothered to follow her.

Slowly, she walked the remaining distance to the pool. At the water's edge, she stopped and tilted her head back. Breathing in deeply, she fought back the deep sense of failure. She fought back her inner fear as well.

Had her own heart truly been stolen by Branded Wolf? She feared so. And it was too late to do anything about it.

She admitted that she was practically mesmerized by him. And yet frightened of the feelings he evoked in her.

A deer stepped into the clearing, and Regan nearly screamed. The animal promptly disappeared as quickly as it had come. She nearly laughed at her foolishness. Frightened by a pretty deer. Here it was probably considered food.

Regan clenched her hands into fists. It was clear to her. She didn't belong there.

She didn't, she reminded herself.

This was Branded Wolf's world. Hers was a lifetime away. Her world was back in Philadelphia with her friends and civilization.

However, that world of privilege seemed almost alien to her. Her heart whispered that maybe she didn't belong in that world either. Maybe she no longer belonged anywhere.

But most of all, she knew she didn't belong with a man who didn't love her. A man who didn't want her.

* * *

The fort was a hum of activity by the time Captain Larkin was prepared to leave. Unfortunately, it was well past sunrise and looked to be a hot day. A meeting with Colonel McBain and a lame horse had delayed his start, sorely testing his patience.

Actually, the colonel had talked, and he had listened. Not a pleasant day's start.

David Larkin grabbed the horse's reins from the private without a word of thanks. He didn't have time for pleasantries. If he was going to proceed with this charade of searching for his dear "fiancée," he'd best get a start on his day's ride.

Not that he had any intention of finding Regan and bringing her back to the fort. However, he would go through the motions. He had to keep up appearances for Colonel McBain.

And if he did by chance find her alive . . . He would have to silence her. Quickly.

He shook off the possibility of finding her alive. He was certain any search for her was pointless. It would prove fruitless.

The Apaches must have had her.

With her poor sense of direction, she had ridden straight into Indian territory when she left him in the desert. No, she couldn't have escaped capture by the Apaches.

If she'd merely wandered around lost, he would have found her body by then. She couldn't have lasted long on her own in the desert, and an eastern lady like her had no sense of survival.

As far as he was concerned, Regan McBain was dead. Or wishing she was.

He smiled widely at the thought. Too bad she hadn't been more amiable to him. He had no doubt she'd proved plenty malleable to the Apaches by the time the savages had finished with her.

His breeches grew too tight at the mental images the thought brought in its wake. Uncomfortably tight.

"Captain Larkin?" a feminine voice called out, halting his thoughts.

He started guiltily and shifted his position to hide his arousal.

He recognized the voice, and it did not bode well for his day. He closed his eyes.

Mrs. Elise McBain.

He cringed but forced his lips into a smile before he turned around to greet her.

He studied the woman as she approached him. Her chestnut hair was swept up in the latest style, and her rose-colored gown was likely the height of fashion back east. And damned if she didn't carry a matching lace parasol.

The woman was as out of place as her daughter had been, and just as useless, except to look at.

He did not like the woman, however beautiful she might be. And he had a disturbing feeling that the dislike was mutual.

She was too intelligent, perceptive, and much too outspoken for his tastes. Not admirable qualities in a woman to him in the least.

He could easily see how Regan came by her insolence. Well, good riddance to her. He considered himself well rid of her.

He surveyed Elise McBain. This is likely what Regan would have looked like in twenty years. The picture wasn't unpleasant; however, he had little use for Mrs. McBain. And Regan had showed every sign of being just as outspoken and spoiled as this woman.

He couldn't see how the colonel tolerated it from either of the women.

If Regan were his wife—

He cut off the thought. There was no use wasting time thinking down that path. It wouldn't happen now. She'd sealed her fate when she rebuffed him.

Actually, he was becoming more and more pleased that the planned marriage to the colonel's daughter hadn't taken place. He had no desire to spend his life tied to one woman—much less to one who persisted in speaking her own mind.

"Good morning, Mrs. McBain. I didn't expect to see you before I left." Actually, he'd hoped not to see her.

"I've been watching for you, Captain. I wanted to speak with you."

"I was on my way to ride out," he said, hoping to dissuade her further.

Elise pointedly looked at the watch pinned to her gown. "I'm sure you have a few minutes for me." She smiled at him.

When he opened his mouth to protest, she quickly added, "Since it is well past sunrise already." Her observation held a hint of accusation.

"Of course I always have a few minutes to spare for a beautiful woman such as yourself," he said.

Her eyes narrowed at his obvious flattery.

"What I have to say will take only a minute, Captain."

"Ma'am?"

"In case the colonel didn't stress it enough, I want you to understand it is *imperative* you bring Regan back."

She held his gaze for several moments, and he had the distinct feeling he'd just been threatened. Very subtly. And very well. Perhaps he had underestimated the lady.

"Mrs. McBain, you have my word that I will see that Regan is taken care of," he told her.

Just not the same way the lady meant, he thought to himself, but no one else need know that.

* * *

Near evening, Regan stared at the meager rations before
her in disgust. More of the impossibly tough meat strips
was about all that remained in the way of supplies. At least
that's all she could recognize as food.

Just then she wasn't about to ask Branded Wolf to explain
to her what the things were called that looked like some
kind of nut. He'd been in a temper all day.

Something was bothering him, she was certain of it.

She wouldn't disturb him now to ask anything. She could
manage one meal on her own without help. Couldn't she?

She frowned. According to Branded Wolf's short remark
earlier, the lack of meat tonight was her fault. He said she'd
made too much noise today moving about, and the snare
hadn't caught anything. And when he'd mentioned hunting
for deer, she'd vehemently objected, picturing in her mind
the pretty creature by the pool.

Sighing deeply, she held up the stringy strips of darkened
meat and studied them.

"Yuck."

From the corner of her eye she saw Sweet Pea wag her tail,
then sit back and bat the air with her paws in supplication.

"Not now," Regan told her.

Sweet Pea whined pitifully.

"Later," she promised. "If this wasn't all I had to work
with, you could have the lot of it."

Sweet Pea barked an answer, and Regan smiled, imagining
what the sound meant.

She looked around the campsite and spotted a pan hanging
from a section of angled sticks. Branded Wolf had put it
together earlier that afternoon from things stored in the
wickiup. But that had been before he'd checked the snare.

Sighing deeply, she frowned at the meat. Tenderizing it
hadn't worked, perhaps cooking it some more would do the

trick. She dragged the pan and makeshift hangings to the fire and set them up above the meager flames.

She dumped the water from a nearby canteen into the pot, then added the thin strips of meat. They floated unappealingly in the lukewarm water. She gingerly stirred the mess with the tip of one finger.

"Yuck," she repeated, wiping her finger on her skirt and staring at the water.

She leaned closer and watched.

And watched.

And watched.

Nothing was happening. The water wasn't making those little bubbles that showed it was cooking or anything. She felt like letting out a wail of disgust. Instead, she kicked at the fire. It flickered and dimmed.

"Oh, stars and heavens," she grumbled.

She'd nearly put the awful thing out. Branded Wolf would be upset if he had to light it again. She'd already put it out twice by accident that day.

She stared again at the water in the pot. It just lay there, doing nothing.

Well, obviously, what it needed was more heat to make it bubble like it should be doing.

Regan wandered off in search of more firewood. After several minutes of looking she deduced there wasn't a stack of cut wood in sight.

"There has to be something that will burn," she said to Sweet Pea, who trotted alongside her.

The little pup bounded over to where a pinecone lay on the ground. Picking it up between her teeth, she brought it to Regan and laid it at her feet.

"I don't have time to play fetch, Sweetie," Regan told her. She patted her pet on the head. "I have to find something to burn for the fire. . . ."

Her voice trailed off, and she picked up the pinecone.

Hmm, if the wood from the pine tree burned, why wouldn't the little cones burn too?

With a cry of triumph she gathered up a pile of the cones, then bundled them in her skirt and carried them back to the camp.

Holding her skirt up in one hand, she picked out one small pinecone and tossed it on the fire. The flames crackled, but that was about all. She tossed in another one with almost the same disparaging result. She didn't have the patience for this.

"Well, Sweet Pea, I guess I'll dump them all in and get it over with. What do you think?"

Sweet Pea yipped, then backed away as Regan stepped closer to the fire.

Regan heard her bark again, this time in greeting, and race off. So, Branded Wolf had decided to return. She hoped he was in a better mood this time. She shook out her skirt, dropping the load of pinecones onto the fire.

"Regan, no!"

His warning came too late.

An instant later, the small sputtering fire gave a *whoosh* and the pile of pinecones burst into flames all at once.

He barely pulled Regan back in time. The spot where she'd stood only a moment before was engulfed in flames that reached over three feet high.

Beside her, Sweet Pea sneezed and rubbed her nose on the ground. Then she began barking at the flames at the top of her lungs.

"Regan, can't I leave for a few minutes without you burning down the camp?" Branded Wolf shouted at her over the din of the dog.

His heart had nearly stopped when he'd realized what she was about to do, but he hadn't been able to reach her in time to stop her. Thankfully, he'd been able to pull her back before she was burned. She had no way of knowing how hot the pinecones burned, much hotter than wood. His hands tightened into fists at the chance of her being hurt, badly hurt.

Regan pushed herself free of his hold. With her nose in the air, she informed him, "I was only cooking our dinner."

He looked from the dancing flames to Regan and back to the fire. "What were you cooking?"

"That tough meat we had in the desert." She waved her hand in the air.

He eyed her thoughtfully a moment, then asked, "You were *cooking* the jerky?"

"If that's what that tough-as-old-shoe-leather stuff is called, yes, I was cooking it."

"Regan, that's jerky. It was ready to be eaten."

"What do you mean?"

"It doesn't need to be cooked." His lips twitched with a faint memory of the first time they'd eaten jerky together. "Or tenderized," he added.

She ground her teeth, remembering the time in the desert when she'd tried pounding it with the rock. She tightened her hands into fists of humiliation.

"Why didn't you tell me that before?" she yelled at him.

"You didn't ask."

She whirled around and her gaze settled on the campfire, or what remained of it. The burst of flames had nearly burned itself out. The sticks that had formerly held the pot had been devoured in the blaze, and the pot lay on its side, blackened with soot.

All in all, it was a disaster.

"Oh, dear," Regan mumbled.

She turned her back on the mess and looked at Branded Wolf instead. He was much more pleasant to look at, even when he frowned.

"I think I ruined dinner," she admitted in a subdued voice.

He raised an eyebrow at her remark. "There's more jerky left and some pinyon nuts."

Regan wrinkled her nose in distaste. "Would it be too much trouble for you to check the snare one more time?"

Unexpectedly, Branded Wolf tipped back his head and laughed.

Suddenly, he pulled her into his arms. "I knew you were trouble the first time I set eyes on you."

She tilted her head back to look up at him. He wasn't angry with her anymore. His good humor was contagious. "Oh, you did, did you?"

"Yes. You had just hit me from behind."

Regan sputtered, "That wasn't my fault."

"Not your fault? I was sitting there peacefully minding my own business, returning from turning in a prisoner, and you—"

Her lips twitched at the recollection of her drawstring bag sailing through the air to hit him. "I was merely attempting to catch Sweet Pea," she reminded him.

"After which your dog attacked my hat, bit the conductor, jumped into my arms—"

"And fell for you, the same as I have," Regan finished in a soft voice.

She remembered clearly how he had looked so handsome with his long black hair and mesmerizing blue eyes. He seemed even more handsome now. His hair trailed his shoulders, his broad bronzed chest was bare, and he smelled of fresh water. He'd obviously bathed in the same pool she'd used. The picture it evoked caused her heart to race.

"Regan?"

She jerked her thoughts back. She couldn't let him guess where her mind had wandered to, she absolutely couldn't. It was too forward, too embarrassing, and too unladylike.

"Then you casually dismissed both of us." She sniffed at him in a remembered tiff of injured pride.

"It didn't do me much good."

She opened her mouth, then promptly shut it again. She resisted the impulse to hit him.

"I wasn't the one who came after you," she reminded him.

"What do you mean?"

"That night you visited the fort."

"I didn't come to see you. I didn't even know you were there."

He gazed over her head into the distance at the towering pines. His eyes cooled with an inner hatred. It was the first time she'd ever witnessed that look on his face. It frightened her, and she was glad it wasn't directed at her.

She didn't know how she knew, but deep inside she knew the hatred was for someone else.

His eyes took on a faraway look, and she knew he was remembering the past. His nightmare.

"Brand, why did you come to the fort that night?" She asked the question hesitantly, but she had to hear the answer.

"To let it be known I was waiting."

"Waiting? For whom?"

"For Soaring Dove's killers."

"Who is Soaring Dove?" she asked in barely a whisper.

"The woman I was to marry." His hands tightened on her arms. "A band of white-eyes killed her and my family."

Regan bit her lip to keep from crying out at his harsh hold. Even worse, she could feel the anguish emanating from him. He must have loved this Soaring Dove very much. A shaft of pain cut through her.

She gazed up at him, seeing the pain of remembering in his eyes. This was his nightmare, she could see it in his eyes. The pain of that night, his anguished cries, had been for the fiancée he'd loved and lost.

She wished someone could love her the way he'd obviously loved his fiancée.

Fiancée.

The word hit her hard. He'd been engaged. He'd loved someone else. Did that woman's ghost still hold his heart? She knew the answer was yes.

Regan swallowed her pain and disappointment. The unfairness struck her sharply. When she at last found someone she could love, he belonged to another. It didn't matter that the woman was dead; her memory still held his heart as surely as if she were standing there between them.

She couldn't stop the question from slipping out past nearly numb lips. "Was she very beautiful?"

"Yes."

The single word said it all to her. Regan couldn't help comparing herself to this other woman in her mind. Soaring Dove had been an Indian. She would most surely have had the same ebony hair and beautiful bone structure as Brand.

Regan's heart caught in her chest. Her own fair skin would look pale and washed out when compared to the beautiful bronze skin of an Apache.

If only she were prettier, she thought to herself. How many times in her life had she suffered that same thought? Perhaps if she were prettier, her father would love her; perhaps if she were more competent in ladylike pursuits— the list had gone on and on, increasing with each time she'd been rejected, until it grew insurmountable.

She bet the other woman could even cook—and do it without almost burning down the camp in the process.

Tears pricked the back of her eyes, but she refused to give in to them.

She was nothing more to Branded Wolf than an inconvenience and a disappointment. Just like to her father. The realization hurt, and she fought back the pain of failure. She wouldn't let it show.

Surely she'd had enough practice with dealing with her father's disappointment with her not to reveal it to Branded

Wolf's observant eyes. She could carry this off without any humiliating tears. Raising her head in defiant pride, she looked past him to a spot over his shoulder.

"If you'll excuse me, I'm not very hungry," she said, struggling to keep her voice even. "I think I'll turn in for the night."

Quickly, before he could see the glint of tears, she turned away and rushed to the wickiup. Once inside, her stomach growled, calling her a liar.

She sank down onto the pine boughs. What had she been trying to do by cooking him dinner? Impress him? Earn his respect? His love?

With a jolt of realization, she saw that she'd been trying to earn somebody's love all her life. Her mother's approval instead of criticism. Her father's acceptance instead of disappointment. And now Branded Wolf.

She slapped her hands down on the ground. She was tired of trying and failing to earn what she couldn't have.

What was wrong with her?

Curling into a ball of misery, she lay down on the makeshift bed. Why couldn't anyone love her? Was she that bad a person?

A gentle touch at her shoulder made her jump. She reassured herself, it was only Sweet Pea coming to comfort her. The little pup always sensed when she needed her most.

"Oh, Sweetie." Regan reached out to the dog.

Her hand came into contact with the bare, muscled skin of a man's chest. She was too surprised to pull her hand back.

"I . . . I . . . thought you were Sweet Pea," she said in a choked voice that gave too much away.

"Hardly."

He leaned closer to her, and the last of the sun's rays shining into the wickiup revealed the traces of tears shimmering on her lashes.

Branded Wolf felt his heart lurch at the sight. He'd hurt her with his sharp words and the hatred that had burned in him by the campfire. It was the last thing on earth he wanted to do.

"Come here, little one," he said in a low voice that sent her nerves skittering.

Without waiting for a refusal, he slid down beside her and drew her into his embrace. He kissed her tenderly, meaning to offer comfort, but at the touch of her lips the heat filled his groin.

Of their own volition, his arms tightened around her. He deepened the light kiss to one of demand, one of possession.

Regan gave in to his kisses willingly. She slipped her hands over the wide expanse of his chest and slid them around his back, pulling him to her. She stole away the last of his faltering resolve.

He pressed her back into the pine boughs and took her lips in a kiss that robbed her of breath. He deftly unfastened the buttons at her bodice, pushed away the barrier of her chemise, and slid his hand inside to cup her breast in his palm.

Wondrous sweet sensation rushed over her in waves. Foremost was the realization that Branded Wolf *wanted* her. Tears of happiness gathered in her eyes, and she blinked them away. She almost feared this was too wonderful to be true.

As she tightened her hold on his back, a groan escaped his mouth. She answered in turn. Her fingers kneaded his muscles, driving him to the edge of a precipice from which there would be no return.

Drawing back for control, he dragged his mouth from her lips, but he couldn't stop himself from returning to sip at the corner of her mouth and drag his tongue across the silken skin of her cheek.

The dampness of tears on her cheeks stopped him from going any further. She was crying.

His passion cooled in an instant, but it took longer to get his body under control. He held himself still, clenching his jaw until it hurt.

He cursed himself. He'd come into the wickiup to comfort her, not to take her.

He reluctantly drew away, unwilling to take advantage of her when she'd needed comfort. He condemned himself for what he'd nearly done. Without a word, he turned and left the wickiup.

Chapter Fourteen

Regan stared after Branded Wolf, confused and strangely overheated. He'd left her, turned away from her and left.

Pulling the gaping material of her bodice together, she fastened the pearl buttons with shaky fingers. What had she nearly done?

Anger, shame, and confusion merged as she fought for a measure of self-control. She clenched her hand into a fist. How she longed to call him back. But she wouldn't. She couldn't.

She pressed her fist against her mouth to keep from crying out. Why had he changed his mind and rejected her?

She longed to go to him, but she knew she couldn't. She'd learned as a child that going to someone in supplication only resulted in painful rebuff. Wasn't that what her father had always done when she approached him after she'd angered him?

She could have overcome Branded Wolf's objections,

could have even faced down an argument, but not this rejection.

Pounding her fist in anger at herself and him, she rolled over and tried to find the dark comfort provided by sleep.

She was worthy of love. Dammit, she was. And she'd set out and prove it to him too. Then he'd see what he'd lost.

If he didn't want her, she wouldn't go running after him like some little girl, seeking crumbs.

She had her pride too.

But that pride was a cold comfort in the loneliness of night.

Branded Wolf watched Regan as she sat under the afternoon shade of a tree and worked out the tangles in the pup's coat. He found himself wishing she'd stroke him the way she did the little dog.

She bent forward, and a tendril of hair brushed her cheek. He shifted on the rock. His breeches were becoming uncomfortable.

He admitted his discomfort was of his own choosing. But his act of honor and nobility of the night before was beginning to make less and less sense in the light of day, especially when he admitted that he still wanted her, wanted her very much. So much that it hurt, far worse than the bullet wound had pained him. He sucked in a ragged breath as he watched her lean forward and drop a kiss on the pup's head.

Unable to stand it any longer without sweeping her up into his arms, he grabbed a stick and surged to his feet in a quick movement. "I'm going to catch some fish for our dinner," he called out over his shoulder as he strode out of the camp.

Regan stared after him in amazement. His footsteps echoed back across the clearing to her. It was the first time she'd heard his footsteps make a sound. He always walked so silently.

She narrowed her eyes on his broad back. Could it be that he was also feeling this same desire that plagued her? She raised her chin in the air and sniffed. She certainly hoped so.

It would serve him right.

Unable to sit still any longer, she jumped to her feet. She stared in the direction Branded Wolf had taken, then turned her back on him and his confusing behavior. What she needed was a nice walk to help her sort out her thoughts.

Not that she'd ever been one to willingly walk any distance if she didn't have to, but she'd been doing a lot of things lately she'd never done back in Philadelphia. She needed time to think over those changes.

Including falling in love, a little voice whispered.

The thought sent her off at a fast walk away from the camp. And away from Branded Wolf.

Captain David Larkin raised the spyglass to his eye for another look. He couldn't readily accept what he'd seen the first time.

Could his luck turn any worse?

In the distance, he watched the cause of his problem stroll leisurely past an aspen tree as if she didn't have a single care in the world.

"Damn."

Regan McBain.

He'd all but celebrated her death, and here she was alive, breathing and walking.

And talking, if he didn't put a stop to it.

Here he'd been, searching the damn hot desert for her, and she was spending her time in the cool of the mountains while he was hot, sweaty, and saddle sore. She looked a little bedraggled but in fine form.

He lowered the spyglass and swore vehemently. She was alive and well from the looks of her.

And not alone.

He hadn't missed seeing the savage she was spending her time with in the camp. He'd been tall, and strong from the looks of him. But he hadn't been beating her, or any of the other abuses he'd been envisioning since she left him in the desert. She didn't have a bruise on her.

He grunted in disgust. Oh, the Apaches had gotten hold of her all right, but it hadn't turned out the way he'd planned it. Far from it.

The Indian wasn't beating her or abusing her. Instead, he was watching over her.

He cursed her luck.

It looked like the high-and-mighty Miss McBain had managed to work her wiles on the fool Indian. The damn savage was treating her like some welcomed guest instead of a prisoner. She wasn't even tied. She was free to stroll around the mountainside, where anyone might find her. Alive and well.

And all too willing to tell about their fateful ride.

If that happened, he'd be ruined. No promotion. No command of his own.

Once the colonel found out the truth—or, even worse, the colonel's wife—it would all be over for him. He didn't relish spending his time in a stockade again. He'd spent too much time there in years past.

No one knew about his true past. Not since he'd come upon the real Captain David Larkin on his way out to be posted at the fort. Then and there he'd taken the guileless young man from back east under his care and learned all about the officer. Then he'd bashed his head in with a rock and disposed of the body where no one ever had found it.

That had been nearly two years ago, and everything had been going his way since. The fool colonel doted on him like he'd found a lost son, and he used it every chance he had. When the colonel told him he was sending for his daughter, he knew his life was set. Marriage, a promotion, his own command, were all within reach. Not to forget the money from his escapades these last four years or so.

He paused to wonder how everything had gone so wrong for him. Why did the woman have to have the good fortune to run into an Indian she could bewitch instead of a band of savages who would abuse her and kill her?

Now it was up to him to take care of her once and for all.

He pulled his rifle from the scabbard. Unflinchingly, he raised the rifle, sighted it on Regan, and smiled. Resting his finger on the trigger, he paused an instant to savor the moment.

He felt the metal beneath his finger and breathed in deeply, drawing out the moment. In his mind he could see the bullet hitting her, could see her body jerking with the impact.

But it wasn't enough.

He wanted to watch her die at close range.

For all the trouble she'd caused him, he deserved that much. Killing her from this distance wouldn't give him the same pleasure as looking into her eyes when he pulled the trigger.

While a shot from there provided him the time to ride away before the Indian could catch up with him, it wasn't good enough. Within himself he longed for the thrill of the kill at close range.

He would not be denied.

If the Indian came running at the sound of the shot, then he'd make certain the Indian met the same fate as Regan.

Smiling, he sighted in on her one more time for pleasure,

then lowered the gun and sheathed his rifle slowly back into the scabbard.

Regan strolled along the trail and wondered how many others had walked this same path through the years. A brief smile crossed her face. She was thinking of other people instead of herself. Yes, she was changing out here in the wilderness.

She looked around the surrounding area, then leaned back her head and inhaled deeply of the fresh air. Lifting her head, she spotted a hummingbird a short distance away. It looked like it was suspended in space. She watched it in awe, hardly daring to breathe, afraid of scaring it away.

Suddenly, the bird took off, disappearing in an instant. She straightened, not realizing in her absorption in the hummingbird that she'd leaned forward. Concentrating the way she'd been doing, she hadn't heard anyone approach. It must be Branded Wolf. Not that she ever heard him walking. Well, almost never, she amended. She smiled at her memory of his earlier noise and the hopeful cause of it.

She turned around to face him, and her heart lodged in her throat. She couldn't make a sound as she stared down the barrel of a rifle pointed right at her.

She slowly forced her eyes up away from the deadly looking gun and came face-to-face with Captain Larkin. What was he doing here? Now of all times?

A sense of unease stirred at the nape of her neck like a chilled breeze. Why wasn't he lowering the rifle? Surely he'd recognized her.

"Captain Larkin—"

"Do you have any idea of the trouble you've caused me?" he asked her, tightening his grip on the wooden stock of the rifle.

She swallowed, taken aback at his verbal attack. "I'm

sorry you had to ride out with a search party, but if you hadn't—''

"There isn't a search party with me."

A brief smile turned his lips but lasted only a second.

"Only me," he added with relish to his voice.

"What are you talking about? I—"

"Shut up."

Regan knew her mouth flew open in amazement. She could feel the air on her tongue. Then anger caught her up. No one ever told her such a rude thing.

"Now, listen—" she began.

"I said shut up."

The words were said with such force that Regan snapped her mouth closed immediately.

"Why couldn't you have died like you were supposed to?" he asked in a low, whiny voice.

Regan stepped back at the quietly spoken question. One look at the hatred on his face, and she knew he meant every word of his question.

As he closed his finger over the trigger, she knew the truth in a flash. He was going to shoot her.

A blur of white flew at him, and Sweet Pea clamped her jaws on his wrist. The shot went wild, thudding into a tree as he dropped the rifle. He yelled, shaking the dog loose. Sweet Pea landed beside a bush and lay still.

Regan screamed and turned to rush to Sweet Pea. Before she reached her pet, Captain Larkin grabbed her arm.

"Oh, no, you don't," he snarled at her. "I want to see your face when I kill you."

She knew he meant it.

Regan opened her mouth to scream, and he backhanded her across the mouth. Her world exploded into a burst of stars, then she tasted blood on her tongue.

As her vision cleared, she heard a chilling war cry and Captain Larkin whirled away from her, shoving her to the ground. She looked up to see Branded Wolf standing, feet braced shoulder width apart. He looked like an avenging angel to her.

Her avenging angel.

As he reached down to pull his knife from his knee-high moccasin, Larkin lowered his head and rammed him in the stomach. Branded Wolf staggered back from the force. Larkin slammed a fist into his chin before he could recover. Pain exploded in his jaw.

Branded Wolf shook off the the blow and struck hard, hitting Larkin in the mouth. The officer's head snapped back, but he didn't go down. Blood trickled from the corner of his mouth, and he wiped it away with the back of his hand, then threw himself at Branded Wolf.

Larkin fought like a man well versed in back-alley fights, throwing punches, dodging, and parrying. This time his skill was born of desperation.

Normally, the two men would be far from evenly matched. Branded Wolf was taller, more firmly muscled, and stronger. However, his wound took away from that advantage.

With an Apache war cry that chilled the air, Branded Wolf shoved the other man back. He landed a solid punch that caught Larkin in the gut.

Regan wanted to close her eyes or look away from the fighting, but she couldn't. Not for a second. She watched each move, each thrust, each hit, flinching each time Branded Wolf suffered a blow. Once she opened her mouth to call out a warning but stopped herself barely in time. What if she distracted his attention and that allowed Captain Larkin the advantage?

Fear kept her silent. She bit down on her lower lip to keep from crying out, until she tasted blood. She couldn't do this. She couldn't.

Standing there watching was driving her insane. She could no longer do nothing.

There had to be *something* she could do to help.

Suddenly, Larkin dove forward, wrapping his arms around Branded Wolf's chest. As he squeezed his grip, tightening harder, Regan saw the flicker of pain cross Branded Wolf's face before he shuttered the look.

His wound. Larkin was squeezing against his injured side. She couldn't imagine the pain Brand was suffering without a flicker of emotion on his face. She swallowed down her cry of alarm. If Larkin kept this up, he might break open the bullet wound again.

Well, she refused to stand idly by and allow that to happen.

Regan tore her horrified gaze away from the two men locked in battle. There had to be something . . .

She spotted the captain's rifle lying on the ground. Grabbing up her skirt, she ran and picked up the smooth wooden stock. Turning, she raised the gun in her hands, then froze.

A knot formed in the pit of her stomach. She didn't know if she could pull the trigger and *shoot* someone. Close on the heels of that thought came another. She didn't have the faintest idea how to shoot a gun.

What if she did it wrong?

What if she missed Captain Larkin?

A shaft of fear so deep and strong pierced her that she trembled with the intensity of it.

What if she shot Brand by mistake?

She lowered the gun, dropping it back to the ground, and shook her head in denial. She couldn't chance it.

In front of her the battle waged on. She could see the strain now showing on Branded Wolf's face. She gnawed on her lip in indecision.

With a grunt Captain Larkin pushed forward, forcing Branded Wolf to stagger back a step. Regan sucked in a breath to call out, but the sound never made it past her lips.

Branded Wolf closed his eyes for an instant, and terror swept over her. She didn't stop to think if he was passing out or drawing on an inner reserve of strength to fight the other man.

She grabbed up the rifle by the long, cold barrel and hefted it in her hands. She rushed forward toward the two men.

Stopping behind Captain Larkin, she sucked in a breath and swung the rifle.

Everything happened all at once.

The next instant, Branded Wolf broke the other man's hold, shoving him away. The gun stock cut through the air with a *whoosh*. And Regan met Branded Wolf's wide-eyed gaze.

A scream on her lips, she tried to pull back on the rifle in her grip. It was too little too late.

The corner of the wooden gun stock caught Branded Wolf on the side of the head and sent him reeling back.

Oh, stars and heavens. What had she done?

Branded Wolf staggered back another step.

Regan watched in horror, the rifle falling harmlessly from her numbed hands to lay at her feet.

Branded Wolf shook his head, attempting to clear his vision. He swung at the figure standing in front of him but missed as the image shifted and blurred. Dazed, he shook his head again.

Regan heard the sound of boot steps thudding on the ground and looked around in time to see Captain Larkin running down the incline. She stood in indecision a moment. Should she go after him? Try to stop him?

The sound of horse hooves galloping away gave her the only answer. Let him go. There was nothing she could do to stop him now.

And Branded Wolf needed her.

She turned back to him. He took one step, then a second. Then suddenly he fell to his knees. This time Regan cried out and rushed to his side. She bent over him. Guilt and fear welled up in her.

Mumbling a prayer that she hadn't killed him, she bent closer to check if he was still breathing.

Branded Wolf opened his eyes as Regan bent toward him. At least he thought it was Regan, except that there were two of her. He blinked, and gradually the world came back into focus. The two Regans he'd seen blended into one. He sighed in relief.

When she brushed her fingers across the top of his head, he winced. It was definitely Regan. No one else had her particular touch for the injured.

"Thank heavens you're alive," she cried.

"Thank heavens you didn't split my head open," he grumbled back at her, although he'd caught only a portion of her swing. He dreaded to think where he'd be if he'd taken the full force of the rifle butt.

"It isn't bleeding," he heard her mutter.

"No thanks to you." He squeezed his eyes shut. He ached. The cavalry officer had a strong fist. He'd—

Branded Wolf shoved Regan aside and surged to his feet, remembering the bluecoat. He looked around the clearing. The man was gone.

"Damn, he got away."

"I couldn't stop him," Regan admitted. She wasn't about to tell him she hadn't even tried.

"You hit me." He looked down at her in puzzlement.

"I was aiming for him!" she shouted back.

"Your aim was off, little one."

"He moved," she whispered, her voice cracking.

"Regan?"

She stepped back and shook her head. "When I realized I'd hit you . . . I—" She gulped. "I was afraid I'd killed you."

He took her into his arms. "I'm a lot harder to kill than that."

''Thank goodness,'' she mumbled, her face tight against his chest.

From the corner of her eye she saw Sweet Pea bounding over to join them. She sighed in relief. Both Sweet Pea and Brand were safe.

''I'm sorry I hit you,'' she whispered into his chest.

Her breath was warm against his skin, and he swallowed deeply. But he had to see to her safety.

''The bluecoat—''

''Is long gone. He rode off,'' she answered. ''I don't think he'll be coming back soon either.'' Her voice hardened.

''Why does the white-eyes want to kill you?'' he asked.

''The white-eyes?'' she asked in confusion. ''Oh, you mean Captain David Larkin.''

''David?''

''Yes, I think he's afraid what will happen if I tell my father what he did to me.''

The white-eyes had better be afraid if Branded Wolf ever got his hands on him again. He'd kill him for daring to lay a finger on Regan. Much less for trying to kill her. For that he'd kill him. Slowly.

He raised her chin to take a look at her face. The man had left a red mark on her cheek. Clamping down on the hatred that soared in him, he placed a tender kiss against the spot.

Regan moaned softly, her breath stirring his cheek. She turned her head so that her lips brushed against his. He kissed her fully, completely. Then, reluctantly, he drew away.

''I want you away from where he hurt you.''

He swept her up into his arms and strode back to their camp.

''Brand, you can't carry—''

A quick, hard kiss cut off what she'd been going to say to him.

Yes, she guessed he could do just about anything he wanted to do.

And he did. He carried her past the wickiup to the clearing beside the pool. There he laid her gently on the grass and followed her down.

The dappled sunlight shined down through the canopy of trees and high rock formations. Regan stared at his dark, bronze skin. She couldn't resist the urge to run her fingertips across his bare chest. The firm muscles rippled beneath her touch.

She stared in awe. She'd never seen a man's chest this close before. Except for when he'd nearly made love to her in the wickiup, but that had been at night with only the moon for light.

Her cheeks heated with the pink stain of a blush.

But this was different.

This was in daylight.

In the middle of the day too.

Branded Wolf leaned back and looked deep into her eyes. Regan thought her heart would surely stop beating at that moment, for time itself had ceased for her. Only the two of them existed.

"Little one," he said, his voice so low it stroked her like the softest of feathers.

It sent shivers of pleasure down her arms and along her back.

She couldn't tear her eyes away from his. She was lost in those blue depths as surely as she'd been lost in the desert. And his gaze was every bit as hot as the sun itself.

His eyes darkened and he spoke. "No more games. For either of us."

Regan scarcely found her voice to answer, "No more games."

She felt his body tense as he tightened his jaw. His shoulder muscles rippled in the sunlight from the effort of him holding back his control.

His words when he spoke were both a warning and a plea. "Little one, say no now if you want, for there will be no turning back for us."

Her heart jumped in her chest at his words. She could no more have said the word no than she could have denied herself her next breath.

She raised one hand from where it rested on his broad shoulder and laid her fingertips over his lips. The heat she felt there nearly stole away the power of speech. She had to draw in a breath before she could answer him.

"Yes," she whispered.

He pressed his lips against her fingers in a kiss, then pressed her hand above her head, holding it captive with one of his.

He cupped her cheek in his other hand a moment, then ran his hand down her throat. Her pulse throbbed beneath his fingers. Smiling to himself, he trailed his thumb along the haughty tilt of her jawline. Her skin was silken beneath his hand, like touching softest velvet.

She curled her imprisoned hand, interlacing her fingers with his. When he pressed his mouth to hers, she thought she'd surely stop breathing. His kiss was nothing less than a brand of possession to come.

Easing away, he slowly stood to his feet, his eyes never leaving hers. He removed first one knee-high moccasin, then the other. Hooking his thumbs into his breeches, he lowered them and kicked them to the side.

She couldn't resist the urge to watch him. His every movement was smooth and sleek, like him. When he stood before her naked, she stared, then swallowed. He was magnificent.

He returned to undress her with a loving tenderness that removed all embarrassment. When at last she lay naked before him, she gazed at him, a nervousness coming over her. Would he be disappointed? Would . . .

His eyes slid over her with a hunger she couldn't miss. His gaze skimmed the swell of her breasts, the curve of her waist, the flare of her hips. It traveled all the way to her toes, then returned to her face. When he smiled, she felt as if she'd been handed a wonderful gift. She knew she was lost to him.

A twinge of old doubts arose, forcing her to ask, "Are you . . . sure . . . I . . ." Her words faltered and her cheeks pinkened with a blush.

He smiled and whispered, "Little one, you are more beautiful than a desert sunset. More precious than life itself."

A flutter of pleasure at his compliment eased her old worries, and she held out her arms to him.

When he came to her, it was with a feeling of coming home. He wanted to crush her to him, possess every part of her, but he forced himself to gentle his touch. The contrast of his dark bronze skin against her creamy body stirred him.

Regan ran her hand down the muscled strength of his arm. His skin was warmed from the sun, and she savored his heat, a heat that seeped throughout her own body at his touch.

Branded Wolf sucked in his breath at the feel of her small hands sliding down his arms. When she returned her hands to his neck, sliding along his shoulders, his breath rushed out.

He pulled her into his arms, and she melted into him, her body fitting perfectly to his, soft curve to hard muscle, as if they'd been made only for each other. He tightened his hands around her tiny waist. Her skin was like silk beneath his roughened hands.

When he kissed her this time, it was a gift of his heart. The kiss was tender, promising so much.

At the sound of a moan of desire deep in her throat, he

lost the battle to be gentle. He pressed his body down onto hers, his chest rubbing against her soft breasts.

Her fingers skimmed his back, her nails lightly grazing his skin. As he slid his tongue past her lips and stroked the recesses of her mouth, every bit of shyness left her, burned away by the heat of his touch, the pressure of his tongue against hers.

Regan tightened her hands in the silken hair around her fingers. She pulled him down closer to her. She wanted to feel his strength, his possession.

He touched her with fire, consumed her with kisses, and branded her as his. He loved her with hands that were both tough and tender.

She ran her hands over the broad width of his back, memorizing each indentation, each tiny scar. She lost herself to his touch as he kissed his way downward from her lips, to her neck, pausing at her breasts. Then down her stomach to her thighs. He brought feelings she'd never felt before, never knew existed. She dug her fingers into his back, crying out. He returned his lips to hers, taking the sound into himself.

He cradled himself between her thighs and whispered words to her in Apache. She savored the melodic, tender words and his kisses as gently, tenderly, he pressed forward and made her completely his.

He swallowed her small cry, kissing it away, then moved with a gentle rhythm that sent her spiraling to the heavens above. He loved her with strength and passion, sweeping her into a place she'd never been before.

Together they crossed the threshold into a land of wonder and starlight in day.

Chapter Fifteen

Regan rested her head on Branded Wolf's shoulder. She knew she'd never experienced such happiness in her entire life. It almost frightened her with its intensity, making her fear that it would be stolen away from her.

A soft sigh of contentment escaped her lips. He leaned over and stole it away with a kiss.

"Rest, little one," he murmured. "We will leave here soon."

Regan's heart took wings and soared to the top of the trees overhead.

He was returning her to the fort.

When her papa saw her and Brand together and witnessed their love, he'd quickly change his mind about his preference for the captain.

She could imagine Brand, dressed in different clothes, perhaps a nice suit, meeting her parents. Her mama and papa would take one look at his handsome strength in a real suit of clothes and see her happiness, and they couldn't help but give them their blessing.

Regan smiled. Life was wonderful. She and Brand would be married at the fort. She ignored the twinge of unease that touched the corner of her mind. Of course, he hadn't *asked* her to marry him yet. But he would.

She snuggled closer to the lean length of his body. Oh, life with him would be wonderful. Everything she'd ever dreamed of, and more.

She couldn't wait to introduce him to her friends back home in Philadelphia. Her mama would arrange a marvelous party for them. Suddenly, a knot formed in the pit of her stomach.

At that point her imagination crashed to a halt. There was no way she could picture Brand in her mama's fancy Philadelphia home, taking tea with the ladies of society. He kept changing to Branded Wolf, the Apache warrior, complete with war paint streaked on his face.

A question sliced through her. Did she love Branded Wolf the Apache, or Brand the white man? Did either man fit into her world back home?

She swallowed, tamping down her fears. He *had* to belong there. Because she most certainly didn't belong here.

Doubts assailed her, rising up to nearly choke her with their intensity.

Branded Wolf slid his hand down her side and drew her more fully into his embrace. Tipping her head back with his thumb under her chin, he looked into her eyes.

Regan took one look at the tenderness shining from his gaze, and all worries fled. This man loved her, that's all she needed.

For now, but what about later? a little voice nagged, but its whisper was drowned in the sweetness of their lovemaking.

* * *

While Branded Wolf packed up the necessary items for their departure and readied the camp, Regan took one last bath in the crystal waters of the pool. Sweet Pea lay beside the bank, refusing to stray too far from Regan's side.

Regan marveled at the change in her pet. Since the captain's attack, Sweet Pea kept a vigilant watch for any danger. At the slightest sound, her ears would perk up and her plume tail would cease its wagging. The little pup had claimed the position of watchdog in earnest.

Regan dressed surrounded by the towering pines. She took extra care with trying to arrange her hair and smoothing out the persistent wrinkles in her gown. She must look a sight, and she longed to look her very best for Branded Wolf.

After patting a reluctant curl in place, she called to Sweet Pea and returned to where she knew Brand was waiting for them. Sure enough, he had finished their preparations and stood waiting beside Wind Dancer.

Regan took one last, lingering look around the mountain camp and the wickiup. She hated leaving it. She'd come to love the beauty of the mountain pines, colorful wildflowers, and the peace there. Not to mention the pool and the wondrous lovemaking there with Branded Wolf.

The thought surprised her. She wouldn't want to actually *stay* in an uncivilized place like this, would she?

Maybe, if Branded Wolf stayed beside her.

She knew her eyes lit up as he approached her, his footsteps as silent as ever. She'd have to get him to teach her how to do that someday.

She smiled at the very thought of her living her life in these primitive conditions, but something about it did appeal to her. Yes, she thought to herself, she was changing.

"Ready?" Branded Wolf dropped his arm around her shoulder and pulled her back to him.

Regan leaned against him, drawing from his strength. She turned into his arms and lifted her face for a kiss. He obliged her until her toes curled in her slippers.

When he at last released her, she was completely breathless. His smile told her he knew it, and the fact gave him pride. She clung to him, her arms around his waist. Tilting her head, she looked into his eyes.

"I don't want to leave," she whispered to him.

He pulled her close again, resting his chin on the top of her head. "We must, little one. I do not want us here should the treacherous bluecoat return."

Regan swallowed her objections. He was right. David Larkin knew where to find them now, and a tiny part of her didn't believe he'd give up this easily. Had he returned to the fort? She doubted it, but the possibility worried her.

"What will you do after we reach the fort?" she asked in a low voice edged with concern.

Branded Wolf stiffened and pushed away to look down into her face. "We are not going to the fort."

His statement caught her off guard.

"What?" She paused to moisten suddenly dry lips. "What do you mean?"

"I told you before. I'm not taking you back to the fort."

"But I thought—"

"You thought wrong."

He stepped back from her, letting her arms fall from his body. His face became a shuttered mask. He looked every inch the warrior, preparing to do battle.

Her temper rose to the challenge. Tossing her head, she crossed her arms over her chest, partially to keep them from reaching out to him again. It seemed her body had developed a mind of its own where he was concerned. She didn't like the new weakness one little bit.

She was losing herself in him.

The thought frightened her more than she was willing to admit. If she allowed herself to be consumed by his strength of will, what would happen to her? She had to retain some small measure of her freedom.

The only way she knew how to do this was to make him return her to the fort. Then staying with him would become her choice. Her decision. Not solely his.

"Brand, you can't do this," she tried to reason with him.

"It's already done."

She gritted her teeth, unwilling to face defeat.

"Brand—"

His jaw tensed. "I've told you before. I am Branded Wolf. Have you forgotten I am an Apache?"

"No, I haven't," she snapped.

They were back to where they'd started with her as his captive. She had to try one more time to make him see reason.

"I don't want to fight with you," she admitted, her voice softening.

"Then don't."

Regan stomped her foot as her temper rose. "It's not that easy. You can't make me your prisoner"

"I already have."

"Fine. If that's the way you want it." She raised her nose in the air and went over to a rock, where she promptly sat down. Crossing her legs, she deliberately turned her head away from him.

She didn't have long to wait for his reaction.

He strode over to stand in front of her. She noted with a burst of pleasure that his footsteps had sounded remarkably like stomps. She kept her face averted from him, trying to focus her gaze on something other than his muscled legs, braced for battle.

For a moment she regretted her hasty decision to give her

temper free rein. She truly didn't want to fight with him, but she would see this through. She refused to back down.

"Regan."

She kept her gaze elsewhere, pretending not to hear him.

"Regan, enough of this. We have to leave."

She waved her hand in dismissal. "Feel free to leave anytime you want to. Sweet Pea and I are going to the fort."

She heard him release his breath in a hiss of obvious frustration. Good. It served him right.

He surprised her by turning away from her. His footsteps crackled the pine needles.

"If you want to wait here for *your captain's* return"— he shrugged in dismissal—"I'm certain he will be back for you. So if you choose to await him . . ."

Branded Wolf let his words trail off, the threat behind them left unspoken. He had no intention of leaving her behind unprotected, but she need not know that.

Perhaps if he gave her a graceful way out to salvage her pride, she would come willingly. Damn, but the white-eyes had enough pride for any three Apache braves.

Either way, she was coming with him, willing or not.

He waited.

Regan jumped to her feet with a huff of indignation. "Oh, all right. I'm coming."

She stomped over to where Wind Dancer stood ground tied. Her slipper-clad feet sent up a flurry of pine needles.

"Aren't you forgetting something?" he taunted.

She stiffened. "What?"

"Your dog." He struggled to keep the laughter from his voice.

She whirled around to glare at him, then turned her head. "Sweet Pea, come here."

The little pup bounded up to her, a stick in her mouth as a play offering. Regan scooped the pup into her arms and tossed the stick to the ground.

He settled her and the pup on the horse in silence. As Branded Wolf swung up onto Wind Dancer's back, he thought he heard Regan mutter something about him in comparison to "the south end of a northbound horse."

His lips twitched, but he didn't let a sound slip past.

He was happy enough that he hadn't had to tie her to bring her with him. He would keep his vow to keep her safe—no matter what it took.

Captain David Larkin sat inside the entrance of the small cave, nursing his bruises with a deep swallow from his ever-present flask of whiskey. The liquor burned his split lip, then seared its way down to his gut.

The whiskey left a warm glow in its wake. Groaning, he set the new silver flask against a rock, picked up a strip of jerky, and absently shredded the jerky into tiny pieces. He reached to lay his palm across the reassuring steel of his revolver and noticed what he'd done with the dried meat.

Standing to his feet, he brushed the litter off his dusty pants. As he raised his head, he hit the back of it on the low overhang above.

He swore long and hard.

The movements made his jaw ache worse. He rubbed it gingerly and slowly sank back to the ground to take another soothing sip from the flask. He was a mass of cuts and bruises inflicted by that savage.

If not for Regan's timely interference, he might have been killed.

He gave a short bark of laughter. If he hadn't known better, he might harbor the suspicion she'd been aiming for him instead of the savage. Foolish thought. But no, she'd hit the savage alongside the head.

Slapping the ground of the cave in glee, he flinched at the pain. Damn, he hurt. Everywhere.

He'd have stuck around to kill Regan himself if he hadn't been certain she'd die anyway. He wasn't about to take a chance of risking his own hide for her, since she had his loaded rifle in her hands. She might just be stupid enough to shoot him.

It didn't matter now. She was dead.

Once he shook off her blow, the savage Apache would skin her alive for sure. His gut clenched into a knot of anticipation. Oh, he'd have liked to stay and watch it.

However, he wasn't a fool. He wasn't taking any chances of that savage Apache coming after him and doing the same. No, he'd executed a strategic retreat like a good soldier. He laid back his head and let the harsh laughter roll free.

Miss High-and-Mighty Regan McBain was dead for good this time.

"Good riddance!" he shouted. He raised the flask in a mock toast to his "fiancée."

The whiskey burned a path down his throat, leaving behind only one regret. He wished he could have watched her die close up. And at his hands. He felt he'd been cheated somehow.

He sighed a guttural groan. The thirst for blood ate at him, gnawing like an unassuaged hunger.

Over the next hours the desire didn't lessen. Ultimately, he would have to do something about it, he thought.

Capping the nearly empty flask, he carefully stood, ducking the overhanging rock this time. It was time to go meet up with his trusted men, then he'd feed this hunger that ate at his insides. And pad his pockets a bit in the process.

Branded Wolf kept a watchful eye for any danger. He guided Wind Dancer over the sloping ground with the pressure of his knees, feeling every shift of the horse.

And every slight movement Regan made in his arms. She

sat snuggled between his thighs, her position threatening to create havoc with his concentration.

He hadn't liked leaving the safety of their mountain hide-away with its ready source of fresh water, but the cavalry officer had left them no choice.

Now that David Larkin knew of the place, it was no longer safe. It could well become a trap.

Branded Wolf tightened his arm around Regan's waist. He would never let the white-eyes have her. Not now. Not ever.

He *knew* he should return her to the fort. To her father, the commander's care. But he couldn't do it. She belonged to him now. He would keep her safe. She *belonged* to him.

No choice remained but to seek the shelter of the Dragoons and old Cochise's stronghold. The numerous caves and can-yons would provide safety. For now.

Branded Wolf suddenly stiffened in alertness. The air carried the smell of smoke. And of death.

He fought off the memory of his nightmare and the past deaths. Reining Wind Dancer to a stop, he raised his chin and sniffed the air.

Smoke.

"What is it?" Regan tilted her head back to look at him.

"Trouble."

She watched in awe as his face hardened and his eyes shuttered, closing out all gentleness. He'd transformed into a warrior, trained to kill. She stared at him for a second in apprehension, but never doubted for an instant that he would protect her with his very life.

With a touch of his knees, he sent Wind Dancer forward. Regan felt his body stiffen behind her. The tension was so palpable, she could almost reach out and touch it.

"Regan," he whispered against her ear. "You will do as I say."

She opened her mouth, then shut it and nodded her head

in silent agreement. This was not the time for arguing. She tightened her hold on Sweet Pea.

They topped a slight rise and could see the scene spread out below. Regan barely cut back her scream of terror.

Smoke billowed from one wagon, while a second wagon had two flaming arrows in the canvas. As a figure stood to beat at the flames, a shot rang out, and the figure crumpled to the ground with a cry.

Regan put her fist to her mouth to hold back her scream. She'd never seen anyone killed before.

A horrible yell split the air, and she saw five riders on horseback charging toward the wagon and its occupants.

"Indians," she whispered, not realizing she'd said the word aloud.

Branded Wolf sucked in his breath. "No, not Indians."

His voice held a chill she'd never heard before.

In a flash, he pulled her down from the horse and pressed her to the ground. He held one hand on Sweet Pea, stilling the dog.

"Stay here. And don't move until I get back."

Before Regan could protest, he swung onto Wind Dancer and rode for the battle.

Her throat closed in terror for him. He was riding straight into the fighting below.

If he thought she was going to sit idly by and do nothing, he had another thought coming.

Chapter Sixteen

Regan raised her head and surveyed the scene below. It looked worse than it had first appeared.

Two bodies lay not moving in front of the farthest wagon. The canvas had burned away to leave a grotesque skeleton of a wagon.

She saw a woman and two children hiding beside one of the rear wheels of the closest wagon. A man lay on the ground. He rose and fired a rifle shot at the attackers.

Regan lay frozen in place for a moment.

The poor settlers didn't stand a chance against the riders bearing down on them.

And neither might Branded Wolf, she thought in fear for his life.

He'd been pretty insistent when he ordered her to stay, but she simply couldn't do it. Not if he was in danger.

He'd be furious with her, but she didn't have a choice. She couldn't let him fight alone.

She spotted a rifle in the dirt behind the closest wagon.

Without giving herself a chance to reconsider or change her mind, she grabbed up Sweet Pea in one hand and her skirts in the other. She ran for the wagon with speed she never knew she had.

Dodging behind rocks and cactus, and keeping as low as she could, Regan pushed herself on. She dove for the protection of the wagon wheel, sliding down beside the woman.

"What—"

"We're here to help," Regan gasped out.

As the woman raised a gun and pointed it at Branded Wolf's back, Regan didn't think, she just acted. She threw herself at the woman. The gun went off, the bullet thudding into the top of the wagon.

"Dammit," she yelled at the woman. "I said we're helping you."

"They're Indians," the woman screamed at her.

"But that Apache is mine." Regan nodded to Branded Wolf.

She yanked the rifle out of the woman's hands and turned to the attackers now approaching. She shivered at the sight of the bare-chested men, feathers in their hair. They certainly looked like Indians to her. Dark, stringy hair greased back from their foreheads, red paint streaked over their cheeks and foreheads, and their chests bared with black-painted streaks.

She frowned. Something about the attackers nagged at her.

Something wasn't quite right.

Suddenly, it struck her. The men's chests were sun-tanned a brownish color, not bronzed copper like Branded Wolf's.

The attackers were white men, not Indians.

"They're white," she whispered in disbelief.

The woman grabbed for the gun, but Regan held her off. "They're not all Indians," she shouted at her. "Just my one. And don't you dare shoot him."

At a chilling yell, Regan turned her attention back to the attackers. One man extended his gun, aiming at Brand's back.

"No!" she cried out, but the man didn't pay any attention to her cry

She raised the rifle in her hands, pointing it at the rider. Her finger found the trigger mechanism, and she pulled it back, hoping she'd worked it correctly. There wasn't time to learn how to shoot now.

The gun roared with a deafening sound that echoed in her ears. It jerked with the force of firing, sending Regan stumbling backward. She tripped and landed on her backside in a cloud of dust.

"Stars and heavens," she said, blinking her eyes and trying to hold on to the rifle.

Nobody told her it would do that!

She leaned forward and sighed in relief to see that the rider was no longer aiming at Brand. The man lay on the ground. Heavens, had she done that?

Branded Wolf caught one approaching rider under the chin with the barrel of his rifle and sent the man flying through the air. Regan smiled in pride.

Two down and—

A third man bore down toward Brand, and Regan called out a warning. She watched in horror as Branded Wolf turned to look back at her. Their eyes met for a second, and she saw shock, fear, and fury in his blue gaze.

She bit down on her lower lip. There'd be hell to pay when this was over. She didn't care if she swore.

She tore her gaze away from his to see the rider still coming. As she raised the gun again, Sweet Pea charged out into the foray. Her high-pitched yips carried through the air above all other noises.

Regan's heart jumped up to her throat, and she couldn't utter a sound. She started to stand, but the woman beside her caught her skirt and yanked her back down to the hard ground.

Regan didn't know who she was the most afraid for, Sweet Pea or Branded Wolf.

All she loved in the world was in danger in that instant.

The scene moved in slow motion for her as she saw Branded Wolf turn barely in time to avoid the rider's shot. Sweet Pea scarcely missed being trampled under the horse's hooves, and then jumped into the air, snapping at the horse's legs.

The horse reared into the air, sending the rider sailing over its back to land on the ground with a hard thud. He lay stunned, and Branded Wolf took the opportunity to knock him out with the butt of the rifle.

Jolted out of her frozen state, Regan grabbed the rifle beside her and aimed it at one of the two remaining attackers. She leaned up and braced herself on her knees to see better and pulled the trigger again. The gun roared, and she fell over backward, hitting her head on the wagon wheel.

The blue sky overhead turned dark for an instant, and stars twinkled in a swirl of circles for her. Then a velvet blackness swept over her.

Regan came to with Branded Wolf's worried face hovering above her. She raised a hand and touched his cheek. He looked so worried and angry.

She ignored the latter and tried to smile to reassure him. Both the enveloping darkness and the twinkling stars were gone, but a headache had taken their place with a vengeance. She blinked, too confused to speak for the time being.

"What in the hell did you think you were doing?" he shouted.

She shut her eyes against his anger for a moment. Then

she opened them slowly. "My head hurts," she whimpered, hating the weak sound of her voice.

"You're lucky that's all that hurts."

Why was he so angry?

She tried to recall what had happened before everything blacked out for her. The attack ... the wagons ... and Branded Wolf charging to the people's rescue.

When he closed his hands around her shoulders, all conscious thought left her. The only thing she could think of was that he was safe.

"What were you doing?" he shouted. "I told you to stay there."

"I hit my head when I shot the gun." She pointed to where the rifle lay beside her foot.

"You could have been killed." Anger blazed in his eyes.

"So could you have," she yelled back, then caught her head in her hand and moaned.

"Dammit, Regan. I told you to stay."

"I couldn't," she explained. "You were in danger."

"I can take care of myself."

Her lower lip trembled. "I couldn't chance it."

Lowering his head and closing his eyes, he drew her close to his chest. "When I saw you lying on the ground, I thought you'd been shot."

"I'm sorry," she mumbled her apology against his chest.

"Why didn't you do as I told you?"

"I couldn't let you fight them alone. You were outnumbered."

He groaned his answer.

Suddenly, she sat up straight. "Where's Sweet Pea? She was—"

He pushed her back down gently but firmly. "She's fine. She wouldn't leave you alone, so I put her in the wagon."

Regan stared into his eyes, afraid he was lying to keep her from knowing the painful truth.

He nodded toward the back of the wagon, and Regan turned her head. For a moment everything spun in an arc but then settled. She saw Sweet Pea sitting on a little girl's lap, being fed a treat.

"Thank you," she whispered to Branded Wolf.

"Why?" he asked.

"Because somehow I know you saved her." She turned to look back at him. Deep in her heart, she knew it for a fact. "Didn't you?"

He shrugged off her question. "We were talking about you."

She looked away. "I—"

"Where did you learn to shoot like that?"

She peeked back at him. "I didn't."

"Didn't what?"

"Learn." She swallowed. "That's probably why I fell backward when the gun went off," she confessed.

He squeezed his eyes shut as though he were in pain. "You'd never fired a gun before, and you came running down here and picked up a rifle?"

His voice rose with his words, and she winced. Put like that, it did sound rather foolish.

"Well?" he demanded her answer.

"Uh-huh."

"Dammit, I—"

"I thought they were going to shoot you. I couldn't let them." She laid her hand on his arm.

"Little one."

He kissed her gently, tenderly, then passionately.

At the sound of someone clearing a throat, they broke apart.

"Pardon me, folks, but I'd like to thank you for your help."

Regan turned to look up at a man with a bandage around his head. Beside him stood the woman from the wagon.

"Me and the missus owe you our lives." He stepped forward and held out his hand to Branded Wolf. "And those of our girls too. Thank you, mister."

Branded Wolf looked at the man's outstretched hand in surprise, then stood to his feet and shook hands. Regan grabbed hold of the wagon wheel and eased herself up. She watched the woman warily, remembering that she'd pointed a gun at him.

"Yes, thank you," the woman added.

Regan smiled at her, liking the older woman with her pale blond hair.

"I'm Robert Duncan, and this here's my wife, Annie." He put one arm around the woman's shoulders. He towered over the blonde by a good six inches, his own blond hair several shades darker than hers.

Annie leaned into his strength. "Your wife explained you were helping us."

"We're not married," Regan blurted out, then wished she could bite her tongue and take back the words.

She stared down at her hands and replied, "We're happy to meet you. I'm Regan and this is Branded Wolf." She said his name with pride, not shortening it to Brand.

Robert Duncan continued with only a slight pause. "We're mighty thankful to you both."

Regan didn't dare look up at Branded Wolf after what she'd said. He'd never mentioned marriage, but surely he would soon.

"Why did the Indians attack us? We didn't do anything." Annie's voice shook with tears, and she held her hands tightly clenched together.

"They killed the Webster brothers first off." Robert gestured to the burned-out wagon. "We were going to be neighbors."

Annie sniffed and grabbed his hand. "Why did they attack us?"

"They weren't Indians," Branded Wolf told the settlers.

Robert stiffened at the denial. "I can understand you feeling some kind of loyalty—"

"Not to the white-eyes."

Regan saw Branded Wolf's chin jut out and rushed to intervene before the men came to blows over the hint of insult.

"He's right," she interjected. "Those men weren't Indians."

"Now, dear—"

Regan cut off the older woman. "They were white men. I saw them too."

Annie's eyes widened in disbelief. "But surely—"

"White," Regan snapped the word like a whip. "Their chests were browned by the sun." She nodded toward Branded Wolf. "The color was different. I saw it. That's how I know."

"But their faces were painted like Indians for a battle," Annie said, then closed her eyes and shuddered.

"No." Branded Wolf spoke up in a cold voice. "The men had paint smeared on them, but they were not painted for battle like the Apache. Their colored paint meant nothing to them."

Regan remembered the paint she'd first seen on his face in the desert. He was right. It had been different. More precise.

"They wanted everyone to think they were Apaches," Regan said in wonder.

Branded Wolf nodded, eyes narrowing.

"Why would white men attack us?" Robert asked.

"To put blame on the Apaches to cover their tracks. To steal your money and goods to sell." His jaw clenched. "These men enjoy the killing too."

"You sound like you know something about them," Robert observed.

Branded Wolf gave a short, perfunctory nod.

"Brand?" Regan whispered.

"I'm a bounty hunter, and I've been tracking them for three years in and out of the Territory. Since they killed my family."

Regan gasped.

"There's a bounty on every one of them." He gave a harsh laugh. "It'll be raised now that someone other than myself believes they're not Apache renegades."

He nodded to Robert. "All but one got away. Go turn over the one who's dead. You'll see he's a white-eyes."

Robert stepped away from his wife and did as Branded Wolf suggested. He returned shortly. "Well, I'll be. Annie, he's right. That ain't no Indian lying out there. Pardon me for saying that."

"We'd be the last to share prejudice. We came out here to get away from it."

Robert stepped forward and clasped Branded Wolf on the shoulder. "Thank you again."

"Would you two join us for dinner?" Annie asked with a smile. "Our way of saying thank-you."

Robert added, "It won't be fancy, but with Annie cooking, it'll be good."

Regan felt Branded Wolf's gaze on hers. Sure enough, when she looked up at him, he grinned.

"We'd like that," he told the couple. "I could use a break from cooking."

"Oh, don't you cook, Regan?" Annie asked.

"I cook," she snapped, sending Branded Wolf a pointed glare.

His only answer was a chuckle.

"We'll stay," he added. "But I think you should move on to a safer spot as soon as you can." He nodded toward the west across the flatland. "I can lead you to a good place for the night."

Robert hesitated only an instant before he responded, "We'd like that."

Regan assisted Annie in putting the wagon to rights and met her two little girls. Julie was six with pigtails and a missing tooth, and Rosie, at four, was a tiny image of her mother. Sweet Pea was in puppy heaven with the two children to fuss over her.

Regan noticed that while she'd been unconscious, the men had gotten the fire out without too much damage to the canvas. She realized she was thankful for that; the settlers hadn't lost anything. However, the other wagon was a total loss, and Annie kept her busy while the two men buried the Webster brothers.

Branded Wolf strode up as soundlessly as usual. Annie jumped, startled, but Regan only turned to smile at him.

"Regan, why don't you ride in the wagon?" He stated it as an order, not a request.

She raised her chin in resistance, but one look at his face made her change her mind. She didn't protest when he lifted her into the wagon.

"I'll ride a little ahead and scout out a safe spot to make camp." He dropped a quick kiss on her lips and walked to Wind Dancer.

Sighing softly, Regan watched him swing up onto the horse's back. She was reminded of when she'd first seen him on the horse. They were still both magnificent. Her lips tipped in a smile.

"You love him a lot, don't you?" Annie observed.

Regan felt her cheeks heat with a blush. She raised her chin in defiance and answered, "Yes, I do."

Annie patted her shoulder. "Well, hold on to him. He looks like a good man."

"He is," Regan whispered more to herself than to the other woman.

The ride was much different in the wagon. Regan found

she missed the comforting strength of Branded Wolf's chest against her back. She missed him, period.

She was relieved when they finally stopped to make camp. The next hour was spent setting the wagon to rights and starting the meal.

The meal was as good as Robert Duncan had promised. Regan could feel Branded Wolf's eyes on her. When she glanced up at him, he smiled, sharing their private joke.

One of these days she might just learn to cook and surprise him, Regan thought to herself.

Afterward the little girls asked if the puppy could sleep with them. Smiling, Regan agreed, and she watched as Annie put her two daughters to bed with Sweet Pea curled between them. A rush of tenderness and longing came over Regan. She wondered what it would be like to have Branded Wolf's children. Would they have a boy or a girl? Would they look like him with his beautiful blue eyes?

The questions brought a lump to her throat. He'd never once brought up the subject of children. Or of marriage, a little voice nagged at her. She silenced it with difficulty.

She looked over at where Branded Wolf sat beside the other man, talking. As if he'd sensed her gaze, he looked toward her. Regan felt warmth and tenderness in his steady gaze.

Branded Wolf stood and walked toward her. Regan suddenly had difficulty swallowing. She could have lost him today. Her heart caught, losing a beat.

When he took her hand in his, she followed him willingly to a spot a distance from the wagon. He settled her down onto a borrowed blanket pallet, then he stretched out a respectable distance away from her.

It took everything he'd learned as a warrior to stop himself from going to Regan, offering her his love. But today had shown him something too terrifying to ignore.

By keeping Regan with him, he was fulfilling his vow of

vengeance, but was putting her life in constant and repeated danger.

The realization shook him to his soul. He could have gotten her killed today.

Could he give up his vow, give up his honor for her?

No, he couldn't do it. He had made that vow on the graves of his dead.

The strength of his vow kept him from going to Regan. Instead, he lay stiff and rigid, listening for every tiny sound, every sigh, every movement from her.

Regan rolled over onto her back, crossed her arms over her chest, and stared up at the sky. The stars shone in the velvet blackness overhead, painting a picture of serene beauty. It mocked her misery.

Branded Wolf lay out of reach, but she could hear his movements in the empty darkness.

She could feel his withdrawal from her. It cut her deeply, more deeply than she wanted to admit.

It was so like the feeling she had each time her father turned away from her in disappointment. She searched deep within to find what she could have done wrong to disappoint him so much that he turned away from her too.

She lay quiet and unmoving, her temper and pride not allowing her to force the issue with him. Well, if Branded Wolf no longer wanted her, then that was his decision. She sniffed.

Although it soothed her wounded pride, it was little comfort when she felt like she was breaking apart inside. If only things could be different between them . . .

Turning her head away from him, she let her mind picture the desolate landscape. Yes, it was that, she thought, but the vast beauty of it tugged at her heart and welcomed her.

She almost groaned aloud before she caught the sound in her throat. Practically against her will, she was falling in love with both the man and the land. If only . . .

However, she knew better than to wish for what she couldn't have. Hadn't her father taught her that lesson well enough?

She closed her eyes and tried to will herself to sleep. It didn't work. The little voice in the back of her mind persisted in repeating that Branded Wolf wasn't her father.

She rolled over, wishing she had a pillow to thump. She was frustrated, unhappy, and in love. And there wasn't a thing she could do about it.

Or was there?

No, she told herself, a lady didn't . . . She didn't give a whit what a lady did anymore.

She'd nearly lost him today; was she going to let her pride stand in the way of giving her love if she chose to do so?

She threw back the covering and stood to her feet in a burst. Then she froze still, uncertainty eating at her resolve.

"Little one?" His low, melodic whisper stroked her, calling her.

Regan stood still a moment, waiting.

"Little one?" Branded Wolf leaned up on one elbow. "Is something wrong?"

She wanted to shout out yes, but she swallowed down her sudden case of nerves and crossed the distance separating them.

She sank to her knees beside him. He stared at her, and she saw him clench his jaw. His breath rushed out between his teeth in that way she loved. It told her he was not unaffected by her. She took her courage in both hands.

"Yes." She leaned closer and answered him in a throaty whisper. "I could have lost you today. I don't want to lose you tonight."

Her soft admission destroyed his hard-won self-control. He pulled her down to him, kissing her with every bit of his heart.

Regan sighed in relief. She knew she'd done the right thing.

She ran her hands over his bare chest, feeling each ripple of corded muscle. Her fingers played over his many scars, and she hurt for him. Pulling back, she lowered her head to his chest and kissed each scar, each hurt he'd suffered.

Branded Wolf felt as if he were being healed by fire. Her lips touched and took away each pain of past battles. He ran his hand along her cheek, her skin like softest velvet beneath his rough skin. He could never get enough of touching her. Of loving her.

Regan turned her head and kissed his palm, then sipped at his thumb, taking it in her mouth. He barely held back the groan in his throat.

Leaning up, she brushed her lips over his in a butterfly's touch, then ran her lips along his jaw.

"Little one," he whispered, his voice hoarse and ragged.

Regan laid her fingers over his mouth. "Shh. It's my turn to love you," she whispered against his throat.

At that moment he knew he had never loved a woman as much as he loved her and never would. She was the other half that made him whole.

Regan moved over him, her kisses branding him as hers. He felt as if his body were on fire. Her lips brushed, feathered, sucked at him.

When he could stand no more, he caught her by the waist and pulled her up. Looking deep into her eyes, his own asked and received his answer. He lifted her, shoving her skirt aside, and slid her down atop him.

Regan bit back her cry as sensations rushed through her too wonderful to describe. He moved and she spread her hand on his chest. She slid her hands up and caught hold of his shoulder as waves of pleasure washed over her. As she reached the peak, he tightened his hands on her hips, pulling her tighter to him, and he joined her at that peak.

The stars exploded in the sky for her, and she collapsed atop him. He held her close, his breath mingling with hers, their lips side by side.

Long minutes later Branded Wolf eased her along his side, holding her close in his embrace.

She waited, practically holding her breath, for him to say the words she needed to hear.

Surely now he'd tell her he loved her . . .

Surely he'd talk marriage . . .

Surely he'd tell her she was more to him than only his captive . . .

She waited in vain.

Chapter Seventeen

Branded Wolf rose before the first light of dawn streaked the sky. The decision he'd reached in the cold of night tore at him.

Regan's sweet lovemaking had nearly broken him apart. He'd longed to tell her what was in his heart. It had taken all his self-control to remain silent. He knew his silence had hurt her, and it hurt him even worse. If only she knew how much.

But he had no choice.

His decision was made, and he would not go back on it. Not now.

Weariness of body and soul ate at him. He'd gotten little sleep that night. He knew he would get even less in the days and nights to follow.

The future stretched long and bleak ahead of him. She would surely hate him for this.

Today he would send Regan back to the fort.

And out of his life.

* * *

Regan awoke alone on the blanket pallet. She reached out for Branded Wolf, missing the warmth of his body next to hers, but he wasn't there.

She leaned up and realized she was lying alone on her own bedding from the night before. She recalled that shortly before dawn he had carried her back. She'd murmured a complaint, but he'd kissed her words away. Then she'd fallen asleep.

She stretched leisurely, rolling her head to the side, arms overhead. She felt wonderful.

The sensible side of her thanked him for attempting to salvage her reputation. She smiled that the handsome warrior would care about it.

Branded Wolf was a complex man. And she loved him completely, totally.

Today she'd get him away from the others and insist they have a serious talk. Her lips twitched. Last night they'd had no time for talk.

But today would be different.

It was over an hour and a half later before Regan had a chance to try to pull Branded Wolf aside for their little talk.

Unexpectedly, he caught her by the hand and drew her back to the Duncan's wagon.

"Robert," he called out.

Regan wanted to stomp her foot. It had taken plenty of maneuvering to get him alone, and what did he do but call the others.

"Brand," she said his name softly.

He turned his head away from her.

Regan felt chill bumps rise on her arms, even with the morning sun shining down on her. She tried to swallow her sudden trepidation, but it remained lodged in her throat like a piece of dry biscuit.

"What do you need?" Robert rounded the wagon, his wife close behind him.

"I don't think you and your family should stay here. Or continue on alone. You'll be safer at the fort."

Robert nodded his agreement.

"I'll lead you and your family to the fort. You'll be safe there. They'll provide you with an escort from there."

"We'd appreciate that," Robert told him.

Branded Wolf raised his hand. "I ask one thing in return."

"Anything you need."

"You will take Regan with you in your wagon—to the fort."

"Brand," she gasped.

"Do you agree?" he asked as if he hadn't heard her speak.

Robert looked from one to the other. "Yes, we'll do it."

"We'll leave as soon as we get the wagon hitched," Branded Wolf ordered, taking over the proceedings.

A burst of anger caught Regan hard. What did he think he was doing? She was getting pretty tired of him making decisions for her. Mama always let her make her own decisions.

Reaching out, she grabbed Branded Wolf by the arm and yanked. Startled, he turned around to face her.

"Excuse me, I didn't hear you ask my opinion." She planted her hands on her hips, chin jutting out in determination.

"It doesn't matter—"

"Like blazes it doesn't!" she shouted.

"It doesn't." He lowered his head slightly. "And would you lower your voice."

"Why? Are you afraid the Duncans will learn the truth?"

He narrowed his eyes. "What truth?"

"That I'm nothing except your captive," she spat out the words as if they had a bad taste.

Catching up her skirt, she whirled away from him and stomped off to where the two little girls sat playing with Sweet Pea.

Regan bit her lip to hold back the tears that burned in her eyes. How could he discard her so heartlessly?

Last night he'd made such tender love to her. Only yesterday they had fought together against the attackers. She stopped in midstep. Did the two events have anything to do with each other, and with this sudden, unexplained decision of his to return her to the fort?

Had he suffered the same terror when she'd been in danger as she'd felt for him?

Of course he had.

Now that she understood his decision, she could do something about it. Whirling around, she stomped back to stand in front of him.

"I'm not letting you do this."

"You have no choice."

"I'm not letting you sacrifice our love because of fear." She raised her chin, daring him to deny her summation.

"You are talking in circles." He began to turn away from her, dismissing both her and her words.

Regan was having none of it.

"Dammit, Brand."

He looked back at her, his brows raised in question. "It is what you've asked for. Demanded."

He started to turn away again, but she couldn't let him.

"I don't want to go back to the fort anymore." Regan took a deep breath and blurted out, "I want to stay with you."

It had taken every bit of her pride to say the words aloud to him. She'd never admitted wanting or needing anyone before, not out loud.

She waited for his response.

"It's not your choice."

"Brand, I said I don't *want* to go back." She spoke slowly and clearly.

He turned to look at her, his eyes shuttered and emotionless. At the look on his face, her breath died on its way to her throat. She tried to swallow, but her mouth turned dry, and she felt as if she'd been hit in the stomach hard.

"No," he stated flatly, and looked away from her, focusing on the wagon.

She gasped, the sound loud in the harsh silence between them.

Branded Wolf clenched one hand into a fist at the sign of her pain. The last thing he wanted to do was reject her love, not when he wanted it more than drawing breath. He'd longed to hear those words from her sweet lips, but not then.

Now those words of love could get her killed.

He had to send her back to the safety of the fort and her parents' protection, while he went after the man who would heartlessly kill her. And he couldn't let her suspect what he was doing.

Once he'd tracked and killed Larkin, he would return to the fort to claim Regan.

If she'd still have him.

"Brand?" her voice wavered.

The sound of it tore at him, nearly ripping his resolve to shreds. He purposely kept his face averted from her. If he looked into her eyes, he might give in to the plea in her voice and change his mind. He could not do that.

"I've told you. It is Branded Wolf."

The words were harshly spoken, and he knew they would hurt. He'd had to force them out past his lips.

"But what about us?" she whispered.

Us.

He swallowed deeply at the vision that one word brought to his mind. If he could change things . . .

He had to send her away from him, no matter how much

he wanted to take her into his arms and hold her and never let her go. He knew his next words would send her away, and she would probably hate him for what he was going to say.

"I've finished with you," he lied.

Her gasp cut through him like a war lance, cutting straight to his own heart. She reached out to him with a hand that trembled. "I love you."

He sucked in a harsh, ragged breath through clenched teeth. "I could never love a white-eyes."

He turned and strode away from her, the sound of her cry of pain slicing through him and shattering his soul. He knew he'd killed her love. And there was nothing he could do to change it now.

Regan sat on the hard seat of the wagon, holding Sweet Pea on her lap and focusing all her attention on the distant horizon. The wheels rolled and bumped, but she scarcely noticed. Neither did she pay any heed to Annie's nervous chatter or Sweet Pea's tiny licks of comfort on her hand.

She felt as if she were breaking apart inside, shattering into tiny pieces. How could love hurt this much? She'd never suffered such pain in her entire life.

Not even her father's rejection hurt as badly as Branded Wolf's last words. Nothing could.

She swallowed, her throat dry and painful with the effect of holding back the tears. However, she'd held them at bay for so many miles that they were now locked away, along with her heart.

Why had no one ever warned her loving someone could hurt this much? If she'd been warned, perhaps she would have guarded her heart more cautiously. But deep down she knew love wasn't something you could control with a thought or a wish.

She had no one to blame but herself, she knew that. She'd willingly given her love and her heart to Branded Wolf; she'd just never expected to have that love thrown back into her face with disgust.

His harsh words returned to haunt her. "I could never love a white-eyes."

She tried to close off the pain, but to no avail. It tore her apart, destroying her girlish illusions.

Branded Wolf was an Apache—a man with honor. He'd given her a choice. He'd warned her with his words about his fiancée. His Apache fiancée. The woman he'd once loved and obviously still loved.

Why hadn't she listened?

It took all her resolve and self-control to try and salvage some small measure of her pride. She would not seek him out. She would not allow herself the luxury of watching him ride on Wind Dancer. To do so would cause her even more pain. And she had more than she thought she could possibly bear. The hurting couldn't get any worse.

She was wrong.

When the fort came into view on the far horizon, her breath caught in her throat. There it was—what she'd asked, ordered, and cajoled him to give her. She wanted to put out both hands and shove the image away.

Branded Wolf rode up alongside the wagon, and Regan couldn't resist the command of her heart to turn and look at him.

He sat straight and tall on his mount's back, pride emanating from his strength. Her chest tightened until she thought she couldn't breathe for being squeezed to death. She couldn't tear her gaze away from him.

Branded Wolf turned, and their eyes locked and held. Hers silently asked, "Change your mind. Please love me? Please want me?"

His eyes changed to the icy blue of a mountain spring in winter. He broke the contact and pointed toward the fort.

"You'll be safe to continue alone from here."

"You're not coming with us?" Robert asked.

"No."

Turning Wind Dancer around, he rode away from them without a backward glance.

Regan stared at the fort, pain chilling every part of her. Swallowing, she raised her chin and kept her gaze faced forward on the future.

It looked as bleak and barren as the Arizona desert to her.

"Regan?" Annie hesitated. "Are you going to be all right?"

Regan smoothed her hand along Sweet Pea's back. The pup whined. Obviously, she hadn't wanted Branded Wolf to leave either.

Annie rested her hand on Regan's wrist. When Regan looked over at her, she read the genuine concern in the other woman's face.

"I'll be fine, Annie. Thank you for your concern." She tried to force a reassuring smile for the other woman's benefit. She wouldn't take her problems out on her new friend.

"If you'd like to come with us, you'd be welcome."

Regan felt a rush of warmth at the words and swallowed down the sudden lump in her throat. "Thank you, no, Annie. But you don't know how much your offer means to me."

"Do you have someplace to go to?" Annie squeezed Regan's hand.

"Oh, yes." She gave a wry smile. "My father will provide quarters for me."

"Your father?"

"Papa is the post commander at the fort."

"Oh." Surprise registered in Annie's voice.

Oh, indeed, Regan thought to herself, wondering at what kind of a reception she would receive at the fort.

Colonel McBain strode away from the stables in irritation. He'd been preparing to ride out, when the wagon of settlers pulled into the fort.

More trouble. Precisely what he didn't need just then. He had more than enough problems on his hands.

He was worried about Elise as it was, with her fretting so much over Regan. His wife was going to make herself ill. He'd almost never convinced her to take the dose of laudanum the doctor recommended. It had taken an argument to accomplish it, but at long last, she was sleeping reasonably peaceful.

Sighing, he walked forward to meet the wagon and get this problem settled as quickly as possible, before Elise awoke. Drawing nearer, he observed the wagon's burn holes and battered condition. It sure looked like Indian trouble.

He stiffened his posture to attention and strode toward the wagon where it had drawn to a stop. Before he reached a man and two women climbed down.

The two women looked weary. The blonde appeared as if she might swoon, leaning against the side of the wagon. However, the woman standing quietly beside her looked to be made of sturdier stock. She set something in the wagon and turned back to face him. She held her head up with pride and self-confidence.

Something about her drew his attention. Her skin was browned by the sun, and she . . .

The woman looked strangely familiar. He resisted the impulse to shake his head.

Realizing his rudeness, he looked away and approached the man. "Welcome, I'm Colonel McBain. It looks like you ran into some trouble." He gestured to the wagon's condition.

"You're right about that." Robert Duncan stepped up and introduced himself and his wife, then reached out and shook hands. "My wife and I were attacked—"

Two little girls clambered out of the back of the wagon and ran around the side with a dirty puppy at their heels. They skidded to a stop at the sight of Colonel McBain, then huddled close to Annie Duncan's skirts.

"Let's discuss this away from the ladies," Colonel McBain cut in. The last thing he needed was a show of hysterics from the women.

"But, your—"

"I suggest our discussion of the Indian attack is hardly fitting conversation for the ladies or children." Colonel McBain nodded toward the two women. "Ladies, I'll have one of my men show you to the doctor's quarters if you'd like."

The dark-haired woman stepped forward. "Aren't you going to ask how I am, Papa?"

He stared dumbfounded at her. It couldn't be. Gone were the fancy airs and fashionable hairstyle. The slightly defiant look on her face had been replaced by a look of confidence.

"Regan?" His voice was barely above a whisper.

She nodded.

"Regan?" he repeated.

She held herself back, resisting the impulse to run to him and throw herself into his arms. He would not welcome her open show of emotion.

"Yes, Papa, it's me," she answered calmly, her chin raised slightly.

He stepped forward and pulled her into his embrace, leaving Regan speechless. Her father had never in all her life done such a thing.

"Thank God you're alive," he said in a low, uneven voice.

As if realizing his lapse, he drew back and set her from him. Straightening, he yanked down his jacket, smoothing it out.

He cleared his throat and turned to Robert Duncan. "Thank you. I owe you a great debt for saving my daughter—"

Robert smiled, looking embarrassed by the remark. "We didn't save her, Colonel McBain. You might say she saved us."

He stared hard a moment at the man's startling comment, not saying a word.

"Your daughter did you proud, Colonel."

Annie Duncan stepped away from the wagon and added, "She helped save our lives."

"What are you talking about?" Colonel McBain looked from the settlers to Regan and back to Robert Duncan.

"She helped fight off our attackers," Annie said, remembered fear edging her words.

"My Regan?"

The colonel turned to stare at Regan for a long while. He took in the changes. Her skin was browned by the sun, and freckles covered her nose. It made her look more approachable somehow. She faced him with self-assurance and an innate calm that made him decidedly uneasy.

While she still held her head high, now it seemed to be with pride and confidence, not insolence. And she met his scrutiny by looking him straight in the eye like a good soldier.

What had happened to her out there?

He'd feared if his spoiled, pampered daughter ever was returned to the fort, she would be a mere shadow of herself, broken. Instead, she'd come back stronger.

"If that's your Regan, then yes," Robert said with finality.

Embarrassed, Regan looked away from her father's study. "I didn't do anything that anyone else wouldn't have done in that spot."

"You shot one of those men," Annie pointed out with pride.

"Regan shot an Indian?" Her father stared at her as if she were a stranger.

"Our attackers weren't Indians," Robert informed him. "They were white men."

The older child peeked out from beside her mother. "Miss Regan and Mr. Wolf fought off the bad men."

"Mr. Wolf?" Colonel McBain asked.

"Actually his name was Branded Wolf," Robert explained.

Regan's stomach tightened at the mention of his name. *Branded Wolf.*

She couldn't face talking about him, couldn't face remembering their time together yet. She needed time to get her turbulent emotions under some semblance of control.

She turned her head and shut out the conversation between her father and Robert. There would be time enough later to answer questions and give explanations.

The adobe buildings looked exactly the same as the day she had left. The fort looked unchanged, and she wondered how so much could have happened and yet everything around her stay the same.

She drew in a deep breath and turned her attention back to her father. He was raising his hand in signal to a group of men near the stables. The men rode up in a column. A sergeant handed the reins of a saddle horse to her father.

Her father turned to the horse, then with his hand on the saddle he paused to ask, "You're certain the men were white, not Apaches?"

"Absolutely," Regan put in.

Her father swung into the saddle and faced Robert, shutting her out.

"Mr. Duncan, if you'd be willing to ride with me, I'd like you to show us where you were attacked."

At the other man's hesitation, he added, "This is important. We were preparing to ride out after a band of Apache sighted in the area. They've been blamed for this series of attacks."

"Of course I'll go." Robert leaned over and kissed Annie on her cheek. "Take care, I'll be back soon."

The sergeant handed him the reins of a horse.

"It may be a day or two," her father informed him.

"I'd like to get back to my family as soon as I possibly can." Robert glanced to his wife and daughters. "They've been through a lot."

"You can fill me in about it on our ride."

Regan couldn't believe her father was riding out just like that. He hadn't even told her good-bye. They had to talk. She couldn't let him leave without telling him a few things. She rushed up and caught his arm.

"Papa, I have to talk to you about Captain Larkin."

"Later. When I return, we'll talk." He leaned down and gently patted her shoulder.

She was taken aback by his gesture of tenderness. And touched by it. He'd never openly shown any kind of concern for her before.

"Now, run along, daughter. I'm sure you want a nice bath and fresh clothes." He straightened, dismissing her and anything she had to say to him.

Regan sighed. Now, there was the father she knew and loved. His brief show of tenderness was over and forgotten. He was more concerned with her appearance than with what she had to say.

But she had to make him wait and listen.

''Father, I need to talk to you about Captain Larkin.''
She planted her hands on her hips.

''Yes, I'm sure you have a lot to tell me, but he's out
with a search patrol.'' He motioned to his men. ''When
he returns—''

''No, I need to tell—'' she interrupted him.

''Of course you want to see him. But it will have to wait.''
He kicked his heels into his horse's side and started out.

The column of men followed after him, blocking Regan's
path to her father.

''I do *not* want to see him.'' Regan ran after him, but
Annie pulled her aside as the men rode past in a cloud of
dust.

''If he returns before I do, he is in charge,'' her father
shouted back over his shoulder, then sent his horse into a
gallop leading the riders.

Regan's mouth dropped open in shock.

Captain David Larkin in charge of the fort?

Over her dead body.

Chapter Eighteen

Regan leaned her head against the back of the tub. The hot bath in scented water was heavenly.

She hadn't realized how much she missed such a luxury. A smile pulled at her lips at the thought that she now considered a scented bath a luxury. Before, she'd deemed it a necessity.

From the vicinity of the floor came a pitiful whine followed by the sound of paws scraping the side of the tub. Regan leaned up and looked over the side.

Sweet Pea sat back on her haunches and rose, her tiny light brown paws batting the air in supplication. Regan laughed at the pitiful picture.

"Poor Sweetie. Would you like a bath too?"

The dog stood and shook herself. A fine layer of dust flew around her, then settled to the floor.

"Yuck. As soon as I dry off, it's all yours," Regan promised her pet.

Reaching for a towel, she wrapped it around her body

and stepped from the fragrant water. She picked up a second towel and dried her hair.

Sweet Pea barked one sharp yip in obvious protest. She sat back and pawed the air again.

"All right. All right."

Regan laughed and scooped her up, careful to keep the pup at arm's length.

"I hope you don't mind smelling like my soap, but anything would be an improvement over the way you smell now." She wrinkled her nose.

Sweet Pea let out another sharp bark. She wagged her ragged-looking plumed tail back and forth several times as if in agreement.

"No insult intended," Regan said. "But, Sweetie, you stink."

She eased her pet into the water, squeezing her eyes shut for the flurry of water that was sure to follow. Surprisingly, nothing happened. She peeked at the tub, then laughed.

Sweet Pea was happily paddling in the water, head up, paws working hard.

"I guess I forgot your daily swims in that mountain pool."

At the memory, a sudden rush of pain swept over her. Branded Wolf had made love to her beside that pool. The remembrance of their lovemaking squeezed her heart until she was sure it would break.

She fought back the tears. She would *not* cry over him. One lone tear slipped free to roll down her cheek anyway.

"Why, Brand? Why?" she whispered.

But no one answered.

The next morning Regan awoke early to the sound of a commotion that would give a horse a headache. She pulled her pillow over her head.

Voices, horses, clanging noises continued, even through

the fluffy pillow. She grabbed up her pillow and stuffed it back under her head.

She missed waking up in Branded Wolf's arms. The admission brought a pang of sorrow. She missed having his broad, comforting chest as her pillow.

The sounds outside blurred together so that she could scarcely separate them out. All the usual sounds of civilization. She turned and buried her head in the pillow again. She hated the din.

She longed for the quiet. It had been so quiet and peaceful in the mountain hideaway with Branded Wolf. She missed it.

Even more, she missed Branded Wolf. But she refused to allow herself to think about him. Later, when it hurt less, she would give in to the thoughts and memories. But not yet.

She sat up in bed, focusing her attention on the softness of the mattress. Compared to the hard ground of the night before, this was heaven itself, she thought.

The noises outside grew louder. In spite of the mix of sounds, she discerned a woman's voice raised in argument outside.

"Mama?" Regan asked in disbelief.

Sweet Pea leapt off the bed in one bound. She ran to the door, barking and wagging her tail until she wiggled from nose to toes to tail.

A second later the door swung open, and Elise McBain stood in the doorway.

"Regan," she called out.

"Mama!" Regan jumped out of bed and ran to throw her arms around the woman. Sweet Pea jumped up and down against her skirts, barking in high-pitched tones of joy.

Her mother hugged her close, then pulled back. "Where have you been? I was so worried about you." She smoothed Regan's sleep-tousled hair back from her cheek. "Are you

all right? Sweet Pea, get down.'' The words tumbled out in
a flurry as she hugged Regan again, then the dog.

Regan wasn't given a chance to answer. She didn't know
if she had spoken if she'd be heard over Sweet Pea's barking.
Elise led the way back to the bed and gently pushed her
down onto the mattress.

''Regan, you shouldn't be out of bed,'' she scolded lovingly.

''Why not?''

''After your ordeal. You need to rest, but I had to see
you for myself. I can't believe you're safe. And alive.'' She
paused and sniffed delicately.

Sweet Pea jumped onto the bed, unwilling to be left out,
and nuzzled Elise's hand for pets. She obliged her, then
picked up the pup and hugged her close.

Regan smiled. It felt good to be fussed over. And her
mother did such a good job of it. She was certain Sweet
Pea appreciated it too, if the constant wagging of her tail
was anything to judge by.

''But let me look at you, Regan.'' Elise set the pup on
the bed and pulled back. ''Why, I—''

''Mama,'' Regan cut in. ''When did you get here?''

Her mother rolled her eyes and waved her hand in the
air. ''Forever ago.''

Regan smiled at the exaggeration. ''Where were you last
night?''

Elise glanced away. ''I . . . ah . . . spent the night in
Carson's quarters. He was out.''

''Mama?''

Elise cocked her head and stared at her. ''Oh, my, your
skin. What have you done to your beautiful skin? It's
browned.'' Her voice was tinged with horror.

Regan laughed out loud. If slightly darker skin was the
worst she'd suffered, she'd have been quite happy. It hurt
a lot less than her shattered heart.

"Oh, dear, no," Elise gasped; "And you have freckles."

Regan raised a hand to her face. She hadn't looked in a mirror since she didn't know when. Last night she'd simply been too tired and heartbroken to care about what she looked like.

Elise rushed to retrieve a silver-backed mirror from a trunk. "Why, just look at them!"

"Where?" Regan smiled at her concern.

"All over your nose."

Regan barely held back her laugh. Her mother made it sound like a plague. She obediently glanced in the mirror at the offending freckles, then wrinkled her nose and dismissed them.

"They'll likely enough fade," she informed Elise, then handed the mirror back to her and got her first good long look at her.

She noticed that her mother didn't look as perfectly coiffed as usual. She blinked at the realization that her usually perfectly presented mother had a button unfastened on the bodice of her day dress and two curls hanging free at her nape.

"Mama, are you feeling well?"

Elise waved a hand as if batting at a ball. "Just a little wooly. Carson made me take some of the doctor's laudanum yesterday, and I slept right through your arrival here."

"Carson?" Regan repeated. "Laudanum?"

What had happened to her mama?

"Mama." She stared at her mother in surprise.

"Oh, don't look at me that way. It was all Carson's idea." She sat on the side of the bed again.

"You've stopped calling him 'the colonel,'" Regan noted. That was all she'd heard her father called for almost ten years.

Her mother actually blushed. She plucked at the lace trim

on her bodice, then tucked a curl into place. "Ah, well. Yes, I have."

Regan didn't think she'd ever seen her mama embarrassed. Something was going on here, and it looked to be between her mother and father. It took her a full minute to take in the possibility.

"Oh."

"Now, dear, it's not what you're thinking." A smile graced Elise's face, and her cheeks pinkened again. "At least not yet." A girlish giggle slipped out.

Regan knew her mouth dropped open. This was the last thing she'd expected to find upon her return to the fort. Her parents? Together? Not arguing fiercely?

"Mama?" Regan began.

"Not now, dear. I want to hear what happened to you."

Regan sighed. She'd known this discussion would be forthcoming, but she'd tried to postpone it as long as possible. She wasn't ready to talk about Branded Wolf yet, much less to discuss feelings for him. It still hurt too much.

"I met your friend Mrs. Duncan," her mother prodded. "We had a nice chat this morning." She fell silent, obviously waiting for her daughter to fill in the missing pieces.

Regan swallowed and folded her hands in her lap. What was she supposed to say to her mother? How could she tell her she'd fallen in love and been rejected by the only man she'd ever love?

"Did you really shoot a man?" Her mama's voice was filled with shock.

Regan nodded and gave her a wan smile. "Yes, I did."

"Oh, dear." Elise fanned herself with her hand, shock and censure on her pretty face.

"But I lived to tell about it," Regan reminded her, her own voice sharpening. "And so did Branded Wolf."

Somehow keeping Branded Wolf from being shot had

mattered a lot more than what her society-minded mama would think about her unladylike behavior.

Elise pounced on her slip-up. "And just who is this Branded Wolf?"

Regan longed to tell her he was the man she was in love with, but she held her tongue.

"The Apache who saved my life."

Her mother studied her closely in silence for a minute, until Regan blushed under her scrutiny.

"Oh, my stars," her mama gasped. "You're in love with him, aren't you?"

Once the words were spoken out loud, she couldn't deny them. "Yes." She raised her chin with her admission.

Elise frowned at her. "If you're in love with him, then what are you doing engaged to someone else? And without telling me."

"I'm—"

"I've met your intended," she announced, her voice on edge. "And I don't care much for him."

"My what?"

Elise leaned closer and took both her hands in hers. "Tell me it isn't true," she wailed dramatically.

Those same dramatics would have sent Regan into a flurry to please her mama at one time. Now they only made her smile with indulgence. Her mother should have been in the theater.

"You'll have to tell me the facts before I can deny them, Mama."

Looking down her nose in dismay, Elise said, "Why, that Captain Larkin, of course."

Regan stiffened and her eyes snapped in anger. "I most certainly am not engaged to him. He tried to kill me."

"What?" her mother shouted.

Regan proceeded to fill in the details for her mother about

her time away from the fort, leaving out selected pieces about herself and Branded Wolf.

"I never did like that young captain. And I told Carson so too," Elise announced when Regan had finished.

"I tried to tell him too, but he wouldn't listen to me," Regan added.

Elise stood to her feet, a light of determination in her eyes. "You need to get some rest, dear." She plumped the pillow and pulled up the coverlet.

Regan was tired of resting already. And she was already beginning to tire of being fussed over so much. If she didn't watch it, her mother would pamper her to death.

"Don't you worry, dear. We will simply have to make Carson listen to reason." Her mama leaned down and kissed her cheek.

"That may take some doing," Regan warned her, holding back a yawn.

"I can take care of Carson." Her mother waved aside her warning. Leaning forward, she studied her a moment.

"What?" Regan asked in trepidation. She'd seen that look on her mama's face before.

"We will have to do something about those freckles before we return to Philadelphia,"

Return to Philadelphia.

The words jarred Regan's thin shell of calm. She wasn't certain she wanted to return to that life now. But she had no future here. Not now.

Her heart had been captured by this vast land and the man she had fallen in love with.

Two days later, Regan was exhausted. She'd never realized before how tiring her mother was to be around. Both herself and poor Sweet Pea had been nearly pampered to death.

Regan felt as if she'd had every part of her body treated, creamed, or mended. Her mama had fussed over her until she thought she was being smothered. How had she ever survived this in Philadelphia?

She wasn't so sure she wanted to return there in spite of her mama's constant planning.

A commotion outside took her to the window, where she saw a column of soldiers riding in. Her father was back at last.

Grabbing up her skirt, she dashed across the room and slipped out the door, carefully locking Sweet Pea inside. Her pet set up an immediate din of barking in protest.

Regan ignored her sharp yipping and smoothed down the skirt of her green muslin gown. She resisted the urge to run across the parade ground to her father, but decided it would be wiser to give him a few minutes to get to his quarters.

She tapped her foot impatiently, looking out across the vast area outside the fort. After several minutes her foot stilled and a lump rose in her throat at the beauty stretched out before her. Memories threatened to swamp her, dragging her down into a pit of despair. Her throat tightened and she forced herself to swallow down the urge to cry.

She didn't have time for tears. She had to explain the facts to her father. Squaring her shoulders, she set off at a ladylike walk to his office, certain that was where he'd go first.

No one stopped her on her approach to the commander's office. She didn't pause to question if her determined steps or new air of confidence discouraged them.

She stepped into her father's office and paused to straighten her shoulders. She wanted to look her most confident when she faced him.

He had his back to her and stiffened at the sound of her footsteps. She'd never had the opportunity to ask Brand to teach her how to walk the way he did without making a giveaway sound. She pushed aside the memory.

"Papa, you're back."

He turned at her voice. "Regan, dear. How are you feeling?"

"I'm fine." She walked toward him farther into the room. "We need to talk."

He raised his chin. "It's not a good time. I've just returned—"

"I know—"

"And there are several things I need to take care of," he continued. "Now, run along. We'll talk later, when I have more time."

Regan gritted her teeth at his patronizing attitude. She wasn't a little girl to be sent out to play.

"Papa, I—"

"Oh, my dear, we ran into the captain's patrol. He's back now. I'm sure he's eager to see you."

"Well, I'm not eager to see him." She fired his words back at him.

"Daughter, that's certainly no way to talk about your fiancé."

"Fiancé? I don't ever want to see him again."

"Of course you do. He's a fine young man. You're just upset."

"Upset?" she repeated his summation. Damn right she was upset.

Her father didn't seem to notice her growing anger. He continued. "Once you've recovered from your ordeal, we can go forward with the wedding."

"There isn't going to be any wedding." She spoke firmly, raising her voice slightly to be heard over his commanding tone. "Not to—"

He patted her arm. "The captain was worried over you,

and quite embarrassed about losing the fight to those Indians.''

''What Indians?''

''Why, the ones who attacked you two on your morning ride—''

''Papa, *he* attacked me.''

''Now, calm down. Think about what you're saying.'' He rocked back on his heels.

''Calm down?'' Her voice rose a level ''I'm telling you, he attacked me. He—''

He held up his hand. ''Now, that's enough.''

Regan sputtered in disbelief. Her father wasn't even going to give her a chance to explain what happened in the desert.

''Now, understand this,'' he said. ''Captain Larkin has served under me for nearly two years. He's been an exemplary soldier and proven himself in battle with the renegade Indians. I've known him well; you I don't know at all, except for what you've shown me here at the fort.''

She narrowed her eyes in determined anger. He wasn't going to get away with brushing her off this way. ''Papa—''

''Captain Larkin is one of my finest officers. In fact, he's like a son to me,'' he said in a firm voice.

''Oh, stars and heavens.'' She threw up her hands. ''Your Captain Larkin is a killer, Father.''

He shook his head at her, looking at her with pity in his eyes. ''I'd expected you to be angry with him. He did fail to protect you.''

''Protect me? He tried to kill me.''

''Now, Regan—''

''You're not listening to a thing I'm saying, are you?'' she asked, her voice tight with emotion.

''Now, dear. I know you're suffering from exhaustion after what you've been through. And I'm sure you're still confused.''

He reached out to pat her shoulder, but Regan stepped back. "I am not confused about this."

He sighed and shook his head. "I'm disappointed, daughter—"

"Disappointed?" She could barely force the word out past her lips. They felt stiff and unmoving.

"Yes, I hadn't expected you to be this vindictive toward the captain."

Regan stared at him a moment in silence. As comprehension dawned, she swallowed down her fury. He wasn't going to listen to her side of it. His mind was made up.

Her father had already accepted his precious captain's lies and fabricated explanations, and nothing she could say was going to sway his opinion. His opinion of her, that was.

She understood at last. Her father had found the son he'd always wanted—in Captain Larkin. And he wasn't going to listen to anything being said against him.

"Father"—she paused, looking him square in the eye—"you are a fool." Her voice was flat, without a hint of anger. But it held disappointment in its depths.

She gave him one long, searching look, then turned away. When he stepped toward her, she walked out the door.

A quarter hour later, Elise McBain slammed out of her husband's office. Muttering under her breath the entire distance, she strode across the parade grounds in a high temper.

Without pausing to knock, she threw open the door to Regan's room and stomped inside.

"The old fool," she said loudly, echoing Regan's earlier comment.

Then she slammed the door with her foot.

Regan jumped at the vehemence in her mama's voice. "What happened?"

"I tried to talk to Carson. Ha! *Listened* is a better word. He talked."

"I tried to talk to him too. But his mind is made up."

"Well, if Carson thinks this is over, he is far from right."

Regan watched in amazement as her mama stomped across the room to her trunk.

"He'll be singing a different tune when I'm finished with him tonight." Elise held up a low-cut evening gown and winked at Regan. "Don't wait up for me tonight, dear. I won't be sleeping here."

Regan stared at her mother in shocked disbelief. Her mama's scheming was getting out of hand. Why, she looked positively set on seduction. Her poor papa didn't stand a chance.

And neither had she against Brand's tender lovemaking, she thought to herself. She let her shoulders slump for a moment, then squared them again. She was tired of keeping up a good front for her mama's benefit.

It was time she faced the truth.

She was miserable without him.

Branded Wolf crouched outside the fort in the shielded darkness of the night and watched. And he waited. Regan was so close, he could feel her. And yet she was so far from him.

He knew which quarters were hers, and even knew she'd gone to bed some time ago.

He told himself he was keeping a watch over her only to ensure her safe return back east, but he knew he was lying to himself, and to her.

He longed to see her with a yearning that was tearing him apart inside.

Would she even want to see him?

Would she listen to the words he so badly wanted to say to her if he came to her?

He closed his eyes and lowered his head. He had to let her go, but he couldn't. He couldn't let her leave with the lies between them. A woman as strong as Regan deserved the truth.

He crouched without moving, and he watched. Finally, a cloud slid across the moon, and he crept forward into the fort.

Regan snapped awake. Her room was wrapped in velvet darkness. She lay perfectly still, listening to figure out what had woken her.

Silence.

She held her breath and heard the faintest of sounds. The hair at the back of her neck tingled. Someone was outside her quarters. She was sure of it.

She swallowed and strained to hear a sound. There it was. A faint scraping at her door. She turned in time to see the door ease open.

Beside her, Sweet Pea raised her head, then thumped her tail on the bed.

Regan nearly sighed out loud with relief.

Mama. She'd obviously failed in her attempt to "cajole" Papa.

Regan feigned sleep, allowing her mama to save her pride by not letting her know she heard her come in so late in the night.

She hadn't believed that her mama's plan of swaying her papa into listening to reason would work. Now here was proof of that. Her mama was sneaking into her quarters after obviously arguing with Papa. Again.

Some things never changed, she thought.

She sighed and snuggled down into her pillow for the night.

The next second a figure lunged for the bed, and a hand

was clamped over her mouth. She snapped open her eyes and opened her mouth to scream, but not a sound passed through the palm over her lips. She raised her hands to fight back, and briefly wondered why Sweet Pea wasn't either attacking the intruder or barking furiously enough to wake the dead.

Her hands came into contact with warm bare skin. A man's chest. She closed her eyes and sighed around the hand over her mouth.

Branded Wolf.

She'd know the feel of his skin anywhere. It seemed she knew it as well as her own. He shifted his hand on her mouth.

She didn't know whether to kiss his palm or bite it.

What was he doing here?

"Regan," he leaned closer, and whispered.

She nodded, staring up at him. Did he truly think she wouldn't know him almost instantly?

As her vision adjusted to the darkness, she could see his eyes barely inches from her own. The pain in her heart melted at the sight of him.

He eased back, sliding his hand from over her mouth. He let it rest along her cheek, waiting to sense her reaction.

Regan lay still, her eyes drinking in the sight of him. He looked wonderful. She wanted to throw her arms around him and hold him close, but she waited.

Sweet Pea yipped once in recognition, licking his arm. He caught up the pup and set her gently on the floor.

He leaned over Regan again, his face inches from hers. Gradually, bit by bit, he lowered his head, giving her time to object. When she didn't push him away, he closed the distance, taking her lips in a breath-stealing kiss that held his heart in it.

Her lips softened beneath his and Regan returned his kiss. She slid her hands around his neck.

He'd come to her.

"Oh, little one," he murmured softly against her mouth. "I had to see you again."

Regan's heart raced at his words, and hope sprang up within her. She cupped his cheek with her hand.

He turned his head, kissing her palm and groaned against her hand. "I had to tell you—"

The door burst open, slamming against the wall.

Two soldiers rushed in, guns drawn.

Branded Wolf pulled away, shielding Regan's body with his own.

Chapter Nineteen

Regan watched in horror as one of the soldiers grabbed Branded Wolf, pulling him away from her and cruelly twisting his arms behind his back. The second soldier kept his gun leveled at Branded Wolf's chest the entire time.

Branded Wolf's gaze was riveted on the last soldier standing beside the door. Regan turned her head to look, and saw that the man had his gun aimed at her, a wide smile on his face. His eyes were locked with Branded Wolf's.

"What do you think you're doing?" she shouted, jumping to her feet.

"Our duty, miss." The soldier holding Branded Wolf's arms twisted behind his back smiled at her. His expression turned to a leer as his eyes raked her standing in her night-gown.

Regan resisted the urge to grab up the coverlet to shield herself. She knew that the only thing protecting her from these men was her status as the commander's daughter.

Sweet Pea snapped at the soldiers' heels, growling fiercely.

Raising her chin in defiance, Regan decided to attempt to use her position to her advantage. She'd *make* them listen to her.

"Let him go," she ordered in clear, firm tones.

The soldier with the gun on Branded Wolf shook his head. "We can't do that, miss. We're following our orders. This here is one of those escaped renegade Apaches—"

"He is not. He's a bounty hunter and—"

"He's the savage who held Miss McBain captive." A familiar voice spoke up from the doorway.

Regan turned her head to meet the cold-eyed look of hatred from Captain David Larkin.

He entered the room, lit a lantern, and kicked the door shut with his foot. She stared at him in openmouthed amazement.

Larkin faced her and continued. "And this savage broke in here to attack her tonight. Probably to kill her."

"He did not," she denied. "And if you don't let him go this instant, I'll scream bloody murder." Her firmly spoken words told anyone that she wouldn't hesitate to carry out her threat.

Larkin shrugged. "Do that, and he's a dead man. Sanders, shoot him if she makes any sound above a whisper. Or if he even moves wrong."

Regan shut her mouth and glared at Larkin. He wasn't getting away with this.

"You see, all we have to do is tell the colonel we shot the savage to protect you. And he'll thank us for it."

"No, he won't, because I'll tell him—"

"Like hell. You'll be telling your dear father nothing." Larkin reached out and grabbed her chin with his hand. "Do you understand me?"

He squeezed his fingers, exerting enough pressure to cause pain, but Regan bit her lip to keep from crying out. She knew he was trying to provoke Branded Wolf. She refused to cooperate in any way with his plan.

Releasing her, he walked over to face Branded Wolf. She could feel the hatred emanating between the two men. Suddenly, Larkin raised his hand and brought his gun butt down on the back of Branded Wolf's head.

As Branded Wolf fell to the floor between the men, Regan screamed and rushed toward him.

Larkin whirled about, caught her chin in his hand, and squeezed. "One more sound and I kill him. And if you so much as touch him, he's dead."

Remaining silent, she looked the captain square in the eyes and spat in his face.

Larkin jerked back, releasing her, and wiped his face with the back of his hand. Sweet Pea lunged for his leg and Regan heard the tearing of material an instant before Larkin let out a bellow.

She snatched up her pet before anyone could do her harm. Perhaps Sweet Pea could aid her later, but not just then.

She needed all her wits about her to deal with this situation. It seemed Captain Larkin had planned for this, then lay in wait to spring his trap. And she'd fallen right into his hands. There had to be a way out of this mess. She wouldn't let them take Brand.

"You've forgotten one thing, Captain."

"What's that?" He glared at her as he rubbed his leg.

"Mr. and Mrs. Duncan," she said with a hint of triumph in her voice. "They will tell my father who Branded Wolf is."

His glare turned into a droll smile. "Wrong again, dear Regan."

Her stomach tightened into a knot. The Duncans were her last chance. They could verify everything with her father. They could identify Branded Wolf.

"No, my dear, I'm afraid they can't. You see, they're

leaving in the morning. Too early for you to speak with them.''

She refused to surrender this easily. She tilted her head in a gesture of false confidence. ''My father will listen when I—''

''Your father will be leading the escort for the Duncans at first light.''

''I—''

''No, I'm afraid you won't be doing anything else this night. Or in the morning. You need your rest, dear Regan.''

She gritted her teeth at his use of her name in that tone.

''As your fiancé—''

''Never.''

''As your fiancé,'' he repeated, ''I've given orders that after what you've suffered tonight, you are to kept protected—''

''Guarded, you mean,'' she snapped.

''You have your words you use, and I have mine. But the result is the same. You will be talking to no one in the morning.''

He whirled around and strode out the door. The soldiers dragged Branded Wolf between them.

Regan rushed up to the men. ''Where are you taking him?''

''To the guardhouse, where he'll be kept until he's sent off to the reservation to die.''

Regan bit her lip to keep quiet. She wouldn't act rashly and endanger Branded Wolf's life.

If they were taking him to the guardhouse, she had time to plan something, to do something. She'd find a way to get to her father and make him listen to her.

''Oh, dear Regan.'' Captain Larkin turned to rake her with his gaze. ''You will remain quiet about all this.'' He smiled and turned away.

Like hell, she thought.

She wasn't about to remain quiet or to let Branded Wolf be sent away to a reservation where he didn't belong. He hadn't finished saying what he had to tell her. And she wanted to hear it.

With every moment passing in slow agony, Regan forced herself to wait several minutes before tiptoeing to the door. She reached out and turned the doorknob.

Locked!

She yanked in anger, and the lock rattled loudly, mocking her predicament.

"Miss, why don't you settle yourself down and rest like the captain said," a man called through to her.

Rest was the furthest thing from her mind. She wanted to scream the fort down, but she remembered Larkin's threats and stayed quiet. He could have Branded Wolf killed long before someone could reach her and hear what she had to tell them.

If Captain Larkin thought for one minute he'd keep her locked away and that she would sit by meekly and obediently and do nothing about it, he most assuredly had another thought coming.

Holding Sweet Pea close, Regan paced the room, trying to come up with a workable plan. After several minutes, she plopped down on the bed.

She would not lose this fight.

Branded Wolf's life was at stake.

Sometime before dawn Regan unwillingly gave in to the exhaustion and fell asleep. The noises of morning awoke her.

She jumped out of bed, deriding herself for falling asleep when Branded Wolf needed her to do something.

But what could that be? she wondered.

She crossed to the door and checked it, just in case. It

remained locked, and she could hear two men muttering outside her door.

Frustrated, she paced the room again. Sweet Pea trotted at her heels, following her steps. Regan thought she had just about worn a path across the room and came up with nothing workable by the time she heard a shout outside her door.

"What is the meaning of this?" her father's voice boomed through the locked door.

Regan wanted to clap her hands in glee. Her father hadn't ridden out of the fort after all. Now was her chance to make him listen to her. She heard a jumble of voices on the other side of the wood.

She was halfway to the door, when a key rattled in the lock and the door swung open. What she saw caused her to stop in midstep.

Her father stood tall and stiff in the doorway with her mother in his arms. She blinked in disbelief. Her father was carrying her mother, and she had her arms wrapped about his neck.

"Regan, get us a chair," he bellowed the order. "She's hurt."

She obeyed without thinking and watched her father carefully lower Elise into the chair. What had happened to her mama?

"Ouch," Elise whimpered.

"What happened?" Regan knelt before her mama, taking in the bright spots of color in her cheeks.

"Oh, there's no need for such a fuss, Carson." Her mama patted his arm.

"Elise twisted her ankle," he informed Regan. "She can't walk a step. You see to her, and I'll go get the doctor."

"No, Carson." Elise caught his arm and held it close. "I told you I'll be fine after a rest. You go see to the fort, and come back and check on me in a little bit." She lowered her eyes and then looked up at him with a half-smile. "Please?"

Regan's mouth nearly dropped open in shock. Her mama was flirting. With her father.

She watched the proceedings in amazement. Were these two people *her* parents? What had happened between them during her absence?

She shook off her amazement and turned to her father. She reached out a hand to him. "Papa—"

"Daughter, what's this I hear about a renegade being captured last night?" he interrupted. "Why wasn't I told about this immediately?"

Her head snapped up in determination. "Because I was under guard. And my door locked."

"For your own protection," he assured her.

"Like hell."

"Regan, watch your language." He snapped the order out. "Your mother is present."

"Now, Carson—"

"Elise, let me deal with her—"

"Will both of you listen to me," Regan interrupted, her voice raised.

"There is nothing to discuss," her father said, rocking back on his heels. "Thankfully, the soldiers got here in time and you were unharmed. And the renegade is safely locked away in the guardhouse, where he will stay until arrangements are made to send him back to San Carlos."

"Except he isn't a renegade, Papa. He's half Apache, and he's a bounty hunter."

"Regan, you don't seem to understand. This man is a dangerous renegade who escaped from—"

"No, he isn't." Regan planted her hands on her hips and faced her father squarely. "His name is Branded Wolf and he saved my life. If you won't believe me, then ask the Duncans. They can tell you about Brand."

"I'm afraid they've already left. I sent Lieutenant Wilson

to escort them past the Sulphur Springs, since your mother had been injured."

"Then either go yourself or send someone to ask the Duncans about him. You're wrong, Papa. Release him." She struggled to keep the pleading tone from her voice. She had to convince him.

He shook his head in answer.

Regan drew up to her full height and met him stare for stare. "You're wrong. At least ask the Duncans."

"I'll look into it," he said grudgingly.

"But you won't release him."

"No."

Regan resisted the urge to stomp her foot. She sensed any display of temper would make her father stand firmer in his decision. It would also give less credibility to her words.

"Papa, if you don't question the Duncans on this, I will send a wire to Washington myself requesting a full investigation."

He stepped back, clearly taken aback by her threat.

She stiffened her spine and faced him without giving quarter. She would not back down.

"Elise, look what you're done to her," he accused, shaking his head. "And living back there in Philadelphia, too."

"Me?" Her mother jumped to her feet and strode toward him, obviously forgetting all about her injury. "You're the one who brought her out here to this wilderness with your lies and deceit."

He stared at her foot. "It seems I'm not the only one deceiving someone. Your ankle seems to have healed remarkably quickly."

She had the grace to glance down at her toes. "Oh, heavens, Carson. I admit I didn't want you riding out again so soon."

"Elise, I'm ashamed of you."

Regan watched as her mama bristled and stood straight,

head held up high. Well, things were certainly back to normal between her parents, with them arguing instead of cooing at each other. She knew the cooing wouldn't last long. It never did.

"You're ashamed of me? As if that's anything new," her mother shouted at him.

"Now, darling—"

"Don't you darling me. That you could say such a thing after last night." She planted her hands on her hips, duplicating Regan's gesture. "But this isn't the first time you've behaved like an miscreant."

"I'm not going to ask what that is." He glared down at her, insulted. "If you'd given me a son who lived instead of the twin girl—"

Elise lifted her hand and slapped him full across face. "You forget, I lost that baby boy too. He was my son as well."

Son. Twin.

Regan stepped back, reeling as the shock hit her full force. She was a twin. And her brother had died.

She covered her mouth with her hand. This explained so much. All her father's comments about a son while she was growing up had been because of this.

Her mama looked her father up and down, then added, "And all you could do from then on was get drunk and carouse with any woman in town who—"

"Enough," her father shouted.

Mama stepped back in obvious shock.

"That happened once, do you hear me? Once. And you never let me explain."

"What was there to explain? You came home drunk and reeking of cheap perfume!"

Regan knew her mouth was open. She stared at her parents as they argued furiously. They'd never reached this stage before in their fights. She didn't think either of them even recalled that she was standing there with them.

"And you condemned me," her father said, his voice heavy with sadness.

"And you destroyed my life," her mama fired back, her eyes blazing with anger.

Papa gave her mother one long look, then spun on his heel and strode from the room, slamming the door behind him. The door rattled on its hinges from the force of his angry action.

"You old fool," her mama whispered.

"Mama?"

Her mother turned slowly, as if just then realizing Regan was in the room.

"Oh, baby." She threw herself into Regan's arms and burst into tears.

It took Regan the better part of an hour to calm her mother and to hear the full story of her father's one act of infidelity that tore her family apart. Following a bitter argument, her father'd had her mama and her removed to separate quarters.

In between tears, her mama had told of the young officer's wife who had taken too strong a liking to her papa. Finally, after coming upon him comforting the woman one evening, Elise had had enough and packed up and taken Regan to Philadelphia with her.

"But, Mama," Regan asked in a low voice, "had he done anything?"

"By then it no longer mattered. Our marriage was over. And I couldn't tolerate the way he treated you any longer. So I took the coward's way out, and I left."

As Elise dissolved into tears again, Regan settled her on the bed and sat beside her. Her mama cried herself out, then, sniffing, fell asleep.

Regan scooped up Sweet Pea and thought about the revelations she'd heard.

It was nearly an hour later when her mama awoke. She remained strangely quiet for several minutes, then began to pace the floor much the same way as Regan had earlier.

"Regan"—Elise faced her with a faint smile—"I've made a decision."

"Mama?"

Her mother straightened her back and smoothed out a wrinkle in her skirt. Then she met Regan's questioning look.

"I want Carson back."

Regan gasped.

"And I intend to get him," her mama announced with finality. "With your assistance, that is."

Regan nodded, then stopped.

"Mama, I'll help in any way I can on one condition." She paused until she had her mother's full attention on her next words.

"What?"

"I need your help to see Brand."

"Are you sure it's safe to see him?"

"Mama, he'd never hurt me," Regan assured her in a decisive voice. "This is all Captain Larkin's lies. The Duncans can prove it. If Papa will check with them."

Her mother patted her hands. "I'll see he does."

"Thank you. Will you help me see Brand in private?"

"Carson will never agree to it."

"I figured that already," Regan admitted in a wry voice. "But I worked out a plan while you slept."

"You love him a lot, don't you?"

"More than life," Regan answered truthfully.

Her mama leaned forward. "All right, then let's hear your plan."

After a few minutes of discussion and arguing over the intricacies, her mama agreed.

The sound of a string of oaths from the guard at the door alerted Branded Wolf to trouble.

He silently stood and stepped to the side of the locked door.

A series of barks, more oaths, and an unfamiliar woman's high-pitched laughter combined to make him unsure of where the danger would come from. His head hurt, and he fought to think clearly. He tensed in cautious anticipation.

The door creaked open, and Branded Wolf steeled himself to remain absolutely still.

Until the right moment to attack.

A figure stepped through the door, then turned to shut it. Seizing the moment, Branded Wolf sprang, grabbing the figure around the throat with his arm and throwing it to the floor. As he brought his hand down to strike, he recognized the figure lying breathless on the ground.

Regan.

He froze, not even breathing for a moment. He stared down into her face in disbelief.

"What a welcome," she whispered, her voice shaky and coming out in short pants of breath.

"Regan."

He bent down on his knees beside her. "What are you doing here?"

"I came to see how you were." The smile she sent him was a bit wobbly. "I wanted to know if you were all right."

He was fine now that he'd seen her, he thought. The sight of her chased the remnants of his headache away.

He helped her to her feet and noticed that his hands were unsteady. He stepped back from her and looked his fill of her. She was incredibly beautiful.

Gone was her ragged blue dress and ripped petticoat. She was dressed in her finery of a cream-colored dress, her hair in perfect curls atop her head, satin slippers on her feet.

Branded Wolf felt his gut clench. This wasn't his Regan from the desert and the mountains. He didn't know her now. This woman was too perfect to touch.

He missed the uninhibited woman she'd been with him. Now she was every inch the fine lady fitting in eastern society. And not for the likes of him.

He had no doubt that this Regan knew what a half-breed was and had no use for one at all.

She had no place in his world, or he in hers.

As he made to turn away from her, she threw herself in his arms, holding tight to him. He stiffened in shock.

Regan responded by sliding her arms around him and laying her head against his chest.

"Hold me, Branded Wolf," she whispered. "Please hold me."

Of their own accord his arms went around her back, pulling her tighter into his embrace. He couldn't have stopped himself from doing it no matter what the cost.

She shivered, and he lowered his head to place a kiss on the top of her curls.

He felt a dampness against his chest and realized she was crying. He'd never once seen her cry before.

"Regan?"

He started to pull away, but she hugged him tighter, burying her head against his chest.

"What's wrong, little one?" he whispered. "Why are you crying?"

She drew in a shuddering breath, and he felt her tighten her self-control.

"Why would you think I'm crying?"

He couldn't help the smile that crossed his face. "Maybe because you got my chest wet."

"Oh."

"Little one?"

"I'm sorry." She sniffed and raised a hand to wipe her cheeks.

Gone was the fine eastern lady. This was his Regan. His little one. No matter how she was dressed, she hadn't changed inside. He was certain of it. Only the outside had changed.

"What is wrong?" he asked, tilting her chin up to look into her eyes.

She stared into his face a moment before she whispered in a broken voice, "You're in here."

He smiled at her words and said, "So are you."

"But I'm free to walk out. They're going to send you to the reservation in New Mexico."

He knew he wouldn't make it far. Not alive. Not if Larkin had anything to do with it.

"Regan, you've got to get out of here. If they find you here with me—"

"Don't worry. Mama and Sweet Pea are keeping the guards distracted." She smiled, and her eyes twinkled with suppressed laughter. "And quite busy. Mama and I planned it all out."

So that explained the unfamiliar female laugh he'd heard, and the barking, and the commotion. He should have known Regan and the pup would be embroiled in any trouble around.

"And they're not going to send you to any reservation," she vowed, her voice quivering.

"Little one, are you fighting for me now?"

"Yes."

She looked up at him, her heart in her eyes. It was his undoing. He pulled her into his arms and his lips swept down, taking hers, branding her. Possessing her.

Regan reveled in his possession.

At last they drew away enough to take a breath. Branded Wolf kept his arms wrapped around her as if he were afraid she would flee him.

"Oh, little one," he murmured, his sigh fanning her cheek and the fine hairs beside her ear.

She shivered in his embrace, clinging to him, and he held her closer. Unable to deny himself the feel of her, he ran his hands down her back and over her slender waist to her hips.

Regan ducked her head, and he felt her lips on his chest. He sucked in his breath between his teeth. She kissed his chest, pausing to brush feathery kisses across the breadth of his chest. His breath rushed out in a ragged sigh of need.

"Regan, how long will your mother distract the soldiers?"

He felt her smile against his moist, heated skin.

"She promised a half hour more at least."

He tipped her chin up to kiss her mouth. "We shouldn't," he groaned against her lips.

Her arms slid around his neck, and she pulled his head down tighter, kissing him back thoroughly. Her tongue slipped between his lips, and any objections or reasoning he might have had deserted him.

He caressed her body through her gown, and Regan felt as if her body were catching fire. His hands fanned the flames until she knew what those pinecones had felt like in the campfire. She arched against him. She was melting in his embrace as his fingers touched, skimmed, loved her.

Regan could feel any distance between them dissolving. Nothing stood between them now. Not words or deeds. Her own touch became bold. She loved this man with all her heart, and she willingly gave her heart to him with her next kiss.

His mouth claimed hers and captured any sound she might

make. She felt his heart pounding against her hand and knew hers raced along with his.

They made love tenderly, passionately, as if it might be the last time.

Chapter Twenty

Branded Wolf stared out the small window and let the memories of his time with Regan wash over him. She'd risked so much coming to see him, and gave him so much of herself.

She lay beyond these walls, out of reach. Oh, that he could keep her safe.

He sighed loudly in the strained enclosure. The closeness of the walls and the stale air nearly choked him. He raised his chin and stared out past the corrals to a distant hill beyond. He breathed in deeply.

"Looking is as close as you're gonna get, Injun."

Branded Wolf whirled around at the sound of the voice on the other side of the door. He tensed, instinctively readying himself for battle.

The door swung open and Captain David Larkin stepped inside, a sneer across his bland features. An armed soldier hurried in to stand beside him, a revolver pointed steadily at his chest.

The time had come. The bluecoats were going to kill him. Regan had been wrong. He tensed, watching the men's eyes, waiting for the giveaway signal for him to fight for his life.

It didn't come.

"Ready to die, are you, Injun?" Larkin taunted. "Well, you're gonna have to wait a little longer. It seems the colonel has sent a rider out after those settlers. Now, we can't have you dying in cold blood, can we?"

Larkin's eyes narrowed and he rubbed a hand across his jaw. "Leastwise not yet."

Larkin turned his head to glance at the bluecoat beside him. The man grinned back.

"Except I don't believe that rider ever made it to the settler's wagon, do you, Jeb?"

Both men shared a harsh laugh. The meaning behind it chilled Branded Wolf's blood. No, he too was certain the rider wouldn't be returning with information that would set him free, as Regan had planned.

Larkin looked back at him and rubbed his jaw again thoughtfully. "No, Injun, I guess you'll live to be taken to that reservation of yours. Mighty nice place, I hear tell."

The bluecoat laughed, then sobered suddenly. He leaned closer to Branded Wolf and stared hard at him.

Branded Wolf remained silent, waiting.

"Come to think of it, I think I'll escort you there personally. Wouldn't want some trooper putting a bullet in you *accidentally.*"

The soldier named Jeb chortled at this, seeming to find great humor in it.

"Don't worry, Injun," Larkin sneered.

The words spoken with hatred hurled Branded Wolf back nearly three years. Those same words had echoed in his mind ever since the day Soaring Dove had been violated and murdered.

He met the other man's eyes and saw the truth within.

As Larkin dropped his hand from his persistent rubbing of his jaw, Branded Wolf saw the scar. It was the one made by his knife that day nearly three years past.

Now he knew he faced the killer of Soaring Dove and his family.

A hot rage swept through his body, heating his blood. His eyes narrowed and he longed for the knife he'd carried in his moccasin. However, his hands would have to do instead. He would take pleasure from killing this white-eyes slowly, painfully.

The other man's lip curled up into a sneer. "You want me, come on, Injun," he dared, throwing down the blatant challenge.

Larkin suddenly reached down and jerked his revolver from his holster. The metal of the barrel glinted in the light from the window.

Branded Wolf held his rage in check, knowing he'd never reach the other man's throat before he fired the gun in his hand. He tightened his teeth together until his jaw ached, welcoming the pain.

Larkin rested his finger over the trigger of the revolver and stroked the gun barrel with the index finger of his other hand. "Like I said, don't worry, Injun. I'll make certain you have a real *pleasant* trip to that reservation of yours." He paused, and then a wide grin pulled his lips. "But before I go, I'll be paying another visit to dear Regan."

Her name was said with a sneer. It turned Branded Wolf's blood cold.

"And I'll make sure Miss McBain forgets all you've done to her."

As Branded Wolf stiffened, the other man laughed harshly.

"Bet you liked that pretty white skin, didn't you?" he taunted. "Well, tonight you can lie here and picture me running my white hands all over that skin of hers. And then

I'll be using more than my hands. You can bet on that, Injun. Is she any good?"

Rage filled Branded Wolf, consuming him, and he took a step forward. The sudden gleam in Larkin's eye stopped him from going any farther.

The man was only seeking an excuse to kill him. Attacking an unarmed officer would be more than enough reason for the bluecoat beside Larkin to shoot him. No one would question the shooting, no one at all.

Except Regan.

He breathed deeply and uncurled his fists. Raising his head higher, he stepped back. As he did so, he read the disappointment in Larkin's flat eyes.

He wasn't going to make it that easy for the bluecoats to kill him.

He knew he'd never make to San Carlos alive, not with Captain Larkin as his escort. But it was a long way there, and anything could happen.

With a curse Larkin holstered his gun. He yanked open the door, then stepped back through the opening.

"Don't worry, Injun," he taunted. "I'll be back. And maybe you'll die today after all."

With this he slammed the door, and Branded Wolf knew the slam echoed with the sound of a death knell.

Branded Wolf stood tall and proud. He would not die alone; he would find some way to take the captain with him in death if it took his last breath to do so.

Captain Larkin straightened his jacket and slicked back his hair. He shook the dirt off the handful of wildflowers he carried in his hand. Anticipation egged him on.

After time with that filthy Injun, Miss High-and-Mighty McBain would welcome a man's visit. She'd probably be feeling the need for one about now. He'd bet that Injun had her real regular like.

His breeches tightened at the thought of lying with her after a savage had bedded her. She'd be real agreeable now. Probably be willing to do anything he wanted her to do. Squaws always did, leastwise that's how he'd always figured it in the past when he'd taken one.

He was halfway across the parade ground when a sergeant hailed him.

"Captain, sir. Colonel McBain wants to see you. Right away," the sergeant informed him.

Larkin swore under his breath, the heat going out of his body.

He tensed, fear eating away at his gut. What had the colonel found out?

Nothing.

He forced himself to relax. He'd covered all his tracks, he assured himself. The old man had nothing on him. No one did, except the Injun, and he was locked away and under guard by one of his own hand-picked men.

Throwing the flowers down, he ground them into the dirt with the heel of his boot. Then he strode to the commander's office.

By the time he reached the door, he'd composed himself and was every bit the fine, young officer the colonel thought him to be.

He knocked on the door, then stood at attention the way that always impressed his commander. He'd learned his part well, and rarely ever let himself slip back into the persona of the worthless illegitimate son of a northern farmer.

He'd never go back to farming. The feel of dirt between his fingers turned his stomach. Looting and then killing had been an easy way to amass the money he'd need to live well. Soon, very soon, he'd have enough.

Then he'd pay off his men with their eagerly awaited

shares. Shortly afterward each man would suffer a fatal accident. A very fatal one from the wrong end of his revolver.

Larkin smiled in anticipation. His life's dream was almost in reach. He had almost enough money. The only thing out of his grasp was the promotion to post commander, and then he could order men out and wipe the filthy savages out of the Territory.

"Come in," a voice bellowed, breaking into his thoughts.

He swore under his breath and resumed his perfect officer pose. If the colonel's daughter had been a little more amiable, he'd be another step closer to his final goal.

Damn Regan McBain, he swore.

Removing his hat, he crossed the threshold and walked briskly to where the commander awaited him.

Colonel McBain sat behind the large wooden desk, and a pang of jealousy hit Larkin. He should be the one sitting in that position, not this old man, who refused to wage war anymore.

With a pretense of respect he snapped to attention. "Colonel, sir, you wanted to see me?"

"Yes, Captain." Colonel McBain smoothed his mustache. "I've spoken with Regan and she has made some serious allegations."

"She's just angry with me." Larkin smiled, brushing off his commander's concerns.

"Are you certain?" the colonel asked, hesitation in his words.

"Sir, if you'll pardon me for pointing it out, I'm sure Mrs. McBain has gotten angry with you a few times over the years." He nodded to the man in sympathy. "As I'm sure you'll agree, women don't always say the truth when they're angry."

The colonel turned an odd shade of red above his collar.

"Your daughter, I must confess, is still angry with me for not defending her better."

When the colonel opened his mouth to speak, Larkin cut him off. "She's right, you know. That savage would have never come back after her if I'd stopped him the first time."

That much was true. If only he'd killed him in the mountains.

"I swear he won't touch her again," Larkin vowed.

"What are you implying?" Colonel McBain stiffened.

"Nothing that everyone else doesn't already know, sir. "Your daughter spent several days"—he paused—"and nights with that savage. Do I need to say the words? I'm sure you see the urgency in an engagement."

He fell silent and let the implication sink in, then added, "She's distraught, sir. Not thinking clearly."

Colonel McBain smoothed his mustache while he studied his officer. "You may be right."

"Sir, I am rarely wrong. She'll come around. You'll see." He glanced toward the door. "Actually, I was on my way to see her."

"Very well, then go on." The colonel waved him off.

"Thank you, sir. And I wouldn't be surprised if we announced our engagement very soon," Larkin said as he left.

Colonel McBain stood beside the window and studied his captain as he walked away from the building. Today Captain Larkin hadn't seemed as much in control as usual. It was as if something had him worried.

A flicker of doubt rose up. Had he possibly been wrong about the young man? No, he couldn't have misjudged his character to that extent, he told himself. The captain had served him well since his time here.

However, Regan's protestation rang loud in his mind. She'd been so sure of her convictions.

Which one did he believe? A man he'd trusted with his life in the past, or a daughter he didn't even know.

Perhaps it wouldn't hurt to have the captain watched. Just to be certain.

Regan tapped her fingers on the windowsill. Frustration ate at her. Sweet Pea whined at her feet, wanting to be petted, but Regan shooed her away. She was far too restless to soothe her pet's feelings.

Regan stomped her foot in a burst of irritation. She hated the waiting. Her mama had once told her she didn't possess a patient bone in her body. Right now she was inclined to agree with her mama.

As he'd agreed, her papa had sent a rider to the Duncans, but he hadn't returned yet with any news. She feared that her papa wouldn't hold much stock in whatever information the rider might bring back.

At a sudden knock on the door, she whirled and raced for any news her visitor might be bringing her. She opened the door to Captain Larkin and barely bit back her groan of disgust.

He was absolutely the last person she wanted to see at the moment.

Unaware of her feelings, or not caring a whit about them, he pushed his way inside.

"Dear Regan, how are you today? Feeling more rested, I hope." He smiled an ingratiating smile at her.

She gritted her teeth. She could ill afford to anger him, at least not until the rider returned with the information that would set Branded Wolf free.

She gave him a wan smile. "I'm still feeling a bit under the weather. You'll understand if I'm not up to receiving visitors."

She put her hand on the door to nudge it closed. He caught the panel with his hand and shoved. She fell backward with the force of his thrust.

"But, dear Regan, I'm not merely a visitor. I'm the man you're going to marry."

Forgetting her role of meekness, she gasped, "Like hell."

"The first thing we will have to work on is your language, my dear bride-to-be. An officer's wife should never—"

"Get out," she ordered him.

"Oh, my, a prewedding argument. How sweet." He leaned toward her until his nose nearly touched hers.

Regan refused to back down or show him any fear. He would only use it against her.

"Now, a wedding between us will make your dear father so happy. Why, likely happy enough to promote me as a wedding gift."

He rocked back on his heels, his eyes pinning hers.

"And I want that."

"Go to—"

"Oh no, Regan. You will get me that promotion. If you want to stay alive."

"I'd rather die than marry you." She spat out the words at him.

"Oh, then perhaps I'm overly concerned with your health. Perhaps someone else's life means more to you." He eyed her steadily.

She forced herself to face him, giving nothing away by a glance or a flinch.

"Perhaps you'd prefer I had your savage lover shot. Ah, maybe in front of you even. Would that be more to your liking?"

"No." She couldn't stop the denial.

"Ah, I thought so."

He caught her arm, tightening his fingers over it until she flinched from the pain.

"You *will* go along with me on this proposed marriage, dear Regan."

She bit back her cry of pain, knowing she'd have a bruise

tomorrow from his touch. Bile rose in her throat at what he wanted from her. However, she'd never let her true feelings show in front of him. Not yet.

She kept her silence until he stormed out the door, shutting it with a decisive click behind him. Then she gave vent to the groan deep within her.

She hated herself for giving in to his demand, but she'd do more than that to save Brand's life. What was a mere engagement?

Engaged. She nearly gagged on the word. She was engaged to a killer who would likely murder her as soon as he got his beloved promotion. Well, he had a surprise coming.

She'd go along with him all right. Only long enough to get Brand safe.

It was past time for waiting.

Her patience had run out.

Regan peered out the door and crossed the fingers of one hand. It was a dark, nearly moonless night. She hoped that was good; she assumed so.

She checked her pocket one last time, ensuring the bottle of laudanum was securely tucked inside. At the last minute she caught up her sturdiest parasol. It wasn't much, but she felt better with some sort of weapon at hand.

"Shh!" she ordered Sweet Pea, who lay on the bed, chewing the corner of a pillow.

Sweet Pea cocked her head and thumped her plumed tail. She started to stand, but Regan held up a hand.

"Stay," she whispered.

Sweet Pea let out a puppy sigh and dropped back to the mattress. She returned to chewing the pillow.

Well, that at least would occupy her pet for a while, Regan

thought to herself. A pillow was a small sacrifice to make this night.

She slipped out the door, closing it silently behind her. Regrettably, she never had gotten Branded Wolf to teach her how to walk without making a sound. She tried to remember the way she'd seen him move, then mimicked his actions.

Softly, she crept across the sloping parade ground toward the guardhouse, keeping in the shadows and moving unbearably slowly. At long last she reached her destination. One guard was posted outside.

Well, it was time, she told herself. She could do this.

Straightening, she adjusted the bodice of her dark green gown, tugging it downward until just the right amount of bosom showed. It was definitely much more than was proper, but there was nothing proper about what she was doing tonight.

And if it didn't work, she could well get herself shot.

Hands demurely wrapped around her parasol in an effort to prevent them from shaking so hard that they gave her away, she sauntered toward the soldier on duty. She made certain to scuff her slipper on the ground to alert him of her approach. No point in getting shot needlessly.

The soldier jerked to attention at her approach. "Miss, you shouldn't be here. The captain—"

Regan put a finger to her lips and batted her eyes at him. She noted he fell silent, seemingly forgetting what he was going to tell her. Quickly, she took in his rank as a private.

"Why, Sergeant," she cooed at him, pausing to send him a tentative smile. "Don't tell on me. It's such a pretty night, and I just needed a breath of air."

He swallowed nervously. "It's Private, Miss McBain."

Her smile widened. Good, he was well aware she was the commander's daughter.

"Papa asked about the prisoner earlier, and I thought

since I was already out for some air, I'd stop by to ask you.''

She looked down in a demure gesture but used the movement to survey the surrounding area. Her eyes lit on a tin cup of dark liquid. Perfect.

"Miss, the prisoner is secure. But you should be moving along now."

She sidestepped closer to the cup. Slipping one hand into her pocket, she grasped the bottle of laudanum. She placed her other hand on the young soldier's arm.

"Oh, excuse me. I have a dreadful pebble in my slipper." She made a face. "Would you help a lady in distress?"

"Ah, miss—"

She fell against him, at the same time tipping a goodly portion of the contents of the bottle into his cup.

"Oh, I am so sorry." She stepped away as if horrified. She lifted her leg and flexed her foot. His eyes followed.

"I do believe that pebble is all gone now." She reached out and patted his arm. "Thank you so much. I will be sure and tell my father of your kind assistance."

Gauging the distance, she stepped back to stand beside the cup. Scooping it up, she raised it and sniffed. She closed her eyes to keep from giving away her pleasure.

Snapping her eyes open, she held the cup out away from her. "Private, I do hope this is not some sort of spirits. My father would never tolerate drinking on duty."

The man reddened.

"Here, you'd best dispose of it before someone comes."

When he reached for it, she pulled it back.

"Oh, my heavens, if you pour it on the ground, won't it smell?" She wrinkled her nose in distaste. "You'd better drink it down right away."

She thrust the cup into his hand and watched as he gulped it down in two swallows.

It was all she could do not to clap her hands.

When he gave a strangled cough, she patted his back. "There, there. Well, I'll be on my way. Now, if you keep my secret, I'll be sure and keep yours," she promised with a wink.

Turning her back, she slowly sauntered away. When she reached the shadowed corner of a building, she ducked back and waited.

Waiting in the shadows, she watched until the soldier at last sat down and slumped against the guardhouse wall. Holding her hand over her mouth to stifle her giggle, she crept back across to the man. She nudged him with the tip of her parasol, and when his only reaction was a snore, she grinned.

Bending down, she withdrew the keys. As quickly as she could, she unlocked the door and slipped inside and out of sight. Speed was of the essence before someone came along and spotted the sleeping soldier.

"Brand?" she whispered.

"Regan? What are you doing here?"

She raced in the direction of his voice in the darkness. She fumbled with the key, and it took two tries to unlock his door.

"Regan?" he demanded in a low voice that sent heat racing along her veins.

When the door swung open, she threw herself into his arms. "I'm breaking you out of here."

She kissed him with a fire that startled him, nearly sending him stumbling over backward. Instead, he wrapped his arms around her and returned her passion breath for breath.

At last he drew back and set her away from him. She worshipped him with her eyes.

"This is crazy."

She leaned forward and kissed him again.

"Little one, you can't do this."

He caught her close in his arms. After being afraid he

would die without ever seeing her again, to hold her close in his arms was like reaching the heavens themselves.

"I hate to leave your arms," she whispered, "but we've got to get out of here."

"The guard—"

"Is sleeping like a baby. A well-sedated baby."

At his puzzlement, she withdrew the bottle of laudanum and held it up. "I gave him a healthy dose. For his nerves."

She giggled softly, the sound doing strange things to Branded Wolf's reasoning. He couldn't seem to think clearly with her in his arms.

"We've got to hurry. I hid Wind Dancer behind the hospital. It's that way." She pointed.

"No."

She snapped her head up, her mouth gaping open.

"What—"

"You're not coming. You have to stay here, where you'll be safe."

"But—"

He shook his head, his hair brushing her fingers where they rested on his shoulder.

"The captain will come after me. After I kill him, I'll come back for you."

"No." Her voice broke with fear. "I'm—"

"You're staying," he cut in. "Or else I'm staying too." With this he stepped away from her and sat on the floor.

"Get up. What do you think you're doing?"

"Will you stay?" he asked, his gaze leveled on hers.

She nodded.

"Your word," he asked of her.

Blinking away the moisture of tears, she whispered, "My word."

"Wait for me." His voice was ragged with things left unspoken.

It was a request, not an order, and it touched her to her soul.

"Forever," she answered.

He lunged up in a lightning-fast move and swept her into his arms. He gave her one long, hard kiss, then slipped out into the night.

Regan closed her eyes and clenched her hands together.

The keys rattled, startling her out of her misery. She had to put the keys back into the soldier's pocket and get out of here before she was found out.

Tiptoeing to the door, she peered out. The only one in sight was the snoring soldier. Branded Wolf had melted into the velvet darkness of the night. Biting her lip, she replaced the keys, then retraced her steps to her room.

She longed to ride out after Branded Wolf, to catch up with him no matter what the consequences, but she would not risk his life.

She crossed to her bed and scooped up Sweet Pea into her arms. Burying her face in her soft fur, she sighed deeply. She was scared all the way to her toes.

Scared for Branded Wolf. And scared of tomorrow.

There would be hell to pay for tonight's act.

Early the next morning, the door of Regan's room flew open and her parents barged in. She stopped her pacing and faced them with her head held high. They both looked angry, furious.

"Good morning, Mama. Papa."

Her father stormed forward, her mama in his wake.

"You let him out, didn't you?" Her father's booming voice held disgust.

Regan ignored it. She did what she had to do, and if need be, she'd do it again without hesitating. "Yes."

"Dear, how could you?" her mother shouted, adding her censure to her husband's.

Regan stared at her parents. Her father had one arm around her mother's shoulders, and her mother leaned back against him. He gave her one long, hard, level look.

For the first time in her life, her parents presented a united front. It was a daunting sight but a nice one.

"What a touching scene," Captain Larkin snarled from the open door.

All three turned at the voice in the doorway. Regan gasped. Captain Larkin held a gun in his hand, and it was pointed at her father.

"Step back, Colonel. And keep your hands where I can see them."

Larkin reached out and grabbed Regan before anyone realized his intention. He pulled her in front of him for a shield, then placed the cold barrel of his gun against her temple.

Chapter Twenty-one

Regan's scream died in her throat. She knew if she called out an alarm, Captain Larkin would kill her without hesitation.

She saw her father pale, and her mama lean heavily against him.

"What do you want, Captain?" her papa asked in a low voice. "I'll give you—"

"It's too late for that."

He pressed the gun harder against Regan's temple, and she let a low whimper slip out.

"Everything's destroyed. And it's all her fault. Her and that savage."

"He's not—"

Larkin tightened his arm around her waist, squeezing hard and effectively cutting off anything she else she might say.

"Keep quiet."

Regan didn't have a choice, since he was squeezing the breath out of her. All she could do was try to draw in enough air to remain conscious. There wasn't enough left for any sound, much less a scream.

Larkin dragged her out the door. Regan's heart sank when she saw the horse saddled and waiting. He'd planned this. Fear hovered ready to pounce on her, stealing her strength to fight.

She might well never see Branded Wolf again.

From the doorway she heard her mama softly sobbing. "Carson, do something," she ordered in a loud whisper that carried outside.

"I can't right now," her papa told her. "Now, shush."

Her mama gasped and fell silent.

As Larkin dragged her backward, Regan stumbled on the step and nearly fell, but Larkin yanked her up roughly. He shifted the gun until the steel barrel prodded her in the back.

He used the horse as a shield, nearly throwing Regan atop the animal. Before she had time to do anything, he swung up behind her.

"Hey, Colonel," he called out. "You send your men after me, and I kill her."

"Let her go." Her father's voice had a pleading tone she'd never heard from him before.

"When I reach Mexico, and not before."

He backed the horse several paces, then whirled and rode out, slapping the reins for more speed. Regan thought about attempting to throw herself from the horse's back but decided it wouldn't be wise to risk a broken neck. She'd bide her time.

He wouldn't kill her yet.

Brand, help me. She kept thinking the plea over and over in her mind and in her heart.

Right now she knew Larkin needed her alive. A wry smile touched her lips, then fled. He *had* to keep her alive to reach safety. But she intended to make every step as slow and miserable as she could possibly do.

Before she was finished with him, Captain David Larkin would regret the day he ever dared to touch her.

Branded Wolf drew Wind Dancer to a stop. He raised his head and studied the hills around him. Nothing out of place. No sign of Larkin anywhere.

Still, something disturbed him.

Wind Dancer shifted uneasily beneath him, then shied to the side.

A cold finger of fear trailed down Branded Wolf's back. Regan was in danger. He knew it in his heart.

He turned his horse back toward the fort and rode like the wind to get there.

As soon as the fort came into sight, he knew something had happened. He could see clouds of dust from a rush of activity inside. When he drew close enough, he recognized that the crowd had gathered in front of Regan's quarters.

He rode straight in and no one tried to stop him. He noticed with surprise that three bluecoats were being led away under armed escort toward the guardhouse. He recognized one of the men from the night in Regan's room.

"Where's Regan?" he called out, drawing Wind Dancer to a halt in front of where the commander sat astride a horse.

Colonel McBain turned to face him. "You," he sputtered.

"She's been kidnapped," an auburn-haired woman spoke up.

He recognized her as Regan's mother immediately. The similarities were there in her eyes and the defiant tilt of her head.

He spoke to her. "What happened?"

"That despicable Captain Larkin took Regan."

Branded Wolf couldn't stop the groan that slipped free.

Mrs. McBain stared at him, then smiled. "So you're him. The man Regan is in love with."

"Yes, I'm Branded Wolf." He met her look directly, unwilling to show any shame.

"Carson, ask for his help," she whispered in a voice loud enough to be heard several feet away.

"No," the colonel said. "He's a—"

"I'm a bounty hunter, Colonel. And I'm going after Regan."

"My men—"

"Will get her killed." Branded Wolf nearly snarled the words out.

"Mr. Wolf?" Elise nudged her horse closer to him. "Can you find her?"

"Elise! He's—"

"Carson, shut up. He's a lot better man than your *nice young officer* who took our daughter hostage and may kill her."

"You're right, Elise. I'll pay you scout's wages to track them for me," Colonel McBain offered him.

"Keep your money." Branded Wolf turned a hard stare on the man.

"Carson, you truly are an old fool."

"Elise, I've had enough of—"

"Carson, shut up. You've just insulted the only person who can save our daughter. He won't take your money because he's in love with her." She turned to Branded Wolf. "Aren't you?"

"Yes, ma'am."

"See, Carson, now apologize and let's *ask* for his help."

"You don't need to ask. Just tell me which direction they rode."

"He said he was going to Mexico. I'm coming with you," Colonel McBain informed him.

When Branded Wolf turned to fix him with a hard stare, he added, "My apologies."

Branded Wolf nodded, then said, "But I ride alone."

"Not this time," Elise put in. "We're both coming with you."

"Ma'am—"

"Elise—"

Both men spoke at once, then looked at each other.

"We're wasting time arguing." She held up one hand. "Let's ride."

She reached down to check that the rifle was secure in the scabbard and kicked her heels in her mount's side.

Branded Wolf sighed in defeat. He knew that look. He'd seen it on Regan's face too many times to forget. The woman would not give in on this.

It seemed the colonel wasn't as knowledgeable. He rode up beside her and attempted to rein in her horse. She reached out with a riding crop and smacked him across the chest. The colonel nearly fell off his mount.

If he hadn't been so worried over Regan, Branded Wolf would have laughed aloud. Instead, he urged Wind Dancer forward, riding between Regan's parents. They'd never reach Regan in time if these two killed each other first. And it looked like that's what they were trying to do.

The McBains fell in alongside him. When he raised a hand and sliced the air, they ceased their bickering and rode in silence.

After a short distance, he dismounted and checked the tracks. He nearly groaned at what he saw. Larkin was headed north toward Apache Pass.

He swung back up onto Wind Dancer and turned north.

"What are you doing?" Colonel McBain asked.

"He's turned north."

"But he said he was going to Mexico," Elise McBain put in.

"He lied."

Branded Wolf kneed Wind Dancer, sending him forward. Larkin's trail wasn't difficult to follow. The man was getting careless. Something told Branded Wolf that the bluecoat had his hands full with Regan. The way the hoofprints kept shying to one side, then the other every so often, gave proof of a far from sedate ride.

Knowing Regan, he never doubted for a minute that she was every bit Larkin's equal. However, fear for her life ate at him, urging him on.

He had to reach her in time. Before Larkin tired of her antics.

Regan pointed her toes down and swung her leg just enough to catch the horse in the front leg. The mount shied to the left.

Behind her, Larkin swore loudly and jerked the reins. The horse followed the lead, kicking up a trail of dust. Regan smiled, knowing they were leaving a path even a fool could follow. And Branded Wolf was no fool.

He was coming. She could feel it deep within her. Somehow, some way, he was coming after her.

All she had to do was delay long enough for Branded Wolf to catch up with them. There was absolutely no way she was going to Mexico, no way at all.

She glanced around, trying to discern any familiar landmarks or scenery, but failed. She didn't know if she'd ever seen this ground before. However, she was certain they were climbing higher. That worried her. If they made it into a canyon, they'd be harder to find.

She cautiously twisted her fingers into her skirt and tore a bow free, then slid her hand down and let the lavender ribbon fall to the ground. Thankfully, she hadn't been dressed in her nightgown or a dress that blended with the landscape. No, she was assured the purple bow would stand out like a beacon.

"What are you doing?" Larkin pinched her elbow.

"Nothing. And quit that," she snapped at him.

"You haven't felt true pain yet, dear Regan," he threatened in a low, smooth voice.

"Neither have you. But once Branded Wolf catches up with us—"

"That savage is far away. Running for his life."

She shook her head. "He's behind us now."

She received the satisfaction of feeling Larkin jerk and look around. So, the cowardly officer was afraid, was he? Well, she'd just have to help him out—by feeding those fears.

"The Apache know things about death we haven't even dreamed of," she said in a voice barely above a whisper, then shivered for added effect.

Larkin stiffened behind her. "He's not coming to save you."

"Oh, yes, he is. I can feel his presence." She sighed and added, "The Apache are like that, you know. They sense things."

She paused to pluck off another ribboned bow.

"And the training they go through is unbelievable." She wasn't sure what she was talking about, but he needn't know it. "They're taught how to use a knife as children." She gave a faint gasp at the end.

"Forget trying to scare me," he sneered, "with talk of your Injun lover."

Regan detected a hint of a tremor behind his bravado. Good.

"He's very good with a knife," she told him. "I wouldn't be surprised if he *scalped* you."

At the harsh sound of him sucking in his breath, she bit the corner of her mouth to hold in her laughter.

"Oh, but that's the white man's custom, isn't it?" she asked. "They took the first scalps."

He answered with a grunt.

"But the Apache perfected it. I hear that an Apache can skin—"

"Shut up," he growled at her.

Regan merely smiled.

"For some reason, it's supposed to hurt worse for darker hair," she elaborated with a lie.

"I said shut up."

She fell silent for then. She'd give him time to think on what she'd told him, and to worry.

Oh, she was far from finished with Captain Larkin. Far from it.

She dropped another lavender bow to the ground.

"Are you certain they headed this way?" Colonel McBain asked.

Branded Wolf gritted his teeth. "I'm a skilled tracker, sir."

"Yes, I'm sure you are, but—"

"What Carson is trying to say is that he's worried about his daughter, isn't that so, dear?" Elise put in.

The man riding beside him seemed to suddenly sag in the saddle.

"Yes, I'm scared to death for her." The words sounded as if they'd been torn from his soul. "If we find her—"

"*When* we find her," Branded Wolf said firmly.

Colonel McBain nodded. "When we find her, I'm going to tell her I love her. Do you know I've never said that to my daughter?"

Branded Wolf looked at him in surprise. How could this man not love Regan? What a poor little child she had been without love and acceptance. He'd had the caring and respect of the tribe in his life. He hurt for her at that moment.

"Well, Carson," Elise said with pride, "that's a start."

Suddenly, Branded Wolf spotted it. He reined Wind

Dancer up and jumped to the ground in a rush. He picked up the purple bow and held it up like a battle prize.

"Regan's," he announced.

"How can you be certain?" Colonel McBain asked.

Elise rode closer. "That's hers. I should know, I paid for that gown to be special made in that color."

Branded Wolf swung up onto Wind Dancer and sent the horse into a gallop. By the time he found the third ribboned bow, he knew where they were headed.

An hour later they reached the canyon.

"Leave the horses," Branded Wolf ordered. "We'll walk the rest of the way."

"How do you know she's here?" Colonel McBain asked, worry edging his words.

"I know."

The older man studied him a second. "You know, I believe you do."

"Regan's spirit is calling to me. I hear her," Branded Wolf told him.

This time when Branded Wolf led the way, Colonel McBain followed without questions. As he glanced back over his shoulder, Mrs. McBain sent him a smile of support. Surprisingly, he knew she had full confidence in him.

Branded Wolf led the way along a narrow trail along the side of the canyon. It was rough going, but the McBains kept up. Suddenly, he stopped and bent down. On the ground lay a deep purple sash, its silk a bright beacon against the dirt.

His chest tightened with the realization that either Regan had run out of bows or the bluecoat had run out of patience.

Let it be the first, he prayed. Desperation made him clench his fists tightly around the silk. Slowly, he released his grip on the sash and tied it around his waist, its ends hanging past his knees. He needed a part of her close to him.

Keeping low, he crawled forward around a rock and froze, his breath going still in his throat.

Regan stood on a small flat space of land, her chin tilted up in brave defiance. He felt a rush of relief as well as pride course through him. She was alive and every bit as stubborn as always.

A breeze caught at her hair, tugging the tangled mass of curls. Dirt streaked her face, and her pretty dress was minus its bows and had a rip the full length of one sleeve. Rage rose up in him, and he vowed to punish the bluecoat for this.

Assured she was well, he turned his attention to her kidnapper. Larkin stood beside her, nervously looking from side to side.

She said something to him, and he backhanded her. When Branded Wolf saw Regan drop to her knees, all he could think of was killing the man who hurt her.

With a loud cry he charged for Larkin. The bluecoat stared for a brief instant, then raised his gun and fired.

Regan threw herself into Larkin's side, knocking him to the ground as Branded Wolf dove to avoid the bullet. It slammed into the dirt beside him.

As he rolled to his feet, Elise fired her rifle, but her shot ricocheted off a rock.

"Elise!" Colonel McBain shouted. "Give me that before you shoot the wrong person!"

Chaos erupted in the next instant. Branded Wolf charged again, catching Larkin in the chest and taking him to the ground. The two men rolled on the ground, trading punches.

Refusing to stand by idly and watch, Regan rushed forward. She grabbed at Larkin's flailing fists. He shook her off as if her light weight were nothing, giving her a glancing blow on the chin, and she tumbled to the ground on her backside.

Colonel McBain yanked the rifle out of his wife's hands

and turned to point it at the fighting men, but he couldn't get a clear shot. Elise made to rush forward, and he caught her arm, pulling her back. They watched the two men locked in battle, each fighting for his life, inching closer and closer to the danger of the ledge as they fought.

Branded Wolf landed a solid blow to the other man's jaw. He drew back his arm to strike again, and Larkin ducked, pulling a knife from his boot. He brought it upward in an arc. Regan's heart stopped, and she knew pure terror.

She screamed a warning and flung herself at Larkin. She caught his free arm, but he shoved her away and turned on Branded Wolf again.

With a cold smile of hatred Larkin faced him. He swung, but Branded Wolf was quicker. He parried the thrust and snapped the knife out of the bluecoat's grip. Larkin stumbled backward, balancing precariously on the ledge that jutted out.

He wavered for a moment, then reached out and grabbed hold of Branded Wolf's arm. The knife flew from his hand to sail over the edge, and Larkin yanked him forward.

Branded Wolf struggled but was pulled toward the canyon's steep ledge. Then Larkin's footing slipped and he fell backward, pulling Branded Wolf along with him.

Chapter Twenty-two

Regan lunged for Branded Wolf. She caught the edge of the purple sash tied around his waist as he slid over the side, and she held tight. The weight of the men dragged her toward the ledge, but she refused to release her hold.

"Brand!" she screamed.

He swung his legs back and caught the corner of a rock. Wrapping his knees around it, he gripped it tightly, levering his weight onto it. Below him, Captain Larkin clung to him like a disease, digging his fingers into his arms.

Branded Wolf felt the satin sash slide, and he remembered his last vision of Regan throwing herself at him.

"Regan!" he yelled.

"Brand." Her voice came out strained.

He knew she was the one holding him. He couldn't let her risk her life.

"Let go!" he ordered.

"No!" she panted.

Larkin's gaze met his, and the man grinned widely.

"You're gonna die with me, Injun. And we're both gonna take her with us." His laughter rang out hollow. It echoed on the walls of the canyon.

"Like hell." Branded Wolf tightened his shoulders and, straining, pulled the other man upward.

"No!" Larkin struggled, kicking out.

He dislodged a cluster of loose rock, and it rained down on him. Instinctively, he raised one hand to shield himself. Too late, he realized his mistake and grabbed for support. Flailing his one arm frantically, his sweat-slickened grip on Branded Wolf's arm slipped.

His fingers raked Branded Wolf's wrist, then clawed at empty air. He seemed to be suspended an instant, then plummeted down. This time his scream echoed from the canyon walls.

"Papa, help me!" Regan cried out, sliding another few inches closer to the edge.

Her father ran forward. Lying on the ground, he reached down, extending an arm to Branded Wolf.

"Grab on!" he yelled.

Branded Wolf grabbed the other man's hand. It was slippery with sweat and he curled his fingers around the colonel's hand.

Colonel McBain leaned over farther and clasped his other hand around Branded Wolf's wrist. He heaved, inching backward. Regan struggled, pulling on the sash as hard as she could.

Finally, after what seemed like an eternity, Branded Wolf clawed his way back over the top of the ledge. He levered himself to his feet, out of breath.

Regan stared at him for a moment, telling herself he truly was alive. She hadn't lost him.

Then she stepped toward him. When he opened his arms, she rushed into his embrace. He held her like he'd never let her go.

She heard her father mumble, "I helped too, you know." Then her mama shushed him.

Regan shut everything out except the feel of Branded Wolf alive in her arms. She heard the rapid, steady beat of his heart against her ear and squeezed her eyes tightly closed. For once in her life, she couldn't utter a single word.

After what seemed an eternity he eased her away from him to look down into her eyes. They glistened with unshed tears. He knew she was too proud to cry. In that instant he loved her too deeply for words.

"Little one." His voice was husky.

It sounded like a throaty purr to Regan. She raised her chin to look into his eyes, those incredible blue eyes that she loved so much.

She opened her mouth, but nothing came out.

Branded Wolf smiled down at her, tender loving in his gaze. He gently brushed a curl away from her cheek, then cupped his hand over her cheek.

"My little one," he whispered, bending closer. A breath away from her lips, he paused. "I love you more than life and death and God's heavens combined."

Her lips parted on a soft oh.

"Will you spend your life with me?"

"Yes," she answered in a barely audible voice.

"Marry me, little one?"

"Yes," she answered, her voice gathering strength.

He smiled a tender smile at her, then added, "Love me?"

"Yes," she shouted. "More than anything. I love you, Branded Wolf."

"Have my babies?" he whispered against her lips.

Her answer was to press her lips against his and kiss him with all the love built up inside her.

Branded Wolf felt like he'd fallen over that ledge again, except this time he was soaring high in the sky.

After long minutes they finally drew apart; however, he

kept his arms wrapped loosely about her waist. A loud cough from her father drew their attention at last.

"It's traditional to ask the father for her hand first, you know." He coughed again.

Branded Wolf faced him, stiff with pride. "And would you have given it?" he challenged.

"Carson," Elise urged him, a hand on his arm.

He looked from Regan's glowing face to the Apache standing at her side. He was not exactly what he would have chosen for her, but somehow it didn't matter as much now as it would have a few days before. Life and death had a way of changing one's outlook.

"An army colonel with an Apache son-in-law," he muttered. Then he looked up at them and nodded. "You have my blessing and my thanks."

"Papa." Regan's voice caught in her throat.

He faced Branded Wolf and held out his hand. "Thank you. I owe you my daughter's life."

Elise cleared her throat loudly.

"And probably my wife's as well," he said gruffly.

Branded Wolf took his hand and shook it.

Her father smoothed his mustache with a hand that shook. "I . . . I'd like to pay a reward if you'd take it. No insult intended," he hurried to add.

Branded Wolf smiled. "It's not necessary, sir."

"But I want to."

Branded Wolf slid his arms down to clasp Regan's hand in his. "I have all the reward I need."

"Regardless, I'm sure you could use the money," her father prodded him.

"No, sir. Actually, I can't."

"But—" her father sputtered.

Branded Wolf held up his hand. "No insult intended." He used the other man's words. "But I've made a good living as a bounty hunter and contributed something to this

Territory. I've more than enough to buy the ranch I've got my eye on outside Tucson.''

Regan gasped. Her father sputtered, and her mama clapped her hands in glee.

"Carson, we're going to have that wedding you wanted after all.''

"Yes, we are." Branded Wolf pulled Regan back into his arms, kissing her until her toes curled.

One week later, Regan walked down the aisle of the town church in a gown of cream silk. Her whole being was focused on the man waiting for her at the front of the church.

Branded Wolf stood straight and proud, his midnight hair hanging to the shoulders of his black suit. He was so handsome that she stopped to just stare at him a second.

"Daughter?" her papa whispered at her side. "Are you all right?"

"Everything's wonderful, Papa," she whispered back, patting his hand to reassure him. Since her kidnapping, he'd become a doting parent.

As they neared the front of the church, her mama stood up and waved, holding Sweet Pea in one arm. Regan wiggled her fingers at them and hid her grin behind her fingers.

Her papa squeezed her hand, then leaned over and whispered, "Daughter, I'm so proud of you."

She missed a step and smiled at him. As they reached the front of the church, he patted her hand and kissed her cheek, then gave her to the man waiting at the alter.

Branded Wolf gazed down at her, and she knew she'd never known true happiness before that moment. She was marrying the man she loved more than life itself, the other half of her.

"Dearly beloved—" the minister began.

A sharp bark interrupted him. Sweet Pea jumped off

Elise's lap and bounded to the front of the church. She skidded to a halt at Branded Wolf's feet and promptly laid her chin on his foot.

The minister stared a moment, then, when neither the bride nor groom protested, he continued.

Branded Wolf took her hand in his, and Regan knew he held her heart as well with that touch. She looked up at him, unexplainably shy all of a sudden. The love she saw mirrored in his blue gaze sent all doubts, all insecurities, away for good.

"Regan, do you take this man—"

"Forever," she cut in, her gaze never leaving the face of the man she loved.

The minister cleared his throat. "Branded Wolf, do you take this woman—"

"Forever," he answered.

The next words flowed over Regan like a gentle dew. All she could see, all she could hear, was the man facing her who made her life complete. Branded Wolf, *her* Apache warrior.

Then he was pulling her to him, his lips slanting over hers, and the world disappeared for her. She clasped her hands around his neck, her fingers sliding through his silken hair. A soft sigh left her lips to be captured by his.

She returned his kiss breath for breath until neither knew where one of them left off and the other began.

It was a kiss that promised a lifetime of love.

Forever.

Epilogue

Outside Tucson, Arizona Territory
One year later

Regan held tight to Branded Wolf's hand. She hadn't an idea why she was nervous. She wasn't the one getting married.

She glanced around at the living room full of guests, and her heart swelled with pride. The home Branded Wolf had built was beautiful, more beautiful than she could have dreamed. The music began, and she squeezed his hand tighter.

Sensing her distress as he always seemed to be able to do, Branded Wolf eased his hand from hers and slipped his free arm around her. He held their three-month-old son close to his chest and nuzzled a kiss against Regan's temple.

She leaned back against his shoulder, all worry gone. He could do that with just a touch, a tender look, a caress. His shoulder-length hair brushed her cheek, and she smiled at the feel of its silkiness against her skin. Her mind rushed back sinfully to two hours earlier. They'd lain naked in each other's arms, making love. Then her outcry of release had awakened their son.

She felt a tug on her hair and turned to disentangle a curl from tiny fingers. Her son cooed at her. Brandon Carson Eagle was the image of his father with raven-dark hair and beautiful blue eyes, except they held a hint of his mother's green color as well. He'd been named for his father, grandfather, and the proud eagle that had flown overhead as he was born.

"Ah, he can't keep his hands off you either," Branded Wolf whispered in the shell of her ear.

"Shh," Regan shushed him. "We're in church. Sorta. It's a wedding."

His chuckle stirred the hair at her temple and so much more within her. She leaned into his warm embrace.

"Regan?" came her mama's loud whisper from the back of the room.

Regan closed her eyes and grimaced. When her mother used that tone, it always—

"Psst! Regan, I need someone to give me away," her mama wailed dramatically.

A titter of laughter traveled around the room.

Branded Wolf handed Regan their son, then stood. "I'd be honored to do so," he volunteered.

"Well, then hurry up before she changes her mind," Carson McBain called out from where he stood waiting in front of the minister. "Or I do."

The guests broke into laughter.

Branded Wolf took long enough to place a lingering kiss on Regan's lips before he strode to the back of the room with soundless steps.

Sweet Pea jumped up from her place at his feet and trotted after him, her plumed tail wagging happily.

Regan turned in her seat, holding her son close, and watched her husband's sleek movements. Today he wore a black broadcloth suit, and he was so handsome, he took her breath away. She loved him more each and every day.

And once he'd told her he loved her that day on the ledge, he'd never stopped telling her. She didn't think she could ever hear those words too much.

Then he was walking back with her mama clinging to his arm. Sweet Pea pranced beside him, one of Mama's gloves dangling from her mouth. Regan bit back her giggle.

At last the trio reached the minister, where Branded Wolf bowed as he gave his mother-in-law's hand to his father-in-law. Then he turned and strode back to join Regan. He sat beside her, slid his arm around her, and kissed her until she was positively breathless. And loving every second of it.

The minister looked at the couple, then at the little white dog with the glove, and back to the couple.

"Dearly beloved, we are gathered here today for the renewing of the vows—"

"Oh, no," Elise cut in. "This is a wedding. Since we've buried old hurts, we need a *new* wedding to start over."

Regan smiled at her mama. At last her parents were together and happy. Papa had left the cavalry to open a business as an attorney, his former profession, in Tucson. Mama had moved her belongings and joined him, and demanded a new wedding. Regan's stifled her giggle.

The minister looked at a loss for words, then he cleared his throat. "Dearly beloved, we are here today for a *wedding.*"

Branded Wolf leaned closer and his breath warmed Regan's ear. She tuned out everything but the man beside her and the child in her arms. Her life was complete, and she couldn't be happier.

As the ceremony ended, her parents kissed, then her mama practically dragged her father to them in her hurry.

"What's the rush?" he mumbled.

"We haven't had time to see our grandson in two days. I want to hold him," she admitted.

He smiled at her in indulgence. "Only if I get to hold him after you."

Branded Wolf's smile widened to a grin. He took his son from Regan's arms and handed him over to the doting grandparents. In seconds they were surrounded by well-wishers and those who wanted to see the baby.

He caught Regan's hand and drew her away from the people. "Shh, come with me."

"What?"

He leaned to her and slanted his mouth across hers for a kiss that most assuredly curled her toes. Pulling away with a groan, he led her out a side door and away from the house. He didn't stop until they reached the wickiup he'd built for them six months ago to hold their memories.

He caught her up in his arms and pressed his lips to hers. It was a kiss that promised, tempted, demanded. And she returned it completely, totally, thoroughly.

In that instant they didn't need words to tell of their love. That single kiss said it all.

It sealed their love.

Forever.